POSSESS

GRETCHEN McNEIL

BALZER + BRAY

An Imprint of HarperCollins*Publishers*

For Mom
(don't kill me)

Balzer + Bray is an imprint of HarperCollins Publishers.

Possess
Copyright © 2011 by Gretchen McNeil
All rights reserved. Printed in the United States of America.

www.epicreads.com

Library of Congress Cataloging-in-Publication Data
McNeil, Gretchen.
Possess / Gretchen McNeil. — 1st ed.
    p. cm.
Summary: Enlisted to help in dangerous cases of demonic possession, a teenaged
exorcist discovers a race of part-demons intent on raising their forefathers to the
earth in human form.
ISBN 978-0-06-206072-3
[1. Demoniac possession—Fiction. 2. Demonology—Fiction. 3. Exorcism—
Fiction. 4. Racially mixed people—Fiction. 5. San Francisco (Calif.)—Fiction.
6. Horror stories.] I. Title.
PZ7.M4787952Po 2011   2010050507
[Fic]—dc22   CIP
                                                                                 AC

Typography by Ann Zeak
12 13 14 15 16 LP/RRDH 10 9 8 7 6 5 4 3 2 1
❖
First paperback edition, 2012

"My name is Legion," he replied.
"For we are many."

—Mark 5:9

ONE

BRIDGET STARED AT THE CLOCK on the wall and cursed its painfully slow progression toward three fifteen. Was the big hand even moving? She slipped her cell phone out of her backpack for cross-reference. Damn. Seven more minutes. It was so like a Catholic school to make Latin the last class of the day. Institutionalized Purgatory.

"Hey," Hector whispered from the desk in front of her. "Want to hit House of Pies after school?"

"Maybe." The last thing Hector needed was another slice of Triple Chocolate pie.

"Maybe?" Hector swiveled his torso around to face her. "You got a hot date or something?"

Before Bridget could tell Hector to shove it, Peter Kim

cleared his throat. "Shut up, you guys. Sister Evangeline's going to kill us."

Bridget glanced at the wizened little nun sitting motionless at her desk, engrossed in a romance novel. "Live a little, Peter. Seriously."

Peter's face was pinched as he slipped his book and pen case into his backpack. "So, Bridge, are you, um, going to the library today?"

A sly smile spread across Hector's face. "Why, Peter? Why could you possibly be asking?"

Peter flushed.

"Because if she's going and you're going, maybe you two could go together?"

Bridget kicked Hector's chair with the steel toe of her boot. She'd known Peter Kim since the second grade and was painfully aware of his decade-long crush on her. And the not-so-secret delight Hector took in torturing him about it.

"Well . . . I mean . . . ," Peter stuttered.

Bridget's cell phone buzzed, saving her from yet another awkward conversation with Peter.

"Who's texting you at school?" Hector said, peering over her desk.

"Um . . ." She looked down at her phone and saw the name "Matt Quinn" blazing back.

Hector's jaw dropped. "He has your cell phone number?"

Crap.

"Who?" Peter asked sharply. "Who has your—"

"'Coaching your brother today,'" Hector read. "'See you after?'"

Bridget couldn't help but smile. She lowered her chin, hoping Hector wouldn't catch it. Too late.

"Oh," he cooed. "So you *do* have a hot date after school. Jealous."

Bridget scowled. "He's not your type."

"Bridget." Peter's cheeks burned the same color as the ridiculous red Windbreaker he always wore, and his dark brown eyes were fixed on her, holding her gaze. "Who are you seeing after school?"

"No one," Bridget said quickly, shoving her cell phone in her jacket pocket. "I'm not seeing anyone."

"The cop's son," Hector volunteered. "The one that sent Milton Undermeyer to—" Hector stopped short as his eye caught Bridget's and she gave him her best "I'm going to rip your heart out through your nose" stare.

Hector swallowed. "Sorry."

"The cop who sent that murderer to see Dr. Liu?" Peter's voice was shrill. "Yeah, I doubt Bridge's dating the guy whose dad got hers killed."

Bridget stiffened. It had been almost nine months since her father's death, yet the raw ache still dug its claws into her heart every time she thought about it. Wasn't it supposed to get better? Eventually the pain would go away, the nightmares would end, and the memories of that day fade to muted colors.

Without realizing it, Bridget reached for the charm brace-let she'd worn around her wrist since she was seven. A First Communion gift from her dad. She traced the familiar, ornate outline of the square cross with her fingers—the weird non-sense letters and the funny scrolling symbols—then closed her hand around the charm and squeezed, letting the sharp corners of the cross dig into the flesh of her palm. She didn't want to forget. She'd rather hold on to the pain than lose him again.

"Dude," Hector said, smacking Peter on the arm. "Not cool."

Bridget released the charm. "It's fine." Her voice was steady. Good.

"Bridge," Peter said rapidly. "I just meant—"

The back door of the classroom flew open, and Monsi-gnor Renault stepped into the room. Latin 201 went silent as the tall, imposing figure of the school chaplain strode quickly to Sister Evangeline's desk, where the nun sat complacently reading her novel. When he placed a gnarled hand on her shoulder, Sister Evangeline jumped and shoved her reading material into an open drawer.

"Monsignor Renault, what a lovely surprise," she squeaked.

He brought his head down and whispered something in Sister Evangeline's ear, then straightened up and handed her a folded piece of paper.

As he turned to leave, his eyes swept the classroom and caught Bridget's. The incline of his head was barely perceptible.

It was time.

"Bridget Liu?" Sister Evangeline called as Monsignor closed the door behind him. "Bridget, I have a note for you."

Bridget pushed herself to her feet. The classroom, her friends, the other students: Everything disappeared from view as she focused her attention on the folded white piece of paper Sister Evangeline held out to her.

She took the note with a shaky hand and returned to her desk.

"What the hell does that old weirdo want with you?" Hector asked.

The bell saved her from having to respond. Hector shot to his feet and swung his backpack over his shoulder. "So you walking to the library or not?" he asked, the note seemingly forgotten.

Bridget shook her head.

"Fine. But I want full details of your date with Matt Quinn, okay?"

She heaved her backpack onto her shoulder. "Sure," she said absently.

It wasn't until Hector turned to leave that Bridget stole a glance at the note in her hand.

2271 18th Avenue

4 p.m.

Suddenly Latin class didn't seem so bad.

TWO

THE HOUSE DIDN'T WANT HER there.

Shocking.

Bridget shivered and zipped her fur-lined bomber jacket to her chin, then pulled Monsignor's note out of her pocket. She read the address off the front of the house, double-checking it against the crumpled piece of paper in her hand—2271 18th Avenue. Yep, this was it. Great. Fog billowed down the street, temporarily obscuring the row house from view. As the haze lifted, she scrutinized the building. Its dark windows stared at her like the cavernous eye sockets of a blanched skull: empty, soulless. The jagged fringe of decorative wood above the garage was a jack-o'-lantern's grin. The fake marble staircase glistened dangerously under a layer of moisture.

What was she thinking? She should turn around and sprint the eight blocks back to the library, where Hector and Peter were hunched over a cozy wooden table, joking in half whispers while they muddled through algebra and history. That's where she belonged, not here.

Get a grip, Bridge.

Maybe what had happened at the Fergusons' house had been a fluke. A hallucination. Some weird family prank. Maybe if she walked up those stairs right now, she could prove to herself that she wasn't really a complete and total freak of nature.

Or maybe her worst fears would be confirmed. Either way, she needed to know.

There was a muffled beep from her jacket pocket. Four o'clock. On cue, a light blazed from the house, illuminating a second-floor bay window through the thickening mist.

With renewed determination, Bridget crossed the street. But as she approached the house, the gooey San Francisco fog swamped her suddenly, blotting out the sun and obscuring all traces of the street, the house, the whole world around her.

Not only did the house not want her there, Mother Nature didn't either. Great.

She couldn't see a thing. The air hung in her nostrils like musty water, and for a panicked moment, Bridget felt like she was drowning. She stumbled forward, unsure if she was even moving in the right direction. Had the entire street disappeared?

Her boot struck the edge of the bottom stair, and Bridget groped for the handrail. House, stairs, rail. It was here; it was real.

Bridget kept the corroded metal railing in a death grip as she plodded up the stairs. The fog was everywhere: in her eyes, in her mouth, seeping into her tights and the deep pleats of her uniform skirt. She felt heavy, weighted, like the fog was trying to pull her down the stairs, away from the house, away from what lay inside.

The handrail ended. She reached out, half expecting that the house had dissolved into the fog, and let out a squeak as her fingertips grazed smooth, hard wood.

The moment she touched the door, the fog retreated, dissipating into nothingness as if it had been sucked up by a giant cosmic vacuum cleaner.

As she glanced back and watched the last wisps vanish behind her, the door flew open.

"Shit!" Bridget gasped.

A young man in black pants and a black short-sleeved shirt stood inside the house. He was squat, with the beginnings of a double chin and stubby, dimpled fingers. A shock of thick black hair was piled haphazardly on his head. His dark eyes gave her a once-over, head to boots and back again, before resting on her face.

"*You're* Bridget Liu?"

If she had a dime for every time she had heard that. Her almond-shaped eyes were blue, and when added to curly brown hair and freckles, they threw everyone off. "Um, yeah."

The young man gave himself a shake. "Sorry, I was expecting someone . . ."

Bridget arched an eyebrow. "More Chinese?"

"N-no," he stuttered. "That's not what I . . ." His voice trailed off. "Er, sorry." He shuffled aside, motioning for her to enter.

Bridget hesitated. Was she really going to do this?

"Come in, come in," the guy said quickly. "He's waiting for you."

Bridget stepped through the doorway. The atmosphere of the house was off. The air was condensed; her ears crackled with the change in pressure, and for a moment she felt dizzy. The room seemed to whirl and pitch like a fun house. She felt the floor tilt, and the ceiling and walls pressed in on her, creating angles that could only exist in a geometry problem or an M. C. Escher print. Furniture bulged, doubling in size. She knew it wasn't real, just a trick of the eye, but still.

The house wanted her out. She could feel it.

Bridget lost her balance and stumbled forward, bracing herself against a grandfather clock. She'd felt this way once before. It wasn't a good sign.

"Are you okay?" the guy asked.

Bridget pressed a hand to her head. "Um, yeah. Yeah, I'm—"

A shriek ripped through the house. Bridget spun around to find an orange tabby cat frozen in the hall, back arched, eyes so wide they practically popped out of its furry little skull. The cat let out a second terrified wail, then bolted past her, through the open door and out into the darkening afternoon.

Smart cat.

"Sorry about that," the guy said, latching the door behind him.

Bridget straightened, trying to shake off the dizziness. "S'okay. Cats don't like me."

He shoved a hand into his pants pocket and retrieved a small wire-bound notebook with a gnarled bit of pencil wedged into the spirals. With a journalist's ease, he flipped open the notebook and began to scribble. "Never or just recently?"

Bridget looked at him sidelong. Why was he taking notes? "Since forever."

"Oh." His head snapped up and he stared at her for a moment, his goatlike eyes locked on to her face. "You're okay now?"

Bridget nodded.

"Because a second ago you looked like you were going to be sick."

"I'm fine."

"Oh. G-good." He nodded twice, made one last flourish of notes on his little pad, and stuffed it back into his pocket. "I'm Father Santos, by the way."

Bridget's eyebrows shot up. A priest?

"Oh, right." Father Santos fumbled around in his shirt

pocket and withdrew a length of stiff, white fabric. "I, uh, came straight from the airport. I take my c-collar off when I fly. So I can sleep."

He dropped the collar, twice, before his plump hands managed to thread it through the opening in his shirt. Bridget eyed him suspiciously. Monsignor hadn't said anything about another priest.

She wondered how much Father Santos knew.

"Where's Monsignor Renault?"

"Right," Father Santos said. He turned and shuffled down the hall. "Follow me."

The coldness of the room hit Bridget even before the smell of burning incense. The vapor of her escaping breath mingled with the swirl of perfumed smoke that hung over a double bed in the center of the room. Monsignor Renault knelt in prayer at the foot of the bed. He didn't stir as they entered, but continued to mutter under his breath before he leaned back on his heels and made the sign of the cross.

Monsignor looked tired, hardly the confident priest she'd seen less than an hour ago. The wisps of white hair scattered across his bald head were pointing in several directions at once, like the Scarecrow showing both ways to Oz. His pale gray eyes seemed sunken, and his skin—gray to match— sagged off his face like raw pizza dough.

With a heavy sigh, he glanced up. At first, Monsignor's eyes didn't register her presence; they just followed Father

Santos with suspicion as he waddled to the far side of the room. Slowly, Monsignor's gaze drifted back to Bridget, and he smiled, instantly subtracting twenty years from his appearance. "Thank you for coming, Bridget."

Bridget smiled in return. Monsignor looked so relieved to see her, and despite her reservations about coming, she knew she'd made the right choice. Monsignor wanted her there. He needed her there.

"I wouldn't miss it," she said.

"I know."

Bridget's smile faded as her eyes drifted to Father Santos. He stood by the window, jotting down notes at a furious pace.

"Father Santos has just arrived from Rome." Monsignor's voice was flat. "He will be working with me for the time being." He didn't sound particularly happy.

"The Vatican is c-concerned with the elevated number of possessions and infestations in the San Francisco area," Father Santos said, without looking up.

"Oh," she said.

"I have explained to him the nature of your unique, ah, abilities," Monsignor continued.

Bridget wondered how that conversation had gone down.

Monsignor Renault cleared his throat and, with a flick of his head, drew Bridget's attention to the bed, where an elderly woman lay on her back, covers pulled up to her chin. She looked to be asleep, though her quick, shallow breaths hinted otherwise.

"Shouldn't we move her?" Bridget asked.

"No."

Bridget crinkled her brows in confusion; then her eyes grew wide as she realized the truth. "Her?"

Monsignor nodded. "Yes."

Oh, crap. She'd thought it would just be the house, not a living, breathing person.

"It speaks through her," Monsignor continued. "But has not yet taken complete control."

Bridget began to inch her way toward the door. "I don't think—"

"Bridget." Monsignor's voice froze her in her tracks. "Bridget, you can do this. I have faith in you."

Faith. Great.

"If she d-doesn't want to be here . . . ," Father Santos started.

Monsignor narrowed his eyes. "She wants to be here, don't you, Bridget?"

"Want" was a pretty relative term, but Monsignor's eyes searched her face, practically pleading for the right answer. She couldn't disappoint him after all he'd done for her. She swallowed hard and nodded. "Um, yeah. Yeah, I do."

"Thank you," Monsignor said, staring directly at Father Santos. The younger priest looked away and shuffled his feet.

Monsignor's face was grim as he looked back at Bridget, but his gray eyes twinkled as if they shared some secret joke at Father Santos's expense. "Don't worry. Mrs. Long cannot hurt you, I promise."

Bridget gazed at the tiny Mrs. Long—she was ninety pounds maybe, but only after she ate a giant burrito or something—and there was no vapor emanating from her nose or mouth. The old woman's breath was frigid.

Bridget bit her lip, attempting to hide the abject terror rising up from her stomach to her throat like bad sushi.

"What is Rule Number One?" Monsignor Renault asked softly.

Bridget swore that man could read her mind. "Do not show fear."

"Do not show fear." Monsignor pulled himself up to his full six-foot height, straightening his back and holding his head erect. Despite his age, his shoulders were square and broad, and he looked strong enough to take on a sumo wrestler. He wore his usual long black cassock piped with red, and a purple sash around his waist. A silver ring encircled the middle finger of his left hand, so thick it was more like a single brass knuckle than a piece of jewelry. Monsignor was old-school Catholic, a spectacle of ancient traditions and beliefs that fascinated Bridget and scared the crap out of her at the same time.

And if he thought Bridget could handle this, then she was damn well going to try.

"Father Santos," Monsignor said. "Please prepare the room."

Father Santos opened a black bag and removed a purple stole, which he handed to his superior. Monsignor Renault kissed the cross on the back of the stole, then draped it over his neck. Next came two small crystal decanters—one of holy water, one of consecrated oil—then a covered bowl of salt, a tray of Eucharistic wafers, and several thick, white candles. After lighting the candles, the young priest took the salt and carefully sprinkled a stripe across the threshold of the bedroom, then deposited a small pile in each of the four corners.

"Bridget," Monsignor murmured without looking at her. She jumped. "Yes?"

"Do you remember what we discussed?"

Bridget's mind fumbled for the Rules he had impressed upon her over the last few weeks. The warnings, the training, the explanation of things she wasn't entirely sure existed. "I guess."

"You guess?" Monsignor turned to her slowly and repeated the question. "Do you remember what we discussed?"

Bridget's mouth went dry. "Yes, Monsignor."

"Excellent." Monsignor raised the crucifix to his chest and stepped toward the figure on the bed. "Let us begin."

THREE

ONSIGNOR'S DEEP VOICE FILLED THE room. "I command you, unclean spirit, along with all your minions, to relinquish your hold on this servant of God."

Mrs. Long's eyes flew open, and black, empty pupils scanned the room, resting briefly on each of its occupants before returning to Monsignor. They were not the soft eyes of an old lady, but hooded, like a snake appraising its prey. Her cracked lips contorted into a grin, and she arched her spine.

"As a most humble minister of the Savior," Monsignor continued, "I command you to obey me."

"Liar," Mrs. Long hissed, her head weaving back and forth. "Liar, liar, liar."

Monsignor narrowed his eyes. "He has given me the power to tread upon the serpents and the scorpions, and to break the dominion of your master everywhere."

Mrs. Long sat up and bounced on the bed. "Liar, liar, liar. He's a liar, liar. Thinks he can lie to us, but we know all about the lies, the lies."

Monsignor stood firm on the other side of the bed. He didn't look scared at all, unlike Bridget, whose stomach writhed and churned with the remnants of her lunch. He gave Bridget a slight nod to reassure her that everything was under control.

The woman pointed a long, crooked finger at him. "We know you. We know you."

"Depart, tempter," Monsignor said. "Depart, seducer, full of lies and cunning."

"We know what you are."

"I am a servant of the Lord."

"Liar, liar."

Monsignor Renault placed his right hand on Mrs. Long's forehead and held the cross directly before her eyes. "Behold the cross of the Lord. Begone, you hostile powers."

Mrs. Long curled her lip and hissed again.

The hair on Bridget's arms stood straight up. Last time there'd been no face to the evil. This was something for Monsignor and Father Santos to tackle. Not her.

"Begone, slave. Return to your master."

With a roar, Mrs. Long's hands shot forward, striking

Monsignor Renault full in the chest. He flew across the room and crashed into the far wall, where he hung suspended, pinned to the wall by an unseen force. Bridget screamed.

"You know nothing of the Master," Mrs. Long said. Or at least Bridget thought it was Mrs. Long. The voice had changed. It was deep, raspy, undeniably male, and it was accompanied by a growl that originated from deep within her body.

Suddenly Monsignor was released, and he crumpled to the floor. Bridget started toward him, but he held up a hand. "I am fine, Bridget. This corrupted spirit and its master cannot harm me."

Mrs. Long ran a parched tongue over her lips. "He has power you only wish to achieve."

Monsignor pushed himself to his feet; he did not look the least bit shaken. "Father Santos, the oil."

The younger priest retrieved the holy sacramentals and removed the stopper from a decanter. Monsignor dipped his thumb in the consecrated oil and made the sign of the cross over Mrs. Long's throat.

"No, no, no, no, no," Mrs. Long cried, writhing on the bed.

"In nomine Patris, et Filii, et Spiritus Sancti," Monsignor bellowed. He moved his thumb to her forehead. *"In nomine Patris. Et Filii."*

"Traitor!" the woman shrieked.

"Et Spiritus Sancti."

"Noooo—" Her scream choked off as Monsignor pressed

his thumb into Mrs. Long's forehead. The old woman's whole abdomen rose off the bed, and then she flopped back onto the mattress, eyes closed, body limp.

All was still in the room.

Awesome.

"Is that it?" Bridget asked hopefully.

Monsignor shushed her. "What is Rule Number Four?"

"Do not let your guard down," Bridget repeated diligently. Out of the corner of her eye, she caught Father Santos scribbling more notes.

What was he doing? Focus, Bridge. She had to keep her mind on the afflicted person, just as Monsignor had taught her. She had to remember the Rules.

Rule Number One: Do not show fear.

Rule Number Two: Do not show pity.

Rule Number Three: Do not engage.

Rule Number Four: Do not let your guard down.

Rule Number Five: They lie.

She closed her eyes and repeated them over and over again like a mantra. Her breath stilled; the pounding of her heart lessened.

That's when she heard it. Not voices this time, but grunts. Animal grunts. Like a herd of pigs running loose inside the house.

Without thinking, she placed her hand on the wall to steady herself.

The noises exploded in her head. A deafening roar, a mix

of snarls and screams at once human and beastlike. She could feel the wall throbbing beneath her palm as if the beings inside were going to burst through the plaster.

"Bridget, are you all right?" Monsignor's voice cracked.

Her breaths came shallow and ragged as the noises pounded through her ears. "Yeah, I—I think so."

"What is it?" Father Santos asked. "What do you hear?"

"I . . ." Crap, what *didn't* she hear? She closed her eyes. "Grunts."

"Grunts?"

"Animal grunts. And screams. They're . . . I don't think they're human."

"They are gathering their power," Monsignor said. He tightened his grip on the cross. "Be ready."

Bridget had no clue what "ready" meant. Ready for what?

Her answer came immediately. The foundations of the house rocked. Bridget lost her balance and staggered a few steps until Monsignor's strong hand gripped her arm, steadying her. Mrs. Long grunted and snarled, then Bridget watched in horror as the old lady's body went rigid—feet flexed, arms plastered to her sides—and began to rise off the bed.

"Jesus!" Bridget said, forgetting who was in the room.

"Concentrate," Monsignor said. "Do not let them distract you."

Yeah, sure. Concentrate with an old lady levitating a foot away? Easy.

The screams and growls filled the room. Father Santos

glanced around, searching for the source of the noises, and made the sign of the cross. "Dear God."

"Concentrate," Monsignor repeated. "They cannot harm you."

As if in response, a barking laugh echoed through the room, followed by a rush of air coming from the wall behind the bed. Photographs and perfume bottles blew off the dresser and crashed to the floor in a mess of broken glass and twisted metal. The candle flames flickered and shuddered, fighting desperately to remain lit. It was a torrential wind, so forceful it sucked the air right out of Bridget's lungs.

Crucifix raised before him, Monsignor leaned into the wind. "I command you—"

"Fool!" It was the voice of many—a dozen voices of different pitch and timbre, all shouting at once—and it came from the walls, the ceiling, the floorboards. *"We fear you not. The Master is strong."*

Father Santos snatched the holy water off the table and joined Monsignor beside the body. He sprinkled Mrs. Long up and down while Monsignor placed the corner of his stole on her neck.

"Begone, you hostile powers!" Monsignor roared.

"The lion of Judah's tribe has conquered," Father Santos replied.

"Heed my words!"

"And let my cry be heard by you."

The wind surged as both priests struggled to stay on their

feet. A print of a Madonna with Child was ripped off its hook and flew across the room, splintering the cheap wooden frame against the wall. The drapes around the window splayed out and rippled away from the pane.

Monsignor shielded his face from the wind with a raised arm. "Every unclean spirit, every infernal power, every legion. We cast you *out*!"

The house lurched again, and all three of them tumbled to the floor. Bridget was thrown against the door, scattering the salt Father Santos had sprinkled across the threshold. The instant the line was broken, the door flew open and the wind rushed in as if it had been waiting outside for the opportunity. It swirled around Mrs. Long like a tornado. The room spun, a chaotic whirlpool that stung Bridget's eyes and lashed at her face. She ducked her head, barely avoiding a crystal vase that had been caught in the roiling air. It smashed into the wall above her head and showered her with shards of glass.

She squinted against the tumult and saw Monsignor vault to his feet and throw his body against the door.

"Bridget, the salt!"

It took her a half second before she realized what he meant. She grabbed the bowl of salt from the table as Monsignor struggled to close the door. With a heavy groan, he lurched forward and Bridget heard the door click. As quickly as she could, she spread a line of salt across the threshold.

The room lay still.

She and Monsignor looked at each other and smiled. One crisis down.

Their celebration was cut short by a deep, grating cackle. It was an ugly sound: a dozen voices laughing at once but without joy, without lightness.

Evil. That was the best way to describe it.

Bridget slowly turned and found Mrs. Long sitting upright on the bed once more, eyes open, a black goo oozing from her mouth down her chin, staining the white cotton of her nightgown. The entities were inside her once again. Bridget could feel them.

Monsignor Renault nodded to Bridget. "It's time for you to try."

Try. Try to talk to them? Try and make them leave the old lady's body? Try to lure them out? She didn't know what to do.

"Bridget," Monsignor said. "Remember the Rules."

The Rules. Right. Do not show fear. Do not show pity. No pity. This wasn't a person anymore. What had Monsignor called them? Demoniacs.

The demoniac laughed again. "You send a child, a little girl, to the sacrifice? Priest, your savior forsakes you."

"You can do this, Bridget," Monsignor said calmly. "Find out its name and you will control it. Do not listen to anything else."

Find out its name. Okay. That should be simple enough. "What's your name?"

"What's your name?" the demoniac mocked. It clapped

its hands and grinned at her. Five minutes into her first official exorcism, and Bridget already felt like a complete failure. What was she supposed to do next?

Father Santos cleared his throat. "Um, maybe . . . maybe try touching her."

Bridget glanced at him. He had the notebook in his hand again. "Touching her?"

"Like you did with the wall."

"Father Santos," Monsignor snapped. "Let her do it herself. She needs to learn."

Right. The voices were transmitted through her touch. With a tentative hand, Bridget reached out and grabbed a skinny, blue-veined arm.

Mrs. Long shrieked at Bridget's touch. It was a cry of rage and pain. "No, no, no, no, no. Impossible!"

The demoniac was scared of *her*?

"Get away!" it screamed. "Get away from us!"

"What is your name?" Bridget repeated.

But Bridget didn't need the demons to speak their names. They formed in her head as if she were reading their minds.

"Ramison," she said.

The demoniac twisted its arm, trying to free itself. "No! Why are you here? How are you here?"

"How can she know that?" Father Santos asked. "That's not possible."

Monsignor held up his hand. "Silence!"

Bridget closed her eyes. "Tulock." Another voice was

screaming out. "And Bemerot. They are servants of—"

"Do not tell him!" the demoniac howled. "He already knows, he already knows."

"Rule Number Five," Monsignor said. "They lie."

There was a fourth presence; it felt weaker than the other three, and yet the others begged it for help. This demon was different. She couldn't feel it, couldn't hear the sound of its voice. It wasn't in the room, but somehow Bridget could sense the demon's rage, its hatred toward Mrs. Long and the priests. Toward her, though, she sensed confusion.

Bridget smiled. It was intimidated by her. Cool.

The riff of one of Bridget's favorite songs ripped through the room. Her cell phone. Dammit. She'd forgotten to tell her mom she'd be late.

The demons took advantage of her momentary lack of concentration. "Traitor!" they shrieked. "You will be punished for your treachery."

"Was that your cell phone?" Father Santos asked.

"Sorry." Her mom was going to be so pissed off.

"Concentrate," Monsignor said gently.

"Oh, right." Time to cut the crap. She needed to finish the banishment and get home before her mom grounded her for the rest of her natural life.

"Who do you serve?" Bridget called out, doing her best impression of Monsignor Renault's stern, commanding voice. She heard Father Santos snicker. "Tell me, or I swear to God I'll . . ."

Her voice trailed off. A tingling sensation emanated from Bridget's fingertips, spreading out through her body in waves. Her lips buzzed, and as she ran her tongue over them, they tasted tangy, metallic. It was like she was drawing energy from the demoniac, sucking it into her body. Totally freaky, and yet it felt . . .

. . . good?

Focus, Bridge! Ignore the weird new feeling and concentrate on Mrs. Long. She tried to think back to her training sessions with Monsignor. He had told her what the demons feared most. Banishment.

"Tell me," she said. "Or I'll banish you?"

The demoniac froze.

"That's right," Bridget said with a smile. She felt a surge of confidence, like she actually knew what she was doing. "I'll banish you."

"Good girl," Monsignor said under his breath.

The demoniac threw back its head and howled. "Noooooooooooooooooooooo!"

Her cell phone went off again, but this time Bridget didn't flinch. She had the upper hand; time to finish it. She grabbed the woman by the sides of her wrinkly old face. "Tell me who you serve!"

The tingling intensified, centering in the pit of her stomach. She loved the way the electricity snapped and crackled over her skin.

"Amaymon," the woman croaked. "We serve Amaymon."

Monsignor Renault and Father Santos gasped.

"Amaymon knows you," Mrs. Long said. "Amaymon knows what you are."

A hot wave rushed through Bridget, starting with her fingers and washing over her body. It moved down from her stomach, lower, and ignited a spark deep within her.

The demon was turning her on.

That was so messed up.

Bridget tossed Mrs. Long away from her and stumbled backward.

"What—what's wrong, Bridget?" Father Santos asked. "Are you okay?"

Her knees felt wobbly, but as soon as she let go of Mrs. Long, the strange sensations stopped. "Yeah. Yeah, I'm fine."

"You must finish the banishment," Monsignor said. His voice was flat, emotionless, but when she glanced his way, his eyes were pleading. "I know it's difficult, but, Bridget, you must continue."

"No, no, no," Mrs. Long muttered. "No, no, no, no, no."

Bridget swallowed hard. She didn't want to touch Mrs. Long again, but at the same time, there'd been a brief flash of something powerful, something she'd enjoyed. What kind of a weirdo did that make her?

"Go ahead," Monsignor prompted. Patience was not his forte.

You can do this, Bridge. Just get it over with.

Bridget reached for Mrs. Long. As soon as her fingers

touched the old woman's wrinkling flesh, the powerful energy came rushing back into her body tenfold.

"All right, servants of Amaymon," she said. Her voice was low and breathy. Not like her voice anymore. It was too confident, too calm to be her voice. "Any last words?"

Mrs. Long's eyes grew wide, as if the beings inside her knew what was coming next. Her mouth opened in protest, then stopped as she began to convulse violently. The convulsions stopped as suddenly as they had begun, and when Mrs. Long opened her mouth, a single voice whispered, "Beware."

The warning totally caught Bridget off guard. "Huh?"

The old lady clutched at Bridget's hands, pulling her close. "Do not trust them," she said so only Bridget could hear.

"What?" Bridget asked.

"Do not trust any of them."

"Who?"

But Bridget never got her answer. Mrs. Long shuddered and fell limp in her hands.

FOUR

BRIDGET'S HANDS TREMBLED. WAS THE old lady dead? Had she killed her? Was Murder in the Act of Exorcism a capital crime?

She let Mrs. Long's body fall against the pillows.

Father Santos dashed to Mrs. Long's side. He felt for a pulse both at her neck and wrist, then pried her eyes open one at a time.

"She's all right," he said. "Sleeping."

Bridget let out a long breath.

"I think," he continued, looking around, "I think they're gone."

"They are." Bridget knew as soon as the words left her mouth that they were true. The chill had lifted from the room, the oppressive atmosphere evaporated.

Monsignor nodded in agreement. "Well done, Bridget."

"They left willingly," Father Santos piped in. "Before you could banish them."

Left willingly? That didn't sound right. "Why?"

Father Santos took the holy water and sprinkled it over the salt he'd laid down earlier. "By leaving of their own free will, they are able to come back. If you'd banished them, they'd be relegated to Hell for eternity."

"We do not know that," Monsignor snapped. "The idea of demons acting under their own free will is ridiculous. I suggest you keep your theories to yourself, Father Santos."

"Y-y-yes, Monsignor."

"You mustn't assume anything with these beings. It will be your undoing." Monsignor replaced his tools in a small leather bag and opened the door. "Come now, Bridget. You should be getting home. Your family will be worried about you."

That was it? She'd scared off a couple of Satan's demons, and now she was just supposed to go home and do her algebra homework?

"But—" she started.

Monsignor rested a hand on her shoulder and bent his face down close to hers, dropping his voice. "I know this is all very strange, but we will talk tomorrow at the regular time, all right?" He shot a backward glance at Father Santos. "We cannot speak freely right now. Do you understand?"

So Monsignor didn't want to talk in front of the new guy. Interesting. She'd noticed the tension between them, but something in Monsignor's tone, something in the hawkish warning in his eyes, hinted at a more serious reason for his silence.

"Do you understand?" Monsignor repeated in a whisper.

Bridget nodded. She'd just have to wait until tomorrow for her bazillion and one questions to be answered.

"Excellent." Monsignor gave her shoulder a friendly squeeze, then ushered her into the hallway. "We'll talk soon, Bridget," he said in his normal, booming voice.

"Okay." She tried to sound natural in front of Father Santos. "Thanks, Monsignor." Bridget walked down the hall, grabbed her backpack, and was gone.

The fog still hung thick in the air, but it was no longer ominous, no longer a threat. Just the normal, depressing San Francisco fog that rolled into the Sunset District 350 out of 365 days a year. Every postcard of San Francisco showed brightly painted cable cars racing up and down sunbathed hills, the picturesque San Francisco Bay dotted with sailboats glistening in the distance. But that wasn't Bridget's San Francisco. Her side of the city—the ocean side—was an organized grid of row houses blanketed in the ever-present fog. It was damp. It was monotonous.

And apparently, it was plagued with demons.

First the Ferguson twins' bedroom, now Mrs. Long. Even

the Vatican thought it was odd if they'd sent Father Santos out to check on things. And here she was with this strange new power, smack dab in the middle of it.

Had it really happened? Had she walked into a stranger's house, confronted a possessed old lady, and forced a pack of demons out of her? Yes, yes, and yes. And what was more, the power she'd felt was . . . exhilarating.

Flip side, she was now a bona fide freak. Not just in the normal "high school outcast" kind of way; more in the "institutionalized for life" kind of way. This wasn't exactly something she could share with people, and last time she checked there was no Most Likely to Banish Demons category in the St. Michael's yearbook. Hell, she couldn't even talk to her mom about it. Telling your mom you're a teenage exorcist wasn't exactly the same as "Hey, Mom, I'm flunking Latin." No, this was something Bridget had to keep on the down low until she could figure out how to get rid of it.

The 28 Muni bus rushed past her as she waited to cross Nineteenth Avenue, but Bridget hardly noticed. Get rid of it. She closed her eyes and tried to recall the tingling on her skin, the crackling of energy pulsating through her in heavy, intoxicating waves. It was warm, almost comforting the way it enveloped her, and she'd only realized after it was gone how much she'd enjoyed the sensation.

She needed to feel it again.

Stop it. No, you don't. It was weird. Weird and wrong. You're not supposed to be jazzed about being able to commune with demons, dumbass. Besides, what if someone finds out? Bad enough she still had half the school whispering about her dad's murder. If this got out, it would be a catastrophe.

A new thought gripped her. What if it was all somehow connected? Could it really be just a coincidence that her new "talent" popped up at the same time the city was overrun with possessions? What if one was causing the other?

Holy crap, that was so not good. She needed to get rid of her power. Go back to being normal, or as normal as she got. Maybe Monsignor could help her? He wanted what was best for her. He could light a candle, give her a blessing or—

"Bridget Yueling Liu."

Bridget snapped out of her reverie. She was right in front of her house on Ulloa Street. She hardly remembered the walk.

"Do you have any idea what time it is?"

Bridget's mom occupied the empty space of the doorway, one hand on the open door, one on her hip. The only time her mom used her full name was when she was in severe, "grounded till you're eighteen" trouble.

"Dammit," Bridget said under her breath.

"Well, do you?"

Actually she didn't. "I just lost track of—"

"Why do I pay for you to have a cell phone? So you can ignore my calls?"

Bridget tramped up the stairs like a death row prisoner on

her last march down the cell block. "I didn't hear it."

"Oh, really?" Her mom barely stepped aside so Bridget could squeeze past. "And why was that? Because you were at the *library*?"

Bridget didn't like the inflection on the word "library." She hung her jacket on the coat rack and stole a glance at her mom. Lips pursed, eyebrows raised in expectation. Her frizzy red hair looked frizzier and redder than usual, and her blue eyes, so like Bridget's own, were combative. Bridget knew this look. This was her mom's patented "I'm about to trap you in a lie" face.

"What did you do, spy on me?"

"It's called being a mother. And for your information, I did not *spy* on you. Matthew Quinn dropped Sammy off and—"

"What?"

"Yes, and he said he stopped by the library to offer you a ride home, but you weren't there."

Bridget pressed her lips together. Matt Quinn. "Oh, so you had *him* spy on me, huh? Perfect."

"I did nothing of the sort. He simply said you weren't at the library and weren't answering your phone. He was worried."

Worried. Matt was always worried about her. It was equal parts sweet and annoying as hell. "You know, it's bad enough his dad's patrol car shows up here every other day to 'check in' on us, now you've got Matt following me around after school? I'm surprised you didn't call his daddy and have half the SFPD searching the neighborhood."

"Bridget and Matt, sitting in a tree. K-I-S-S-I-N-G."

Bridget's eight-year-old brother, Sammy, stood in the kitchen, kicking the door rhythmically with his foot.

"Thanks, Sammy," Bridget said with a limp smile. "That's helpful."

"Sam," her mom said, steering her youngest child back into the kitchen by his shoulders, "finish your chicken."

"Annie?" a male voice called from the kitchen. "Is everything all right?"

Her mom flushed scarlet. "Fine, Hugh. It's just Bridget."

Bridget's stomach clenched. Hugh Darlington? Again? This was the second time in a week. There was no way her mom could pretend he was still "just a friend" checking up on them. Her mom was dating less than a year after her husband's death. It was seriously messed up.

"What's he doing here?" Bridget whispered.

Her mom dropped her voice. "Hugh wanted to borrow one of your father's books, so I invited him for dinner."

"One of Dad's books? Really?" Was her mom that stupid? "You really bought that line?"

"Watch your tone, young lady."

"Hi, Bridget. It's good to see you again." Hugh Darlington's tall, slender frame loomed behind her mom. From the perfectly coiffed blond hair that looked like he had a hairdresser on staff for daily blowouts, to the meticulous manscaping of eyebrows, Hugh Darlington always looked like he just walked off the set of a makeover show.

Bridget wrinkled her nose. She'd known him almost her whole life: Along with Sergeant Quinn, Hugh Darlington had been one of her dad's best and oldest friends. But somehow Bridget had never warmed up to Mr. Darlington, even after her dad went to work for him—something she'd always felt vaguely guilty about.

Especially after her dad's murder. Mr. Darlington had gone out of his way to make sure the Lius were well looked after. But as the weeks and months passed, and Mr. Darlington started to spend more and more time with her mom, Bridget couldn't shake her resentment.

And then there was his daughter, Alexa. Alexa had been in Bridget's class since kindergarten and had spent most of that time making Bridget's life a living hell. It had taken a few years for Bridget to catch on. Outwardly, Alexa was all smiles and laughs, but then the rumors started to spread. At first they were stupid: *Bridget Liu eats her boogers. Bridget Liu doesn't wash her hands.* They got nastier as Bridget got older. *She's too Chinese. She's not Chinese enough. Her dad's not her real dad. Her mom's a slut.*

Then one day Bridget lost it and punched Alexa in her perfect little face on the playground. Alexa had screamed bloody murder and carried on like Bridget had lit her face on fire. As if. But from then on, Bridget was labeled a "troublemaker" and had "anger management issues."

And almost no friends.

Her dad's murder may have made Bridget the center of gossip at St. Michael's Prep for the past year, but thanks to Alexa Darlington, Bridget had been a social pariah for a long, long time.

Maybe Bridget hadn't given Mr. Darlington a chance, but the idea of her mom replacing her dad with Hugh Darlington made her physically ill. And the thought of having Alexa as a stepsister made her downright homicidal.

Her mom shot Bridget a look that said, "You're being rude," and Bridget forced a smile. "Hi, Mr. Darlington."

"Are you enjoying St. Michael's this year as much as my Alexa is?"

Considering that Alexa had screwed half the junior and senior boys since they'd started at St. Michael's last year, Bridget sincerely doubted it. "Yeah, it's, um, great."

Her mom pursed her lips, obviously displeased with her daughter's lack of enthusiasm in answering their dinner guest, then turned to Mr. Darlington with a smile. "Could you wait for me in the kitchen?"

"Actually, Annie, do you mind if I have a look in David's office now? For the book I mentioned?"

"Yes, yes, of course, Hugh."

He gave her mom a wink and slipped down the stairs to the garage where Bridget's dad had kept his home office.

Ugh. The last thing Bridget needed to see today was the two of them flirting. She rolled her eyes and headed down the hall to her bedroom, but she didn't even make it halfway before her mom came after her.

"I'm not finished with you."

"Of course not," Bridget muttered. "I couldn't be that lucky."

"What was that?"

Bridget threw open her bedroom door and flopped down on her bed face-first. She was too tired, mentally and physically, to care about this argument. "What do you want me to say, Mom?"

Her mom was close behind her. "Where were you today?"

Bridget pulled a pillow over her head. *You don't want to know*, she thought.

"Answer me, Bridget."

Should she tell her mom the truth? After all they'd been through in the past year, would her mom be able to handle it?

Doubtful.

Bridget tossed the pillow aside. "I was at Hector's, working on my history paper."

"You told me you finished that paper last night."

"I did. He didn't."

"Why don't you have any girlfriends?" her mom asked. "Why is it always Peter and Hector and that Brad?"

Bridget snorted. "They're about as close to girlfriends as I'm gonna get."

"That's not funny."

"It wasn't meant to be."

A gentle tapping interrupted them, and Bridget's bedroom door creaked open far enough for Sammy to stick his head through.

"Is Bridget in trouble?" he asked. Typical Sammy—go right for the jugular.

Her mom sighed. "No, Sammy. We're just having a disagreement."

"That was a loud dis-a-gree-ment," Sammy said, hanging on each syllable.

"I know, but it's nothing, Sammy. Go watch your cartoons."

Sammy didn't budge. "Bridget?"

Bridget winced. It was a sore spot in the family that Sammy always looked to Bridget first. "It's okay, Sammy."

"You're not mad?"

"I'm not mad."

"You're not sad?"

"Not at all," Bridget lied. She smiled and gave him a wink. "Now go watch your *Justice League*, okay? I'll join you in a minute."

Sammy grinned, exposing a row of crooked teeth, then slowly withdrew his head. As soon as the latch clicked into place, Bridget heard her mom exhale slowly, then felt the weight on her mattress shift as her mom sat down on the edge of her bed. "Bridget, I was worried."

"Would you have been worried if Matt Quinn hadn't called you?"

"If you didn't answer the phone when I called? Yes. I need a bit more responsibility from you, especially now that . . ."

Her voice trailed off, and Bridget was suddenly sorry that she'd been the cause of more stress in her mom's life.

"I'm sorry, Mom."

"Sorry isn't good enough."

Bridget sighed. It never was.

"And sorry or not, you're grounded."

"Fine." She had figured as much.

Her mom stood. "You'll come straight home after school from now on."

"For how long?" Two weeks? Three weeks? She could handle it.

"Forever."

Bridget snorted. "Funny."

"I'm serious. Until you can prove you're responsible enough with your time after school, you'll be spending it here. Starting tomorrow."

"That's not fair!"

Bridget's mom glanced over her shoulder as she walked out of the room. "Life isn't fair, Bridget. Get used to it."

FIVE

HECTOR THREW HIS HALF-EATEN snack bar on the table in disgust. "So you're grounded again?"

Bridget rolled her eyes. "Don't sound so dramatic."

"What about the Franz Ferdinand concert Saturday night? I already bought the tickets."

Bridget choked on her soda. "Dammit. I forgot."

"Forgot what?" Brad Hennessy slid his heavily laden lunch tray into place next to Hector's and straddled the bench with his long, skinny legs. "History paper?"

"Done," Bridget said, dabbing drops of Diet 7Up off her sweater with a napkin.

Hector eyed the stack of sandwiches on Brad's tray. "What are you, eating for two?"

"No, dude," Brad said, two-fisting turkey sandwiches. "Baseball conditioning started last week."

"Oh." Hector's eyes moved from Brad's sandwiches to his own diet snack bar, rice cakes, and celery sticks. "I hate you right now. I hope you know that."

"Don't worry about the history paper." An elbow jostled Bridget's right arm as Peter stepped over the bench and took a seat next to her. He was wearing the ridiculous red Windbreaker again over his uniform shirt, and the cowlicks in his thick, black hair made him look like he'd just rubbed a balloon over his head. As Peter slid his tray forward, it tipped Bridget's soda can, spilling the remainder of its contents all over the cafeteria table.

"Peter!" Bridget and Hector said in unison.

"Sorry! Sorry!" Peter squeaked, frantically searching for a napkin.

Brad calmly stretched his lanky arm across the table and mopped up the pooling liquid with a napkin while Bridget tried to pretend that the whole cafeteria wasn't staring at them.

"Oh my God, Bridge," Peter said, turning crimson to match his Windbreaker. "I'm so, so sorry. Can I get you another one?"

"It's fine, Peter," she said, pushing her tray away. "I'm not thirsty."

He dropped his eyes to his tray. "Sorry."

She caught Hector making kissy faces at her from across

the table and gave him a swift kick with her boot.

"Ow!" Hector grunted. "What was that for?"

"So what did you forget, Liu?" Brad said, diving into sandwich number three. She'd given up trying to get him to use her first name; can't teach an old jock new tricks.

"Franz Ferdinand concert," Hector answered for her. "She's grounded."

"Again?" Brad shook his head in disbelief.

It was like they thought she was some sort of delinquent. "Don't you guys ever get grounded?"

A look of horror spread across Peter's face. The mere concept of being grounded by Mr. and Mrs. Kim was paramount to public flogging. Brad shook his head, mouth full of turkey and canned cranberry sauce, but Hector was smiling.

Bridget knew exactly what he was thinking. "Getting sent to Catholic school because your parents think it'll beat the gay out of you doesn't count as getting grounded."

"Please," Hector said. "That's the ultimate grounding."

Peter cleared his throat. "Um, Bridge, why did you get grounded this time?"

"Duh," Hector said. "She had a hot date with Matt Quinn."

Peter's eyes grew wide. "But you said . . ." His lower lip trembled.

"Dude, no, she didn't," Brad interrupted. "I was at Riordan Prep for a scrimmage yesterday and Quinn was practicing with the varsity team."

Hector's jaw dropped. "YOU STOOD HIM UP?"

Bridget threw up her hands. "There was no date!"

Hector ignored her and pointed at Brad. "Maybe he was trying to throw you off by *pretending* to practice."

Brad smiled and played along. "She could have been in his truck the whole time . . ."

"In his truck?" Poor Peter. Now they were just torturing him.

". . . taking a break from sucking face!" Hector finished. "That's totally what happened."

Brad and Hector fist bumped while Bridget shook her head. "You guys need therapy, you know that?"

She felt Peter stiffen. "Bridget, were you really with Matt—"

"Hey, Kim," Brad said, tactfully changing the subject. "What did you mean about the history paper?"

Bridget could have kissed him.

"Huh?" Peter asked.

"You said not to worry about the history paper."

Peter grudgingly turned his attention from the Archbishop Riordan Prep varsity baseball team and Matt Quinn. "Right. Mr. Singh took a leave of absence. We have a new history teacher."

"What?" Bridget said. "From Monday to Tuesday he needs a sabbatical?"

"Yanno," Hector said. "You'd think he'd have the decency

not to assign that hot mess of a paper if he was going to bail on us."

Brad shrugged. "Oh, well. At least I don't have to explain why I'm not turning it in." He gathered up his tray and nodded at Peter. "We still on for tutoring tonight?"

"Yeah," Peter said. "But if it's after practice, you'll have to come to my house. My mom won't drive in the dark."

Hector bit his lip so hard trying to suppress a laugh, he practically drew blood.

"No, worries, dude." Brad stood up. "For help with algebra, I'll take it."

"I'm sure Peter can help you pass algebra this time," Hector said. Bridget caught a faint tinge of pink in his cheeks. Hector might have been able to hide his crush on Brad from everyone else on the planet, but not from her.

"Let's hope," Brad said with a grin. "Catch you guys later."

"Bye, Brad," Hector said with a wistful sigh as Brad's tall, lanky form sauntered away and disappeared into the lunchroom crowd.

"Why does he hang out with us again?" Bridget asked.

"Other than the fact that Peter keeps him from flunking math?"

"Yeah."

"Probably your hag factor."

Oh, yes, Hector's favorite topic of conversation: Brad's closeted gayness. Of course Hector was the only one who actually thought Brad was gay. Not that it stopped him.

"It's the only reason I can think of to explain hottie Brad hanging out with us social lepers," Hector continued.

"Hottie Brad?" Bridget teased. "I thought you told me he wasn't your type?"

Hector flushed. "Yeah. He's, um, totally not."

Bridget realized she'd hit a little close to home. Time to change the subject.

"So who's the gaysian of the week?"

Hector glanced up at her from beneath his heavy fringe of eyelashes and grinned. "Ah, there was a gorgeous barista at the Grind this weekend. I think I'm in love."

"You're always in love," Peter said.

Hector smirked. "So are you."

Bridget picked up her bag and tray before the subject of Matt Quinn could be resurrected. "Come on, Hector. Don't want to be late for the new history teacher."

All Bridget could think about as she and Hector threaded their way through the hallway was Matt Quinn.

How many times had she told him she didn't need a guardian angel? But try as she might, she just couldn't shake her old childhood playmate. Sometimes she wasn't even sure that she wanted to. It didn't help that he was so kind to Sammy. Bridget was grateful for anything Matt could do to help keep her little brother from getting picked on at school. The thought of Matt teaching Sammy to play baseball made her smile.

Then he'd do something annoying, like get her grounded, and she was over him.

Matt's dad had been the referring officer in the Undermeyer case that landed in her dad's office. Sergeant Quinn thought Undermeyer, the St. Michael's facilities manager and a suspect in a breaking-and-entering case at the parish, was a certifiable whack job, and he'd asked Dr. Liu to give a professional opinion. Two of them had entered her dad's office at Hugh Darlington's Fallen Angels Clinic that afternoon—Dr. Liu and Milton Undermeyer—but only one walked back out. There were no witnesses, and the audiotape Dr. Liu had been running during the session had mysteriously clicked off just five minutes in.

Sergeant Quinn threw himself into the murder investigation. There was no weapon, and no suspect other than the straitjacketed Undermeyer, who managed to get off with an insanity plea. Since that day, Sergeant Quinn had elected and inaugurated himself protector-in-chief of the Liu family.

Bridget was pretty sure that her mom's hotness didn't hurt.

Matt had followed in Sergeant Daddy's footsteps. She remembered him at the funeral, his light hazel eyes fixed on her from the other side of her father's open grave. She hadn't seen him since they were kids, but his eyes held all the sadness Bridget felt, as if he was suffering her anguish right along with her.

Bridget had felt sick during the whole funeral, but there at the grave site, she thought she was going to pass out. Matt had walked around the grave and stood beside her, quiet and calm. He reached out and took her hand, and in that moment Bridget wanted to cry, to let all the pain and anger pour out while Matt held her.

Then Sergeant Quinn had come up beside them. Her mom collapsed into his arms and wept uncontrollably while Sergeant Quinn stood strong and sturdy, stroking her mom's hair. Bridget saw in Sergeant Quinn the same thing she saw in Hugh Darlington: They wanted to replace her dad.

After that she had hardened herself against Matt. Sure they'd played together when they were kids, but they'd lost touch after Matt went to live with his mom. And now that he was back, he was different. Matt Quinn, star pitcher for Riordan Prep's varsity baseball team, was Mr. Popularity. Mr. Perfect. They had nothing in common.

No, that wasn't quite true. She and Matt did have one thing in common: Alexa. Matt had dated her most of last year. And Bridget hated her with the intensity of a thousand burning suns.

"Are you even listening to me?"

"Huh?"

Hector darted in front of her and stopped dead, hands folded across his chest. "Did you hear anything I said?"

Bridget took a wild guess. "Asian barista, should you ask him out or not?"

Hector's eyes narrowed as he fell back into step beside her. "Lucky guess."

"I was totally listening."

"Sure you were. Thinking about Matt Quinn?"

Bridget tried to control the hot flush spreading across her face. Damn half-Irish blood. "Don't be stupid."

Hector opened the door to room sixty-six. "Whatever."

Bridget brushed past him and stomped to her desk, dropping her bag on the floor. The new teacher wasn't there yet, but the room was all atwitter about Mr. Singh and his replacement. Bridget didn't care. She felt tired and old and completely disinterested in the goings-on at St. Michael's Prep. She folded her hands across her desk and sank her forehead on top of them.

"G-good afternoon, class," a familiar voice said from the front of the room. "I'm your new history teacher."

Bridget's head shot up, and she found herself staring at Father Santos.

It wasn't until the bell rang that Bridget realized a whole hour had slipped by.

"B-Bridget," Father Santos called from the whiteboard as students filed out of the room. "Um, Bridget Liu, can . . . can I see you for a moment?"

"What the hell did you do?" Hector whispered. "Fall asleep?"

"I'll catch up with you after school," she said, waving

Hector off. She didn't want any witnesses.

"Bridget," Father Santos began once the room was empty. "I was wondering if I might have a chat with you after school today."

"Sorry, can't," she said, relieved to have an excuse. "I'm grounded."

"Oh." He paused for a moment and slipped a little-smoky-link finger between his collar and his neck. "Um, well, can you meet me in my office tomorrow morning before class? Around seven thirty? It's—it's important."

It always was with these priests.

SIX

EVERY TUESDAY BRIDGET HAD SIXTH period free. Her stint as the second accompanist for the St. Michael's show choir satisfied her elective credit, and since the choir spent Tuesdays working on audition solos, Bridget was free to (a) sit in the back of the church and work on her homework, or (b) sit in the library and work on her homework.

Exciting options. How about . . . neither?

Bridget rapped softly on the door of Monsignor Renault's office in the rectory and was answered with an immediate "Come in."

Bridget smiled to herself. He'd been waiting for her.

She slipped into the office to find Monsignor scribbling away at his ornately carved desk. "Hello, Bridget." He glanced up and gave her a quick nod. "I'm glad Mr. Vincent could spare you today."

"Me too." Any excuse to get out of choir practice.

With the tip of his pen he pointed for her to sit, then continued with his writing. Bridget eased into a brown leather chair and patiently waited for him to finish.

Monsignor's office was close and cramped, yet over the last few weeks Bridget had come to find it comforting. The dark green carpeting, the heavy reddish brown wood of his desk and bookcases, the Pietà paperweight, the small Tiffany lamp of purple, green, and orange stained glass. Even the heavy scent—a mix of furniture oil and candle wax—marked a place of refuge, a place where someone understood exactly what she was going through. Monsignor was the only one who did.

Her eyes drifted to the portraits of the three archangels that adorned the walls. Traditional Catholic-y stuff, just what you'd expect to find in the office of a semiretired priest, but they were like familiar friends now, observing Bridget's weekly sessions with her mentor. Raphael, beautiful and cherubic in flowing burgundy robes and matching wings, guiding the young Tobias through the desert. Gabriel the messenger, almost girlish with his strawberry blond locks, bringing the news of the Annunciation to the Virgin Mary. Michael with his sword, his foot on the neck of a cartoonish serpent as he vanquished Satan before the Fall. They seemed to be watching over her, the only witnesses to her weekly meetings with

Monsignor, shepherding her into a strange, new world.

Monsignor finished up, carefully closed the leather-bound journal in which he'd been writing, and slipped it into his desk drawer. Bridget heard a lock click into place, then Monsignor tucked the key into the pocket of his cassock and turned his attention to her.

"Shall we discuss yesterday's banishment?"

He always used that word—"banishment"—instead of exorcism. Bridget kind of liked it. Banishment sounded less icky, less Linda Blair's spinning head and green puke.

"Please."

"You did very well with your first possession."

"Thanks."

"You remembered the Rules, you followed your instincts." He paused. "I was impressed."

Bridget beamed. It was high praise coming from Monsignor. It was why she'd been working so hard, struggling through the Rules and the training, hoping she would remember what to do when the time came. She wanted to leap over the desk and hug him.

"But you still need to work on your focus before we can tackle a more complicated possession."

Focus. She hated that word. "Oh."

"These are powerful entities, Bridget. They are not just evil spirits, things of fairy tales and nightmares. Demons cannot manifest of their own accord. They must be summoned into our world through a curse or a satanic ritual, and such summoning only increases their power, as you witnessed yesterday. If you are to succeed in this career, you must learn focus."

Whoa, what did he say? "Career? I don't think I—"

"That said," Monsignor barreled on, ignoring her protest, "you possess a remarkable talent. I've never met anyone with your unique abilities."

"You haven't?" Bridget hadn't thought to ask if there were others like her. She'd just sort of assumed that there were. Was she really all alone in this?

Monsignor shook his head. "I have never seen anyone lay hands on a demoniac with the results you achieved yesterday."

That wasn't particularly comforting. "Why?" she asked. "Why me?"

"That is difficult to say. Obviously, you've been granted a gift."

Banishing demons was a gift? Some gift. Like getting underwear from Santa.

"Your talents could serve a great many people. Think of all the Mrs. Longs you could help. It would have been many sessions, many painful exorcisms before I would have been able to free her."

All her fears about her new power bubbled to the surface. "What if it's not a gift? What if . . ." Bridget bit her lip. "What if I'm somehow *causing* the possessions?"

Monsignor looked confused. "I don't follow."

"You said it yourself: Father Santos was sent here because the Vatican is concerned about the rise of demonic activity in the area."

"Yes. And?"

"Well, I've been babysitting for the Ferguson twins since I was thirteen, and nothing weird or demonic ever happened before. Then suddenly I can do . . . things." Bridget swallowed hard. She was almost afraid to say it. "This power I have—what if I summoned the demons into their house with it?"

"Have you been performing satanic rituals without my knowledge?" Monsignor asked.

"Um . . . no."

He smiled. "Then I don't think you have anything to worry about. Besides, I've never heard Mrs. Long mention you before. Do you have a relationship with her I don't know about?"

Bridget shook her head.

"See? You're not causing these events. And both the Fergusons and Mrs. Long are quite lucky that you discovered your new talents when you did."

Bridget tried to smile. *They* were lucky. Not *her.*

"As for Father Santos, I think the Vatican is overreacting. Throughout the years I've witnessed dramatic fluctuations in demonic possessions. It's a natural occurrence."

"Oh. Good."

"So don't worry."

Monsignor smiled. He looked so pleased, so proud of her. And yet . . .

"What if I don't want this power?" she blurted out. "What if I just want to go back to being what I was before?"

Monsignor cocked his head to the side. "And what, exactly, was that?"

Bridget sighed. "Normal."

"Normal? Oh, Bridget." Monsignor fell silent. He pressed his lips together until their pink line disappeared into a threaded white blur. He seemed at a loss. "I thought you were enjoying our sessions," he said at last. "Learning the Rules. I thought you enjoyed the banishment."

Bridget slumped back in her chair. That was the problem. She *did* enjoy the banishment. Too much. The sensations, the power—what did that make her? Some kind of weirdo that got off on talking to demons? There were cults for that kind of crazy.

"I guess," she muttered.

Monsignor stood up and moved to the corner of his desk nearest her. "Bridget, I don't want to force you to do anything you're not comfortable with, but I feel a sense of responsibility toward you. If I hadn't cancelled my appointment with your father to consult on the Undermeyer case that day, I would have been there, might have prevented the tragedy." He reached out and placed a firm hand on her shoulder. A frown tugged at the corners of his mouth, but his gray eyes were soft. "I hold myself personally responsible."

So many apologies. She knew Monsignor really meant it too. He'd been so patient with her over the last few weeks, trying to help her understand what she was, what she could do. But there were only so many times she could say "It's not your fault" before the words lost their meaning.

Bridget sighed. "It's not your fault."

"Yes." Monsignor patted her shoulder. "But I intend to keep a watchful eye on you, guide you in this new world you've discovered. Together, we can be a force against the Enemy."

Woo hoo.

Monsignor bent his face down close to hers. "I believe in you, Bridget. I believe you can do wondrous things." Monsignor returned to his chair. "Now, let us discuss Mrs. Long."

Bridget dropped her eyes to her lap. "Okay."

"There were three presences, correct?"

Bridget paused. Three demons that had told her their names, but right at the end, the last one who gave her a warning had seemed . . . different? New? How could she tell that it wasn't part of the others? These things didn't exactly wear name tags. And yet . . .

"Bridget?"

"Sorry," she said with a start. "Yeah, three demons."

"And they said they were servants of Amaymon?"

The names were fuzzy. "That sounds right."

Monsignor leaned forward over his desk. "And you

sensed this demon, you felt Amaymon's presence?"

"It was there but, um, not." Bridget looked up at the ceiling, trying to recall her encounter with the demon. "Like it was watching what was happening from the end of a long tunnel or something. But it sensed me, knew I was there. It seemed really surprised. They all did. I don't get it."

Monsignor twirled his silver ring around the third finger of his left hand. "Perhaps they could sense your power."

"I don't know. It seemed like they remembered me somehow."

"Be careful, Bridget," Monsignor said. "You cannot always trust your instinct with these entities. What is Rule Number Five?"

"They lie."

"Exactly. It is their primary objective to sow doubt and strife among their adversaries. You must remember that."

"Okay." Monsignor was probably right. After all, he'd been doing exorcisms for, like, a hundred years or something.

Monsignor leaned back in his chair. "One more thing. I want to talk to you about Father Santos."

"Yeah?"

"By now you've discovered that he is the new history teacher at St. Michael's."

"Yeah."

"And I'm guessing he has approached you? Asked to meet with you?"

Bridget nodded. "Yeah!" How did he know?

Monsignor slapped his hand against the desk. "Exactly as I suspected. When?"

"Tomorrow morning. Monsignor Renault, who *is* he?"

"Father Santos? A Vatican pawn. On the surface, they are concerned that I'm not capable of dealing with the increased number of possessions. Though to be frank, I believe word of you and your abilities has reached Rome."

"Rome?" Bridget was horrified. "They sent someone to spy on me?"

"In a word, yes." Monsignor ran a hand over his mostly bald head. "Bridget, I would like you to keep your meeting with Father Santos."

Meeting the new Vatican spy was the last thing she wanted to do. "Um . . ."

"And tell me everything he says. Can you do that?"

"Do I have to?"

"It could prove helpful."

Ugh. "Okay."

"Excellent. Just be careful."

Be careful? Of Father Santos? "I'll try."

Bridget glanced at the clock on the wall. Five minutes until the end of the period. She sat motionless in her chair, waiting for Monsignor to say something else, but he just stared at her, through her, while she fidgeted with the zipper on her sweater. There was one more question she wanted to ask, but she was afraid of the answer.

"Monsignor?" she said at last.

"Hmm?" He seemed like he'd forgotten she was there.

"Do you think it will just go away? This new ability of mine?"

"Go away? Why would it do that?"

Because I want it to? "I don't know."

"No, Bridget. It will not just go away. This is who you are now. You need to accept that."

The final bell rang, and Bridget forced herself to stand up. Her legs felt weak. She'd been hoping for a different answer.

"Next week then, shall we?" Monsignor said as she shuffled toward the door. "Unless something comes up?"

"Sure." Unless I throw myself in front of a Muni bus before then.

"Have a blessed day, Bridget."

Yeah. Blessed.

SEVEN

BRIDGET PLANTED HER FOREHEAD AGAINST her locker as she slowly dialed the combination. She felt deflated. First Father Santos showed up as her new history teacher, then Monsignor basically told her that she'd be stuck hearing demons for the rest of her life. Hell, getting grounded was like the best part of her week.

She banged her head rhythmically. *Bam, bam, bam.* Yeah, it was all perfectly wonderful, her life at the moment. What else could happen? What else could possibly go wrong?

"What was that all about?"

Bridget snapped her head up to find Hector leaning against the next locker, arms folded across his chest, eyebrows raised. She'd made it to Latin class just in time and had darted out as soon as the bell rang, avoiding conversation with Hector and Peter. She just wasn't in the mood.

"Um . . ." Had he seen her coming out of Monsignor's office? She wasn't sure how she could explain that one away.

"Are you in trouble with the new history teacher already? Is that why you ditched me after class?" Hector continued.

Bridget let out a breath. Oh, *that*. She opened her locker door casually. "It's nothing."

"Nothing? You looked like you'd seen a ghost when he asked to talk to you."

"Don't be stupid." Bridget positioned her locker door so Hector couldn't see her face. Not a ghost, silly. He just wants to know how I can exorcise demons.

"Well?" Hector prodded.

"Your eyeliner is smudged," she lied, hoping to change the subject.

"No, it's not." He waited for a moment, just like her mom did when she was expecting a lie but hoping for the truth. "Why are you acting all weird?"

Bridget rolled her eyes. "I'm not acting weird." I am weird.

"Then what did he want?"

Bridget peered at Hector through the slats in her locker door. "You don't want to know."

He grabbed the door and swung it open so he could see her face. "Try me."

Bridget pursed her lips, weighing her options. On the one

hand, she could just lie to him. He'd know, of course, but he'd also let it go. Hector avoided confrontation like it was a herpes flare-up. On the other hand, if there was anyone she *should* tell, anyone who would believe her, be on her side no matter what, it would be her best friend.

She took a deep breath. "He wants to talk to me before school tomorrow," she said, dropping her voice. "About this thing I can do." Wow, did she really just explain her freaky new exorcism skills as "this thing I can do"? Like she was going to tie a cherry stem into a knot with her tongue or show off a double-jointed thumb?

Hector turned his head to the side. "What *thing*?"

Hope you can handle this, Hector. "I can, like, kinda hear things. Voices that aren't there."

It wasn't until the words came out of her mouth that she realized how utterly and completely lame they sounded.

Hector shook his head; the gelled spikes of his hair stood firm and immovable. "Fine, Ghost Whisperer, don't tell me. You walking by the library, or do you have to go straight home?"

Bridget blinked. He thought she was being a smartass. Not that she blamed him. It was probably for the best.

She hauled out the last of her books and swung her backpack over one shoulder. "C'mon, I'll walk you as far as the park."

Hector and Bridget dodged the last stragglers in the hallways and headed out into the dull, gray afternoon. Heavy fog had rolled in—again—blotting out the rays of the sun. It didn't help her mood.

"I love this weather," Hector cooed, zipping up his black Misfits hoodie.

"Blech. Hate it."

Peter was sitting on the front steps; he popped to his feet as soon as he saw them. "Hey, Bridge," he said, jogging up. "Can I walk you home?"

Hector camouflaged a laugh by pretending to sneeze.

Shocking. Peter Kim waiting to escort her home. Prince Not-So-Charming was always at the ready. Was this really all she had to look forward to in her dating life? Bridget sighed. "Yeah, whatever."

A swift elbow to the ribs from Hector knocked her off balance. "Look," he said, nodding toward a group of girls swarming in front of a red pickup truck across the street. "Isn't that your boyfriend?"

"Boyfriend?" Peter squeaked.

Matt saw her before Bridget had a chance to retreat back inside. "Bridget!" he yelled. His *Teen Beat* fan club turned their heads in unison.

"Dammit," she said under her breath.

"But I thought you said he wasn't your—"

"Shut up, Peter!" Hector and Bridget said.

Matt crossed the street, his admirers following in his wake. He still wore his Archbishop Riordan Prep uniform—black polo shirt and khaki pants—with his purple-and-gold varsity jacket zipped halfway up. His floppy sandy blond hair blew across his forehead in the afternoon breeze.

"Hey," he said, walking right up to her. "I want to talk to you."

Bridget rolled her eyes. "Can't. I have to get home." She started to walk away. "I'm grounded, or haven't you heard?"

Matt followed. "Bridge, I want to explain."

Bridget whirled on him with every intention of letting rip a string of profanities that would make Chris Rock blush, but his eyes—those hazel eyes she remembered from her dad's funeral—caught her off guard. So full of concern. They riveted her to the pavement and froze the snarky words in her throat.

It only lasted a moment.

"Matt!" A head of perfectly curled auburn hair emerged from the gaggle of girls behind him. The others parted for her like the Red Sea with Moses. She stood before Bridget, hands on her hips, emerald green eyes fixed on Matt's face. Bridget hated those eyes. She swore Alexa Darlington wore colored contacts to make her eyes that green. And Bridget was pretty sure that wasn't the nose she'd punched back in sixth grade. Alexa was definitely vain enough for a nose job. And rich enough.

"Matt, weren't you going to take me for a ride in your new truck?" It was not so much a question, as a command. "I don't have all day."

She must get up at five in the morning to get her hair

rolled perfectly. Who does that?

Matt dropped his eyes and shifted toward his ex-girlfriend. "Alexa, I . . ." He ran a hand through his hair. "I don't remember offering."

Alexa swiveled her hips in a wholly unnatural way and snaked toward him, placing a manicured hand on Matt's chest. "Sure you did. We were talking about the past . . . and the future and you mentioned your truck—"

Bridget had heard enough. The idea that Matt might be thinking about getting back together with Alexa made her stomach churn. "Later," she said, turning on her heel.

Matt's hand gripped her arm. "Bridget, wait."

She froze but didn't turn around. She didn't want to see Alexa standing there behind him. "What? What is it? Don't you have better things to do?"

"I'm sorry, Bridge. I didn't mean to get you in trouble."

Alexa emitted a noise that sounded startlingly like a dog's growl. With a sigh, Bridget turned around. She didn't get the territorial display. It wasn't exactly a secret that Alexa had dumped Matt before the start of the school year, effectively making him the most sought-after high school bachelor in town. So why Alexa cared about Bridget was beyond her understanding. Wasn't she dating some college douchebag anyway?

The green eyes narrowed on Bridget. "What are you staring at?"

Could she be any more of a *Mean Girls* stereotype?

Unbelievable. Bridget rolled her eyes. "A harpy, apparently."

"A what?"

"Seriously, crack a book once in awhile." Bridget shook free of Matt's grip and stalked down the street before Alexa could get in one of her standby "You're ugly" or "You're lame" comebacks.

"Jesus, Bridge," Hector panted, trotting up alongside. "Why not just commit hari-kari on the front lawn? That was social suicide back there."

Like she had a social life. "Don't care."

"Bridget, slow down." Peter, with his overloaded back-pack plus the four textbooks cradled in his arms, struggled after them.

"Maybe if you weren't taking twenty classes so you can graduate early, you could actually keep up."

Peter's eyes welled up. Ugh, why was everyone such a pain in the ass today?

A car horn made her jump. Matt's truck pulled alongside, pacing her.

"Bridge," Matt said through the open window. "Can I give you a ride home?"

"Nope."

"Please?" He smiled, exposing perfect rows of sparkling white teeth.

Bridget stopped and Matt slammed on the brakes. "Why don't you drive Alexa home? You guys looked pretty cute and cuddly back there."

Matt flinched. "There's nothing going on between Alexa and me."

Bridget shrugged, trying to look casual. "Don't care."

"Liar," Hector said under his breath.

"Come on, let me give you a ride home." Matt leaned over to the passenger window. "Please?"

Bridget thought of Alexa and set her jaw. "What part of 'no' do you not understand?"

"Bridge," Hector whispered from behind her. "Let the man drive you home. Maybe he'll give me a lift too."

"Walking to the library," she said out of the corner of her mouth, "is the only exercise you get."

"I have a bad back."

"You have a lazy ass."

Hector rested his chin on her shoulder. "Do it for me, lady."

"Well?" Matt asked.

Yep, this clinched it. The day was made of fail.

"Fine. But my friends need a ride to the library."

Matt's face lit up, then clouded again immediately as Peter went straight to the passenger door, yanked it open, and started to climb in.

"Dude," Matt said, giving Peter a frat-boy-in-training staredown. "No."

Hector grabbed his friend by the backpack and dragged Peter to the truck bed. "This way, lover boy. Haven't you always wanted to ride in the back of a truck?"

Bridget stared out the window and tried to ignore Matt's fidgeting while they waited for the light to change. In thirty seconds he had adjusted his rearview mirror, turned on the radio, checked his cell phone, readjusted the mirror, and changed the radio station. Twice. Now Coldplay was blasting through the subwoofers. Really? Coldplay? Holy crap, this was her own personal nightmare: trapped in a pickup truck with Matt Quinn and Coldplay. Add some spiders and a porcelain doll or two, and she'd be curled up on the floor of the cab in the fetal position.

"I'm sorry, okay?"

She refused to look at him. "There are a lot of things I can forgive, but bad taste in music isn't one of them."

"Coldplay?"

Bridget wrinkled her nose.

"Will you forgive me if I change the station?"

"I'll try."

Matt switched to the local indie station as the light changed. "Perfect. So you forgive me for getting you grounded. Awesome."

Bridget swore under her breath. She had walked right into that one.

"You know," he said, turning onto Sunset Boulevard. "You know, if you weren't so much trouble, I wouldn't worry about you."

"If I weren't so much trouble?"

"Yeah."

"And how would you know anything about my life?"

Matt shrugged.

"Because unless you've been talking to the two dorks in the back of your truck, I'm guessing you don't know jack about it."

"I've heard about where you go on the weekends. Clubs and stuff."

Clubs and stuff? She and Hector hit the occasional concert south of Market or in Berkeley, but it was hardly "stuff"—and not on her mom's radar. What the hell was he talking about?

Bridget shifted her hips to face him and immediately noticed the flush spreading up his neck. Suddenly she knew exactly who had been spreading the rumors about her. Bridget dug her fingernails into the faux leather seat. That bitch.

"For your information, the only words Alexa Darlington's spoken to me since the sixth grade are the ones you witnessed this afternoon, and as far as her or you knowing anything about my life, let's just say you're both clueless, okay?"

"But that's what I mean."

"Right. I'm sure you'd be perfectly happy if I spent my time beerbonging it at the football team's latest blowout. Or perhaps you'd prefer it if I just partied with Kappa Sig like your ex-girlfriend? You'd be comfortable with that, right? Because that's the world you know? As long as I'm letting some college sophomore ply me with Keystone, it's all good."

Matt's tanned face flushed a deep shade of scarlet, and Bridget knew she'd hit close to home. But she didn't care. She was tired of everyone sticking their noses in her business. She'd done fine for years without Matt Quinn in her life, and just because her dad was dead didn't mean she needed any help from Mr. Perfect Grades, Perfect Body, Starting Pitcher, no matter how cute he looked when he smiled.

How cute he looked when he smiled? Whoa, did she really just think that?

A movement from the flatbed caught her eye, and she saw Peter's face plastered against the cab's window, his quick breaths fogging up the glass. Peter always seemed to be watching her these days. It was getting a little creepy.

Matt slammed on the brakes, and Bridget snickered as Hector rolled into Peter. Matt rapped his knuckles against the cab window. "Library."

The shock absorbers bounced as two bodies scrambled over the tailgate—first Hector's fumbling, then Peter's slow, careful tread. Peter's face was at her window instantly, trying to ask a question through the glass, but Matt didn't wait; he peeled away from the curb with an ear-shattering tire squeal.

As they drove in silence, Bridget stole a glance at Matt. His mouth was clamped tight, the muscles of his jawline bulging out from below his sculpted cheek, and his eyebrows were scrunched low. He ran his hand through his sandy blond hair, and the longish strands stood up straight for a split second before flopping down over his ear.

"I worked with your brother yesterday," Matt said, switching gears.

Bridget softened. Sammy was her Achilles heel.

Her brother was hardly an athlete and cared about sports about as much as Bridget cared about Latin class. But Sammy got teased mercilessly about being horrible at sports, and Bridget had comforted the devastated eight-year-old on more than one occasion. Enter Matt Quinn to the rescue.

"He's getting a lot better," Matt continued. "You know, I think once he gets over his fear of the ball, he could be pretty good."

"Yeah?" Bridget said, despite herself.

"Totally." Matt turned to her with a grin. "His timing is pretty impressive."

Bridget couldn't help smiling. Anything that might help Sammy get along better at school made her happy. "Thank you."

Matt slowed down for the stop sign. "No problem. I like Sammy."

Bridget laughed. "You and I might be the only two people on the planet who do."

They smiled at each other, and Bridget couldn't suppress the warmth spreading over her. There was something so familiar about Matt. Homey. Comfortable. Something that reminded her of a happier time in her life.

A honk from the car behind them snapped Matt's attention back to the road, and he accelerated through the intersection. As they drove in silence, the radio DJ bumped out of a commercial break into the next song, and Coldplay blared through the speakers once more.

Without thinking, Bridget reached to change the station. At the same time, Matt's hand shot forward and his fingers grazed the top of hers. Bridget was surprised how soft his fingers felt; she'd assumed a pitcher would have rough, calloused hands. Matt let his fingertips linger, and even though Bridget's first instinct was to pull back, she didn't.

What the hell was wrong with her? Bridget shook herself and whipped her hand away from the radio. Matt's hand fell to his lap.

"Why are you so difficult?" he blurted out.

"Me?"

"Yeah. You know, I've tried really hard to be your friend since I moved back to San Francisco. But you're so prickly all the time. Always looking for a fight."

"I am not!"

"See?"

Bridget threw up her hands. "What?"

That look of concern crept back into Matt's face. "You weren't like that when we were kids. You were more fun. You used to smile. And laugh."

His words struck a chord. At one point in time there'd been a happy, laughing Bridget Liu, content to wear her school uniform and play peekaboo with her baby brother, or hide-and-seek with the son of her dad's best friend. But somewhere along the line, that Bridget had been lost, masked by a hard, sarcastic shell complete with steel-toed boots and a don't-mess-with-me scowl.

Bridget sighed. She was so tired. Tired of fighting with everyone. Tired of having no one to confide in. Hector wasn't exactly a confidant, and Peter would only get two seconds into a serious conversation about her feelings before the words "I love you" came spilling out of his mouth. Her dad had been her best friend. Now that he was gone and her mom had a revolving door of boyfriends, it was like she had no one to talk to.

She glanced sidelong at her chauffeur. Maybe Matt understood? They'd been close once, a long time ago, and in a way, he'd also lost a parent. Although in his case it was to a dot-com millionaire who moved his mom to Dubai. Still, they must have been close since he'd lived with her for all those years after his parents divorced. When she left, it must have felt like she'd been ripped from his life too. Just like her dad.

The truck slowed as Matt pulled into her driveway.

"Are you going to Winter Formal?"

His question caught her so off guard, she burst out laughing.

"What's so funny?"

"I don't do dances."

"Why not?"

"Well, the lameness factor for starters."

"You ever been?"

"Hell, no."

"Then you can't judge."

Bridget shook her head. "Dude, are you applying for my mom's job?"

Matt ignored the jab. "You should go."

"To Winter Formal?"

"Yeah. You should go with me."

Did he just invite himself to her school dance? "No way."

"Are you afraid?"

"Of a dance? You're kidding, right?"

Matt looked right at her. There was a hint of a smile he couldn't suppress. "Then prove me wrong."

Bridget wasn't a complete moron. She knew when she was being played. Matt had found her sore spot: her inability to refuse a challenge.

"Fine," she said, meeting his steady gaze. "Hope you don't mind a date in combat boots."

Matt smiled, flashing that lethal combination of perfect teeth and hazel eyes. "I wouldn't have it any other way."

EIGHT

BRIDGET DRAGGED HER BACKPACK THROUGH the front door and dropped it on the spiral carpet, then sank to the floor herself and leaned back, clicking the door into place. She reached up and bolted it. The way her day was going, it was only a matter of time before someone else showed up at the house: Monsignor, Father Santos, Matt Quinn. Nope, she was locking them all out.

Bridget closed her eyes and sucked in slow, deep breaths. The house was so quiet. A-freaking-men.

Maybe being grounded wouldn't be so bad. It gave her an excuse to spend her time at home doing whatever she wanted. Yeah, this could be awesome. Like a break from everything. No chiding about Matt Quinn, no training with Monsignor, no voices in the walls . . .

The silence was broken by the patter of feet—paws, to be exact—trotting across the hardwood floor in the dining room.

Bridget's eyes flew open and swept the room. She thought for sure she'd see an animal of some sort disappearing down the hall. But there was nothing. Just a gentle *swoosh swoosh* from the swinging door that led into the kitchen, as if something small had just pushed its way through.

Bridget scrambled to her feet and crept to the kitchen door. Had the neighbor's cat gotten in somehow? Bridget cringed. She hated Mr. Moppet, the Shaughnessys' long-haired Burmese. Or maybe it was a rat? Bridget wasn't sure which was worse. She slowly pushed the door open and heard the sound of scurrying feet again, this time more of a clacking sound as the animal padded across the cushiony linoleum flooring. It had to be Mr. Moppet, who was always wandering into open garage doors in the neighborhood. But how had he gotten inside the house? And more importantly, how was Bridget going to get him out?

Bridget peeked around the door, hoping not to scare the stupid cat, but there was nothing there. No cat, no rat. Nothing.

What the hell?

She tiptoed into the kitchen. "Mr. Moppet," she said, trying to sound nonthreatening. "Here, kitty, kitty. Here, stupid kitty who hates my freaking guts."

Silence. She checked the pantry, but the door was firmly latched. She checked under the table, behind the recycling bins, even under the sink. No Mr. Moppet. No nothing.

Had she imagined the footsteps? Possible, but then why had the door been swinging back and forth like something had gone through?

A sickening thought hit her. She'd heard animal noises in the walls at Mrs. Long's house, grunting pigs and stomping hooves. Could this be the same thing?

See? She was right. Demonic activity *was* following her around.

Okay. She could handle this. She was a trained exorcist, after all. Bridget stilled herself and took a deep breath, trying to sense the room, just as Monsignor had taught her. Twice before in the presence of a demon, she'd been able to feel it in the air—the heaviness, the oppression, and that strange dizzy sensation of the walls stretching and skewing. Not this time. Her kitchen felt exactly like her kitchen.

There was one other test, one other way to know if there was an entity in her house. She reached a tentative hand toward the wall. If there was something there, she'd definitely hear it.

BRRRRRRRRING!

Bridget let out a muffled yelp as the telephone broke the silence. Out of breath, her heart racing, she picked up the receiver.

"Hello?" she panted.

"Bridget?" her mom asked.

"Yeah."

"Are you okay? You sound like you just ran home from school."

"I'm fine," she lied. "I was in the bathroom."

"Oh." Her mom sounded less than convinced. "Well, I left you a note on the refrigerator. Do you see it?"

Bridget scanned the fridge door and saw a list in her mom's neat, schoolteacher print, held up by a San Francisco Giants magnet. "Yeah."

"It's your list of chores for today. You're grounded, not on vacation."

Perfect.

"And the last one is most important. Put the roast in at four forty exactly. I'm taking Sammy to math club, so we'll be home after six and I want dinner ready to go, okay?"

Pat pat pat pat pat. Bridget spun around, searching for the source of the footsteps. Still nothing. Was she losing her mind?

"Bridget, did you hear me?"

"Roast. Oven. Got it."

"Okay. See you soon."

Bridget held the receiver to her ear even as the dial tone buzzed. Her eyes were frozen on the kitchen door, swinging madly back and forth. From beneath the sleeve of her sweater, Bridget felt the charm on her bracelet give one violent lurch.

Bridget stumbled backward, holding her arm as far away from her as she could. Animal footsteps, maybe, but she sure as hell didn't imagine *that*.

Bridget dialed the number for the St. Michael's rectory from memory.

"St. Michael's," the little old church lady who volunteered in the kitchen croaked forth. "How can I—"

"Monsignor Renault, please," Bridget blurted out.

"I'm sorry," she drawled. Was she talking this slowly specifically to piss Bridget off? "Monsignor is not to be disturbed this afternoon."

She always said that. And he always took her call. "It's Bridget Liu."

As expected, the church lady grumbled something incoherent and put Bridget's call on hold. A peppy rendition of "City of God" blared as hold music just long enough for Bridget to start to sing along with the chorus. Catholic brainwashing at its best.

"Bridget?" Monsignor said. "Is everything okay?"

"Um . . ." How exactly did she bring this up? There's a ghost in my house? My jewelry's moving by itself? She was going to sound like a lunatic.

"Is something wrong?"

"Kind of." Monsignor was silent, waiting for her to explain. "I think there's something in the house."

"What kind of something?"

"I don't know. It sounds like a cat, but I can't see

anything. Just footsteps and doors swinging like something went through them."

"Did you calm yourself? Take a breath and try to sense the room?"

Bridget smiled. "Yeah, just like you taught me."

"And the house feels normal?"

"Totally."

"Interesting." Monsignor paused. She could almost see him twirling that massive silver ring around his finger as he drifted into thought. "You don't hear anything? No voices?"

"Nothing."

"Very interesting."

For him, maybe. Bridget was freaking the hell out.

"I suggest," Monsignor said after a pause, "that you try to ignore it. If it *is* an entity, giving it attention will only serve to strengthen it. Try and go about your afternoon as normally as possible."

Normal for a girl who can banish demons. Awesome. "That's it?"

"I'm afraid so."

"Oh."

"But call me if anything changes or the contact escalates, okay?"

Bridget's eyes crept toward the kitchen door that still hadn't stopped swinging back and forth. "Okay."

"Excellent. Good luck."

Bridget's mom hunched over her plate, trying to get some leverage as she cut a piece of pot roast with a flimsy table knife. Eventually she was able to tear a chunk of the overcooked meat free and get it into her mouth. Bridget couldn't help but smile as she furtively watched her mom chew the meat for a full minute before she could swallow.

"Excellent job with the pot roast, Bridget," Mrs. Liu said with a big, kind grin. "Really, really great."

Her mom was a horrible liar. "Thanks."

"Isn't it great, Sammy?"

Sammy stuck out his tongue and made a slobbery motorboat sound.

"Sammy!" her mom snapped.

Bridget touched her tongue to the tip of her nose—one of Sammy's favorite tricks—and sent him into a paroxysm of laughter, spouting bits of overcooked pot roast all over the table.

"Samuel Michael," her mom said, wiping up bits of food with a napkin. "That is not something we do at the dinner table. How old are you?"

"Square root of sixty-four," Sammy said, pushing the meat, potatoes, and carrots around on his plate in concentric circles.

"Yes, Sammy." Her mom sighed. "Now finish your pot roast."

"Gross," he said.

Bridget couldn't help but agree. She'd meant to take the

roast out after exactly an hour and twenty minutes, just like the note said, but she'd gotten distracted. She had been at the piano, working her way through a Chopin prelude and trying to ignore whatever it was haunting her house, just like Monsignor said to do, when she heard the same scampering paws across the dining-room floor. She continued to ignore it, but every few minutes she'd hear that damn cat again, each time with the same quick trot, scooting down the hall toward her room.

The fifth time, she got up and closed every single door in the house: her mom's room, her room, Sammy's room, the bathroom, and the door that led downstairs to the garage. Closed tight, locking the cat in one of them. It wasn't supernatural; it was just some poor, dumb animal trapped in the house. Mr. Moppet could just stay put until her mom came home.

As soon as she sat down at the piano, she heard the footsteps again, pattering down the hall toward her room.

She bolted from her chair and ran down the hall only to freeze in her tracks halfway. The door to her room was wide open, and from inside she heard a muffled sound.

MEEEEEEOW.

That's when the panic set in. All her training, all Monsignor's words, went right out the window. Bridget attacked her room, desperate to find the source of the noise. She pulled her bed apart, threw her closet open and dug through piles of shoes and old school uniforms. She hauled her desk away from the wall and even yanked the grate off the heating duct, just in case the cat had gotten inside.

Still no Mr. Moppet, and the only result of her mad search had been a disgustingly overdone pot roast.

"I think Mr. Moppet got in the house again," Bridget said. That cat loved her mom and Sammy, so maybe they'd have an easier time finding the thing.

Her mom glared. "That's not funny, Bridget. You're going to upset Sammy."

Had everyone gone insane? "Why would Mr. Moppet in the house upset Sammy? He loves that stupid cat."

"He's not stupid!" Sammy screamed. He shot up from the table, face red as a well-done lobster, and launched his fork right at Bridget's head. She ducked just in time; the fork barely missed.

"Sammy?" she said. Tears streamed down his cheeks.

"He's not!" Sammy continued. "He's not! He's not!"

Without another word, Sammy dashed from the kitchen. Bridget could hear his sobs as he ran down the hall to his room. Dammit.

"Mom, what's going on?"

Her mom sighed. "I forgot. You weren't here yesterday when Mrs. Shaughnessy stopped by."

A lump rose in Bridget's throat as she realized what her mom was getting at. Oh, please, oh, please, oh, please don't say the stupid cat is dead.

"They had to put Mr. Moppet down."

Shit.

Bridget stared at the ceiling in the darkness of her bedroom. Mr. Moppet was dead. Could she have imagined it all? She wasn't insane; she'd heard an animal. She'd seen the door moving. And she was pretty sure there was no demonic presence in the house. Yet a phantom cat and her self-propelled bracelet charm hinted otherwise. Was there another explanation?

A light tapping at her door made her jump.

"Bridge?" Sammy poked his head into her room. She could see his mess of dark hair in the soft glow of moonlight. "Are you asleep?"

"Nope," she said.

"Good." She heard his bare feet pad across the floor, and with a sigh, she scooted over and held up the comforter for her little brother.

"What's wrong?" she asked to the back of Sammy's head.

"Nightmare."

"Elephants again?" Sammy had been terrified of elephants ever since he'd seen the psychedelic dream sequence in *Dumbo*.

"No."

Phew. Getting him back to sleep after one of his elephant nightmares was almost impossible. "Was it about school?"

She felt Sammy shake his head back and forth, then he pulled the comforter up to his ears and his body shuddered with a sob.

"Sammy?" He rarely cried, or showed much emotion at all. What was wrong with him tonight?

"Mr. . . . ," he began, then his voice choked off.

Ugh. The damn cat. "Mr. Moppet? You had a nightmare about Mr. Moppet?"

"Mmhmm." Sammy scootched toward her until his frigid feet just touched her knees. Bridget froze. Sammy *hated* being touched.

"I'm sorry, Sammy," she said. She laid a hand on his back, but he flinched away. "I didn't know. I wouldn't have said anything if I'd known he was . . ." Dead? Stone-cold dead and *haunting our freaking house*?

"Had a dream," Sammy said. His voice cracked. "Had a dream about Mr. Moppet."

Bridget stiffened. "A dream? Was he . . ." Flail, how did she bring it up? "Was he in the house?"

"In the house," Sammy repeated. "Running in the house."

Yeah, not a dream, kiddo.

"Running up and down the hall," Sammy continued. "I could hear him."

Bridget wasn't sure if she was happy someone else could hear the phantom cat or sad that Sammy was plagued with this nightmare. "It was just a dream." Bridget hoped her voice sounded convincing. "Mr. Moppet was sick, and now he's . . . he's in Heaven. He's happy there."

Sammy glanced back at her. "Cats don't go to Heaven," he said. "Sister Monica said so."

Stupid freaking nuns. "Well, he's in a better place, okay?"

"Promise?"

"I promise. Now try and get some sleep, Sammy."

He snuggled down into the pillow next to her. "Okay."

So Sammy could hear the footsteps too. Ugh.

Good news, Bridget wasn't crazy, although having Sammy as her sanity touchstone wasn't exactly the most comforting thing in the world. Bad news, she couldn't pretend the footsteps weren't really there. Something was in the house. Something she couldn't see.

She rolled over and stared at her alarm clock, the deep red glow of numbers telling her that she'd be lucky to get five hours of sleep before she had to get up for her meeting with Father Santos.

Blech. She was looking forward to that meeting about as much as a trip to the dentist. There was something weird about Father Santos. He wasn't like Monsignor Renault, whose very presence demanded respect. Father Santos was more like a doddering professor than an apprentice exorcist, and she hated the idea that he was watching her all the time, writing down every detail of her existence.

Sammy's breathing slowed, the deep rhythm indicating that he'd fallen asleep. That made one of them. Bridget yawned, and her eyes flitted closed. She'd worry about it all tomorrow: the mystery cat, Father Santos, the Winter Formal. Tomorrow, tomorrow, tomorrow.

She was just drifting off when her breath caught in her

throat. The charm on her bracelet tugged at her wrist, standing up of its own accord and pointing toward her closet door. Before she could even turn to look at it, she heard a noise. From inside her closet came a distinct scratching.

Claws against wood.

NINE

FATHER SANTOS WAS WRITING IN his little spiral note-book when Bridget arrived at his office. Classic.

She had knocked—twice—and hadn't gotten an answer, so she decided to peek inside and see if the new History teacher had ditched her. No such luck.

Bridget didn't see the priest at first. Even though the office was small and narrow, like a long broom closet, Father Santos had lined the room, ceiling to floor, with heavy wooden bookcases.

Empty bookcases. The intended occupants were half unpacked from an endless number of uniform cardboard boxes plastered with preprinted white and black labels that read PROPRIETÀ DELLA BIBLIOTECA APOSTOLICA VATICANA, followed by a number written with a fat-tipped Sharpie marker in a smooth, unhurried hand. The boxes were everywhere. Some had been ripped open, their contents searched through and stacked on the floor. Most hadn't been touched.

The desk was pressed into a corner, jutting out at a diagonal like an afterthought. The only other furnishings were two chairs: the one at which the priest sat and another in front of the nearest bookcase.

And Father Santos.

He sat forward in his chair so the tips of his toes just reached the ground. His writing pace was frantic, as if he was afraid his thoughts would disappear if he didn't get them on the page fast enough. She wondered if he was writing about her, about what had happened with Mrs. Long. She wondered if his account of what she and Monsignor had been doing would end up on some cardinal's desk back in the Vatican, or worse, the pope's. Could she get excommunicated for practicing unlicensed exorcisms? Her mom would kill her.

Father Santos paused, scratched his upper lip with the cap of the pen, and scrunched his eyes, trying to capture some fleeting detail before it escaped. She thought maybe he'd notice her then, but with a quick intake of breath, he dove back into his writing. He reminded her of Sammy when he was fixated on a problem, his little genius mind utterly incapable of multitasking.

Bridget cleared her throat. "Father Santos?"

She might as well have shot a gun off in the office. Father

Santos let out a shriek like a twelve-year-old girl at a Jonas Brothers concert and knocked a large pile of books off the corner of his desk.

"Bridget!"

Why was he surprised to see her? "Yeah."

"What time is it?"

Bridget glanced around the office, quickly registering the lack of clock or window. "Seven thirty. Like you said."

"Really?" He pushed back his chair and fumbled around with the pile of books on the floor. "Already?"

Sheesh, how long had he been there? "Yeah."

"Come in, come in," he said, wiping his brow with a dirty handkerchief. "Sorry about the mess."

With a heavy sigh, she closed the door behind her, edged her way past piles of ancient tomes, and dragged the empty chair to the desk. Bridget clutched her backpack to her chest and stared at a spot on the wall.

Father Santos cleared his throat several times while he shoved his notebook into a drawer. "So," he said at last. "I suppose you know why I asked you here?"

What did that mean? "I take it you don't want to talk to me about my history grade."

A wry half smile sprung from the side of his mouth. "That was a joke, right?"

"Yeah." Was he for real?

"I thought so," he said with a wink.

Lame.

Father Santos took a breath, then exhaled on a *whoosh* and blurted, "I, uh, want to discuss what happened with Mrs. Long."

Bridget had to fight to keep from rolling her eyes. Yeah, like it took a brain surgeon to figure that one out. Was he going to give her an official scolding from the Vatican? Or accuse her of being a witch? Did they still do that? She said a silent prayer that she was in no danger of getting burned at the stake in twenty-first-century California.

She stared at him blankly.

"What you did," he continued quickly. "W-with Mrs. Long and the, uh, the entities. That was highly unusual."

This time Bridget couldn't suppress a laugh. Father Santos raised an eyebrow. He clearly didn't see the humor.

"Sorry," she said, drawing her backpack closer to her chest.

"Like I said, it was highly unusual. I've been scouring the histories for two days trying to find a similar case of divine grace, and I must say that I've—"

"Of what?"

Father Santos did a double take. "Divine grace. A touch from the hand of God, usually bestowed on those of exceptionally pure and vigorous faith. But I've been unable to find any cases involving someone so . . ." He paused, grasping for the correct adjective. "So young."

"Oh." Bridget doubted very much that was what he was thinking. "Is that what I have?"

Father Santos dropped his eyes. "Perhaps."

Huh? "Perhaps?"

"I . . . I, uh, I thought Monsignor would have discussed this with you."

Bridget shook her head.

Father Santos pushed his chair back from his desk and laced his fingers together around his belly. "Hmm. So he didn't give you any explanation for your unique abilities?"

Bridget shrugged. "He just said I had a gift and that I had to be responsible and use it to help people."

"Very good."

"And then he started teaching me the Rules."

"His rules of engagement during an exorcism?"

Bridget cringed. She didn't like the E word. "He calls it a banishment."

"Yes. Yes, of course. But he didn't . . . he didn't mention anything about the Watchers?"

Watchers? "I don't think so."

"Interesting."

"Really?"

Instead of answering, Father Santos pulled his notebook out of his desk drawer and grabbed a pen from the caddy. He flipped to an empty page and looked at her expectantly. "Why don't we start at the beginning? Tell me exactly what happened at the Fergusons'."

That came out of the blue. "The Fergusons'?"

"Your first exor— Er." Father Santos scratched his chin.

"Your first banishment, wasn't it?"

"Um, I guess."

"Then let's start there." Father Santos poised his pen over his notebook and looked at her expectantly. "You were baby-sitting, right?"

Bridget nodded.

"For the Ferguson twins?"

Bridget nodded again.

Father Santos laid his pen down on the desk. "Why don't you tell me exactly what happened?"

"Didn't Monsignor already fill you in?"

"He did," Father Santos said quietly. "But I want to hear it in your own words."

Ugh. She so didn't feel like going over this again.

"It's important."

"Fine." She cast her mind back to the last night she'd baby-sat for the Fergusons. The night that changed everything.

It had taken three readings of *Curious George Goes to the Hospital*, but Bridget finally got the Ferguson twins to bed. Remote in one hand, tub of Ben & Jerry's in the other, she'd just settled in front of the TV when she heard the footsteps.

At first Bridget thought it was one of the twins. But the steps were plodding and heavy, and echoed out from the upstairs hall like boots marching down the parquet floors. *Clop. Clop. Clop.* Definitely not the patter of bare feet.

"Danny?" she called, her voice more casual than she felt.

Clop. Clop. Clop. They were coming down the stairs.

"Manny?"

No response, just plodding footsteps. They reached the bottom of the stairs and came down the hall toward the living room. Steady, unhurried.

Bridget's stomach backflipped. There was someone else in the house.

She slid her legs to the floor, cursing the creaky sofa, and tried to keep her voice calm. Maybe she could fake out the intruder. "Funny, guys. Go back to bed." She tiptoed over to the fireplace and carefully pulled the metal poker out of the stand. "Your parents will be home any second, and they're going to be pissed if you're still awake."

The footsteps grew louder, stronger, so forceful she could feel their vibrations through the floor. They were almost to the living room, and Bridget positioned herself behind the door, poker raised over her head like she knew how to use it.

How the hell did someone get into the house? She had seen Mr. Ferguson set the security system when he left—an intruder would have set the alarm off.

Unless he was already in the house.

Okay, don't panic. The phone's in the kitchen. Just hit him as hard as you can and run for it.

A shadow slid across the floor, black and massive. Definitely not the twins.

Oh, shit.

The footsteps stopped. Bridget held her breath. Did he

know she was waiting for him? Her arms ached as she held the poker overhead, and blood pounded in her ears. Just as her arm muscles were about to give way, the shadow withdrew and the steps retreated down the hallway. Where was he going?

Bridget bit her lip and peeked around the living-room door. The light in the hall was on, but there was no one there. Huh?

She crept out of the living room, expecting at any moment for Jason or Freddy to come at her with an array of cutlery that would make an Iron Chef drool.

The footsteps continued up the stairs; she could hear each step straining under the weight of an invisible body.

Hear, but not see. What the hell was going on?

A door slammed from upstairs. Then the silence of the house was pierced by the terrified screams of Danny and Manny Ferguson.

Poker in hand, Bridget sprinted up the stairs to the twins' room. She had no idea what was up there with them, only that she had to get the boys out of house. They were her responsibility.

She reached the top of the stairs: Their bedroom door was closed. Bridget dropped the poker and gripped the handle with both hands, but it wouldn't turn.

"Mommy! Mommy!"

Bridget pounded on the door. "Guys, it's me. Open up!"

All she got was more screaming.

"Danny, listen to me," she pleaded to the more level-headed of the six-year-olds. "Open the door."

The door flew open so violently that it knocked her across the hall. Her skull smacked into the wall, and as she crumpled to her knees, Bridget caught sight of the twins through the open door, huddled together on the floor in the corner of their room.

"Guys, run!" she yelled. Too late. A cacophony of slamming doors filled the hallway, and Bridget froze in horror: Every door in the house was opening and closing by itself.

They needed to get the hell out of there. Like, now.

Bridget scrambled to her feet, waited for the door to swing open, then sprinted into the twins' bedroom. She grabbed one of the boys with each hand and hauled them up, ready to make a beeline out of the house. Whatever was in there with them wouldn't be scared off by a babysitter wielding a poker, that was for damn sure.

The bedroom door slammed shut before she could drag the hysterical twins out of the room. As quickly as it had started, the banging doors stopped and the house fell silent.

Then the closet door slowly creaked open.

Bridget turned. An imposing black mass filled the entire closet from floor to ceiling. It seemed to be made of shadows and darkness, sucking light, energy, and hope right out of the room. It seethed, growing larger and smaller as if taking deep breaths, yet it made no sound.

Sweet cartwheeling Jesus! This couldn't be happening. She backed up to the wall, keeping the twins behind her. She had to protect them as if they were her own brothers. As if they were Sammy.

The mass glided forward, blocking the door, and Bridget could sense its hate. Dark, focused hatred. As it came toward her, the room began to pitch, and Bridget was swamped with an overwhelming sense of dizziness. She staggered and placed a hand on the wall to steady herself.

That was when she heard them.

"There's no escape from us. No escape. We own it. We own this place. We were summoned and we won't go back."

"Back?" Bridget asked without thinking.

She felt a collective gasp, a hundred people inhaling at once.

"She hears us."

"No, she doesn't. She cannot."

"She does. Look at her."

"Impossible! The Master protects us. They cannot hear us unless we take their voice."

"I . . ." Holy crap, what the hell were these things? "I can hear you."

This time the voices in the wall shrieked like they'd just been set on fire.

"No, no, no, no, no, no!" they all screamed at once. Then gibberish filled her ears as the voices broke into a language she didn't understand. The black mass wavered.

It had to be a hallucination. Maybe they all had food poisoning? Food poisoning from pepperoni pizza. Sure, why not? It was the only way this made sense.

Bridget took her hand off the wall to brush a strand of hair from her face. As soon as her palm left the rough, stuccoed surface, the voices stopped. She held her hand an inch from the wall and could hear them again, muffled in the background.

She could hear them. They could hear her. Maybe she could use that to her advantage? Bridget placed her hand flat against the wall.

The voices were still speaking nonsense, louder now, arguing among themselves. They seemed less terrifying when she pictured them as bickering old church ladies. The thought actually made her smile and gave her the courage to speak.

"Get out," she said.

"It is speaking to us? Is the traitor speaking to us?"

"Get out of this house." Her voice sounded strong, even if she felt like she was going to ralph her vanilla ice cream all over the rug.

"We don't listen to you."

"We don't listen to her."

"We were summoned. The Master wants us here."

"Well, I don't want you here."

"Bridge?" Danny (or was it Manny?) sniffed.

"It's okay, boys. It's going to be okay."

"This is our home now."

"Don't talk to her. The Master wouldn't like it."

"I want Mommy," the other twin said.

Bridget inched toward the door, keeping one hand on the wall while she herded the twins with the other. "Leave us alone."

The black mass shrank into the closet. *"We'll never leave. Never, never, never."*

Bridget's hand was on the doorknob. "Let us out of this room."

"We won't! We won't! We won't!"

"Now!"

With another painful shriek from the voices, the bedroom door swung open. Whoa, they did what she told them to? Amazing. Somehow, she had power over them.

She shepherded the boys through the door. "Get out. Get out of this house."

"How are you here?"

"We only obey the Master."

"Her words burn like the white flame."

Bridget planted her feet on the floor and clenched her fist. "Get out of here!"

The house moaned. The lights in the hallway flickered, and the voices in the walls let out a soul-wrenching wail.

Then all was still.

TEN

B RIDGET PAUSED. FATHER SANTOS FURIOUSLY scribbled notes, flipping new pages with mechanical precision. He seemed unaware that she'd stopped talking.

"And how did Monsignor Renault learn of the incident?" he asked without looking up.

"Can't you ask Monsignor?"

Father Santos still didn't look at her. "How did he find out?"

Bridget sighed. "Mrs. Ferguson called Monsignor and told him the whole story."

He glanced in her direction. "I take it they know each other?"

Bridget shrugged. "They're in the parish."

"Interesting. And Monsignor never mentioned anything about the Watchers or divine grace?"

Was he serious? "Pretty sure I'd've remembered that."

Father Santos stopped writing and looked at her. "Are you sure?"

Bridget returned his stare. "Someone tells me I've been touched by Jesus, I remember."

"Not Jesus," he said in all seriousness. "The hand of God."

Bridget was getting tired of all the Bible talk. "Whatever."

"No, not whatever. There is a grave difference." Father Santos bounced to his feet and scurried over to a pile of boxes in the middle of the room. He shifted the top two onto another pile, then drew a set of rosary beads out of his pocket. In a swift, clean motion he made the sign of the cross over the box, then used a sharp corner of the metal crucifix to break the seal on the packing tape, running it down the length of the box.

Well, that's something you don't see every day.

As he slipped the rosary back into his pocket, he caught Bridget's eye.

"Can't seem to find any of my supplies," he said, the color rising ever so slightly in his brown face. "You know, any port in a storm and all that."

Bridget nodded and hoped her face didn't reflect what her brain was thinking, namely that Father Santos was a whacka-doo.

After a few moments digging through the sacrilegiously opened box, Father Santos pulled out a large volume, thick as a dictionary and encased in a crinkly plastic cover. He resumed his seat and placed the book carefully on the desk in front of him. As he flipped open the cover, the stench of damp newspaper wafted upward.

"You are blessed, Bridget Liu," Father Santos said as he carefully turned the worn, fragile pages.

That was hardly what she would call it.

"You are blessed with an exceedingly rare gift."

"So I've heard," she said under her breath.

"A divine gift," he continued. "The touch of the hand of God."

Bridget fought back a laugh. "Um, sure."

Father Santos cocked his head. "You don't believe me."

"Look, no offense, but that's not possible."

"According to the Bible, it's quite possible."

"But—" How exactly was she supposed to argue with that? The old "It's in the Bible" was about as irrefutable as her mom's "Because I said so, that's why." "Look, even if that's true, it wouldn't happen to me."

"Why not?"

"Because God and I aren't exactly on the best of terms." Bridget decided not to mention that she'd told God to piss off after her dad's murder. "If he was making a gift list, I'd be at the bottom. Trust me."

Father Santos smiled. "I think you underestimate yourself."

I think you're out of your freaking mind.

Father Santos found the page he was looking for and swung the book around for her to see. It was an etching of angels exposed to an enormous light, the beams drawn as lightning bolts coming from a central point. Most of the angels looked rapturous, their heads thrown back in ecstasy, arms reaching up to the unseen source of light. But some cowered, clamoring over one another in an attempt to flee the rays, their faces twisted in pain, rage, and fear.

"The divine grace of God," Father Santos said, his voice lower now, reverential. "Signified by the hand of God."

"You mean it's not really his hand?"

Father Santos sighed. "God doesn't have a hand, Bridget. Or a body. What are they teaching you in Catholic school?"

Bridget narrowed her eyes. "History?"

"Hmph. Divine grace," Father Santos continued, ignoring her. "It's not just God's favor, it's the spark of life itself. And God has not offered his grace to man directly since the time of Adam."

"That's cool and all," Bridget said, stifling a yawn. She was so ready to blow this taco stand. "But I don't see what it has to do with me."

"Well, that's not a talent most people have, Bridget. Not even an experienced exorcist like Monsignor Renault can communicate with the entities unless they are in possession of a human, and even then, well, they tend to be unreliable."

"Rule Number Five," Bridget said.

"Rule Number Five?"

"They lie."

"Yes, they do. It is their nature to do so. To lie and to take possession of our souls by any means possible. And you, Bridget. You are a great weapon against them."

Bridget got to her feet. "Look, I'm sure you're an expert and all, but Monsignor would have told me about all this if it was true."

Father Santos cleared his throat. "Really?"

Bridget's face grew hot. She didn't need to justify Monsignor's actions to Father Santos. She swung her backpack over her shoulder and headed for the door. "I'm out of here."

She didn't make it halfway across the tiny office before Father Santos grabbed her right hand and spun her around with such force that her backpack whipped off her shoulder and slammed into a bookcase.

"What is this?" Father Santos said. His beady black eyes were trained on her wrist.

"Let me go." Bridget yanked her arm away, but Father Santos held firm with a strength that surprised her. He drew her arm close to his face.

"Where did you get this?"

What the hell was he doing? Bridget tried to pull away again, but Father Santos only tightened his grip. She could feel her fingers going numb from the pressure. Suddenly, Bridget was painfully aware that (a) no one knew where she was and (b) the only person around the rectory at that hour was the little old church lady working in the kitchen, who probably wouldn't hear her screams.

"Let me go or . . . I'll scream."

"V R S N S M V," Father Santos said, reading the letters that circled the square cross charm. "Do you know what this is?" His eyes darted back and forth between it and her face; his upper lip glistened with perspiration. He almost looked as if he was frightened. "Do you?"

"No."

"Don't lie to me."

Bridget was officially freaked out. This wasn't the Father Santos she'd seen so far. His stutter was gone. His absentminded-professor persona had vanished. And as he held her there in his office, his face hardened with suspicion and fear, Monsignor's warning against the new priest from the Vatican raced through her mind. *Be careful.*

"Well?" Father Santos said, giving her arm a shake.

"It was a gift," Bridget said. "From my dad."

Instantly Father Santos released her. "Your dad?"

Bridget rubbed her wrist, easing circulation back into her fingers. "Yeah, it was a First Communion gift from my dad, okay? What the hell is wrong with you?"

"Oh. I—I see." The old Father Santos had returned. He dropped his eyes to the floor and shuffled his feet. "I—I—I'm sorry about that."

Sorry? Bridget snatched her backpack off the ground and

bolted for the door. "Stay away from me."

Father Santos trotted after her. "Bridget, wait. I—I—I need t-to explain."

She hauled the door open and stepped into the hall-way. "Explain why you practically ripped my arm out of my socket? No, thanks."

"That's a little d-dramatic, don't you think?"

"Whatever." She turned and headed toward the stairs. She couldn't wait to get as far away from Father Santos as possible.

"Wait, please!"

Bridget ignored him and flew around the railing and down the stairs. She was already at the front door when he called her name from the upstairs balcony.

"What?" She was going to be so late for class.

"I—I'm sorry. I didn't mean to . . . to upset you."

"Uh-huh."

"But I have something that might, er, make it up to you." Father Santos held up his hand, asking her to wait, then dashed back into his office.

Bridget folded her arms across her chest. Make it up to her? Oh, this should be good.

Father Santos waddled down the stairs and held up a small white envelope, which he placed in Bridget's hand. "This might help."

"Help what?"

"Help you deal with . . . everything."

"I don't need your help."

He motioned to the envelope. "Please?"

"Fine." Why was she humoring him? Bridget flipped the envelope open and pulled out a laminated prayer card. One side had the image of a sword in each of its four corners, with the Latin text of the Prayer of St. Michael, which every St. Michael's Prep freshman was forced to memorize. The back had a weird picture of an angel, Michael, sword in hand on a rocky island, doing battle with a dragon. Beneath, the words *"Vade Retro Satana"* were printed in a strange, medieval-looking font.

"St. Michael and the serpent in the battle for Heaven."

"I know what it is," Bridget snapped. "Catholic school, remember?"

"Right." Father Santos's tone was lighter than it had been since she arrived. "It's . . . it's a talisman of sorts. It might help."

Bridget tossed the envelope into her backpack. "If you say so." Like a prayer card was going to help her through the nightmare that was her life.

"Just promise me you'll keep it, okay? Maybe say the words to yourself once in a while?"

The text on the card jumped into her head. *Vade retro satana*. Her fingertips began to tingle. Bridget shook it off. "I'm going to be late for class."

Father Santos planted his hand against the front door. "Promise you'll keep it? Please?"

Why did he have such a burr up his butt about this? "Fine."

"And the bracelet."

Bridget took a step away from him. "What about it?"

"You wear it all the time?"

"Yep."

"Good. Promise you won't take it off."

"Fine, whatever." Just let me out of here.

Father Santos opened the rectory door for her and stepped aside. "Good. Good. That's good enough for now."

ELEVEN

B RIDGET HURRIED DOWN THE STEPS of the rectory. What just happened? Father Santos's split personalities spooked her. One minute he's a stuttering clown, the next a violent psychopath. And then he gave her a gift? Maybe he was off his meds or something.

Almost against her will, the Latin words from the prayer card popped into her head. *Vade retro satana.* Her fingertips tingled again, just a teeny bit, like when you come into a warm room from the bitter cold. She felt lightheaded, giddy, kind of like she'd felt when she laid her hands on Mrs. Long.

Vade retro satana. The sound of the warning bell drifted across the courtyard, but Bridget barely registered it.

Vade retro satana. Why couldn't she get those words out of her head? It was seriously annoying. Like a Lady Gaga song. What did it mean?

Crap. Latin was her worst subject. "*Vade*" from the verb "*vadere*," to go? Maybe.

Students brushed passed her as they scurried to class, but Bridget didn't care if she was late to homeroom.

Vade retro satana. She couldn't stop saying it, repeating it in her mind. Each time the vibrations in her hands got stronger, spreading up through her arms. The charm on her bracelet vibrated violently against her wrist as if it was absorbing the energy that raced through her body.

She froze and held her arm up before her face. The charm hung there innocently enough, twisting back and forth on its clasp. "*Vade retro satana,*" Bridget said out loud. The charm leaped to life and flapped back and forth several times against her wrist.

The words were linked to her charm bracelet? Kill me.

Okay. Her Latin wasn't that bad. She could do this. *Vade.* Go. Go where? *Retro*: That was easy. Back or backward. Go backward.

Go backward *satana*.

Go back *satana*.

Step back *satana*.

Step back, Satan.

Step back, Satan. Bridget's stomach sank. No wonder the phrase had triggered that humming sensation in her body. It was practically an exorcist's mantra. She didn't care what

Monsignor or Father Santos said, there was definitely something wrong, something unnatural about the way she could communicate with evil. Worse, the way she enjoyed it. The giddy tingling vanished as a new, horrifying thought flooded her mind.

She *liked* the power she had over the demons.

This was so not good.

The hallway was clear as Bridget rounded the corner next to her locker. The last bell must have rung, but she never even heard it. Her hands shook as she fumbled with the combination lock.

"Come on, Bridge," she said out loud. "Get a grip."

"Who are you talking to?"

Bridget screamed and spun around to find the slight figure of Peter Kim staring up at her.

"What are you doing here?" she asked.

"What are *you* doing here?"

Bridget returned to her locker. "Getting my books, Peter. Locker equals books."

"You're late for class."

Bridget didn't like his tone. "Yeah, I know. And you're making me later."

"You're never late for class."

Bridget slammed her locker door and wheeled on him. "How would you know? What are you, my stalker?"

He didn't answer, just stood there and stared. Peter held himself rigid, like he'd been injured and was keeping his body in a certain position to minimize the pain. His face was blank and pale. Paler than usual.

"Peter, what's going on?"

"I need to talk to you."

"You're supposed to be in homeroom. Zero tolerance policy for tardiness? Detention, your mortal enemy?"

"I don't care."

Bridget's mouth fell open. Peter Kim didn't care about detention? Peter Kim? Had the whole world gone mad?

"I need to talk to you," he repeated.

"Peter, I see you every day. We have homeroom and first period together, for chrissakes."

She started down the hall toward homeroom, but Peter stepped in front of her, blocking her way. His eyes were hard and flat. "I need to talk to you *alone*."

She sighed and leaned back against the row of lockers. He'd been acting so weird lately. Well, weirder than normal weird. Like, creepy serial killer weird. How many times did she have to tell him that they were just friends?

"All right, Peter. What? What do you *need* to talk to me about?"

"Are you going to the Winter Formal with Matt Quinn?"

Bridget's jaw dropped. "What the hell?"

His voice was very calm. "I said, are you—"

"I heard you, Peter. I heard. How did you know about that?"

"It's true?"

"Well, um . . ." A quick montage of the various times Peter had asked her to the same dance flashed through her mind: at the library, walking to the library, walking home from the library. Flail.

"You lied to me."

Bridget cringed. "I didn't lie to you."

"Liar," he growled. She'd never heard such rage in his voice before.

Was everyone in her life ganging together to put her on trial? Questions, accusations, apologies—she was sick of it. Bridget covered her eyes with her hand, rubbing her now-throbbing temples with thumb and forefinger. She didn't need to justify herself to Peter Kim. This wasn't any of his business.

"Well?" Peter's voice was a harsh whisper.

"Look," she said, dropping her hand to her side in a gesture of defeat. "I wasn't planning on going. Then he asked and I—"

The sight of Peter's face froze the words of explanation in her mouth. He was red, deep cherry red, and shaking.

"I. Asked. You. First!"

His shout filled the empty hallway, bouncing off the tile floor and metallic lockers before fading to a hollow echo. He took several steps toward her, backing Bridget up against a row of lockers. His lip curled up over his teeth and he grabbed her roughly by the shoulders. "You lied to me, Bridget Liu. You lied to me."

She'd never seen Peter like that. The one constant, the

one lovely thing about Peter Kim was that he was as passive as a freaking kitten. She said no, he backed off. That was the pattern.

Bridget pressed her body against the cold lockers, trying to get as far away from Peter as she could. This wasn't the friend she'd known since she was seven. His features were contorted and his small eyes were black with rage.

"How did you know I was going to the dance with Matt?"

The question seemed to shake him for a moment. His eyes flickered away from her face and the redness drained from his features.

"I, uh . . ." Peter's voice died away. A spell had been broken. "I don't remember."

Bridget sensed the power swing. She shimmied out from between Peter and the lockers. "You don't remember who told you?"

"Um . . ."

The old Peter was back. Timid, unsure. He wrung his hands in front of him, and his eyes wandered around the hall like he had no idea how he'd gotten there. Poor guy.

"I have to go," he said. His feet stumbled forward like he was a marionette propelled on strings, pigeon-toed and jerky. "I have to go."

"Peter?" She couldn't help feeling like she'd wounded him. She tried to touch him, but he flinched from her hand.

"Leave me alone!" he screamed, then broke into a full sprint and disappeared around the corner toward the gym.

Bridget stared after him. She couldn't decide which was stranger: Peter's rage or the fact that he willingly ran into the gym. It was Bizarro Peter.

"Bridget!"

Bridget jumped and turned to find a breathless Monsignor Renault marching down the hall, his heavy, purposeful footsteps filling the void left by Peter's retreat. "You weren't in homeroom. I've been looking for you."

"Sorry." She wondered how much of Peter's conversation Monsignor had overheard.

Monsignor's eyes were fixed on the door to the gym. "You're not usually late for class, are you?"

"Yeah, I was just—" Had he forgotten about her meeting? She decided not to bring it up. The last thing she wanted at the moment was to rehash her unsettling conversation with Father Santos. "I'm just running late today."

"Hmm," he said, still gazing over her head.

Bridget was officially so late for class that even her lax homeroom teacher would have to write her up. She cleared her throat and pulled her cell phone out of her backpack to pointedly check the time. "What's up?"

"Yes," he said with a shake of his head. "Yes. We have another, eh, situation."

"Another one?" Three cases of demonic possession in a month? That had to be a record, right? "Isn't that kind of weird?"

His eyes shone. "Yes!"

"Oh."

Monsignor clapped her on the shoulder. His hand trembled, and there was a hint of a smile about his mouth. He looked like Sammy on his first trip to the Academy of Sciences.

"We are so lucky to have another opportunity for you."

Lucky wasn't the word that came to mind. "Um, yay?"

"We'll need to get over there as soon as possible. After school today?"

That was going to be a problem. "I can't. I'm grounded."

"Grounded?" Disappointment swept across his face.

"Yeah. I'm really sorry. You'll have to go without me."

Monsignor threw up his hands. "I cannot go without you. It would be pointless."

Bridget's eyes flitted down to her phone again. Fifteen minutes late, and Monsignor just stood there, rubbing his chin in thought while Bridget pictured detentions piling up on top of her grounding. This week was a horror show.

"I'll talk to your mother."

Bridget's eyes grew wide. "My mom?"

"Yes, I'll call her after school. She teaches at St. Cecilia's, correct?"

"Um, yeah, but she's not going to—"

"Perfect. Then we'll go tomorrow."

Obviously Monsignor Renault had never dealt with Annie Liu, First Grade Teacher. She wasn't exactly a pushover. "What if she says no?"

"She won't." He patted her head just like her father used to, then turned and walked away with quick, long strides as if he suddenly had someplace very important to be. "Meet me in the rectory parking lot after school tomorrow," he called over his shoulder.

"No?" she said halfheartedly. But the word fell on an empty hallway. Monsignor Renault was gone.

TWELVE

JUST WHEN BRIDGET WAS SURE her day couldn't get any worse, she found Sammy and Matt Quinn sitting on the front steps of her house after school.

"Really?" Bridget made no attempt to hide her exasperation. "Are you following me everywhere I go now?"

"Calm down," Matt said, pushing himself to his feet. "Just bringing Sammy home."

Bridget eyed her brother, who was working on a word puzzle at the top of the stairs. "Is everything okay?"

"He's fine. He didn't want to practice today. Kept going on about coming home to see the cat."

"Perfect."

"Yeah, your mom seemed to have the same reaction.

What's wrong with the cat?"

Other than that he's dead and apparently haunting my bedroom closet? "Nothing," Bridget said, starting up the stairs. "We don't have a cat."

"Bridge!" Sammy squealed, clambering to his feet. "Is it time to see Mr. Moppet now? Is it?"

Matt laughed. "You sure about that?"

"Er . . ." Bridget changed the subject. "Thanks for bringing Sammy home."

"No problem." Matt followed her up the steps.

"Don't you have practice to go to or something?"

"Not till four."

Kill me. He was expecting her to invite him in, wasn't he? She fumbled with her latchkey. "Um, I'd invite you in, but—"

"Your mom said it was fine if I hung out for a little while."

Gee, thanks, Mom. "Oh. Great."

Sammy pushed passed her as soon as she opened the door and sprinted down the hallway to his room. "Mr. Moppet! Time to play."

"You know, you could look a little more excited to see me," Matt said.

"What are we, best friends?"

Matt shrugged. "We used to be."

Low blow.

"Don't you remember, we used to play hide-and-seek downstairs? But I'd only have, like, a minute to find you because you were so scared of the spiders in the garage you'd pop out of your hiding place and give up."

"I was six. I don't give up as easily now."

Matt grinned at her. "I know. That's one of the things I like about you."

"One of the things?"

He smiled, pushed open the kitchen door, and sauntered to the refrigerator. "What does a guy have to do to get a glass of water around here?"

Bridget sighed and pulled a glass out of the cupboard. "Promise you'll be out of here in five minutes?"

"Deal." He grabbed the Brita pitcher and poured himself a glass. "If you still want me to."

"Four minutes, fifty-three seconds."

Sammy ran back down the hall. "Mr. Moppet? Bridge, I can't find him. Can I go downstairs and look?"

Bridget shook her head. Yes, Sammy. Please keep bringing up the dead cat in front of Matt. "Sure, Sammy. Just be careful of the spiders."

Out of the corner of her eye, she caught Matt smiling. "Shut it," she said, before he could remind her of her phobia.

"I didn't say a thing."

Bridget sat down, rested an elbow on the table, and cradled her head in her hand. Matt sipped his glass of water, watching her carefully.

"You look tired," he said.

"Thanks."

"Bad day?"

Let's see, she'd gotten assaulted by both a priest and one of her oldest friends, and then found out she was going to have to perform another exorcism. "You could say that."

"Anything I can do to help?"

The question should have annoyed her, but it didn't. "No. Thanks, though."

"Is it about the dance?"

"The what?"

"The Winter Formal. Are you upset because we're going?"

It was so far from what was actually worrying her, Bridget laughed out loud.

Matt set his glass down on the counter. "What's so funny?"

"Nothing. Sorry." With some effort, Bridget got herself under control. "Sorry, I just wasn't expecting that."

Matt sat down next to her. "But something *is* bothering you, right?"

Sammy's muted voice drifted up from the garage. "Mr. Moppet, where are you?"

Bridget sighed. She wished it was just "something" bothering her rather than the nightmare she was up to her neck in. "I'm okay."

"You can talk to me, you know. If you want."

Bridget closed her eyes. Not about this, Matt. Sorry.

"I know it's important for you to be tough. I totally respect that. But you used to trust me, you know."

"It's not that," she said, opening her eyes. "It's just—"

"I mean, I know we didn't see each other for a long time, but I'm still the same seven-year-old who used to protect you from spiders."

Bridget laughed softly. "This isn't as easy as killing spiders."

Matt bent his head close to hers. "So there is something? I knew it."

Bridget opened her mouth. For a moment, she was tempted. Tempted to spill everything that had happened to her that day, that week, everything since the night at the Fergusons'. It would have been so easy.

"I want to help. I want to be there if you need someone." He smiled slightly, just enough to make her breath catch in her throat. "I want you to let me in."

Bridget looked into those soft hazel eyes. "Matt, I—"

"Bridge!" Sammy burst into the kitchen. "Bridge, I can't find him."

Bridget straightened up. "What?"

"Mr. Moppet. Help me, Bridget. Help me find him."

Matt got to his feet. The moment was gone. "I should go."

"Right." Bridget stood mechanically and followed him to the door. "Um, thanks. You know, for bringing Sammy home and everything."

Matt opened the door, turned around, and smiled. "My offer still stands. If you want to talk, I'm here."

"I'll remember." *Don't hold your breath.*

Matt stood there for a moment. He made a move like he was about to hug her. But then he thought better of it and stepped outside. "Bye."

"Bye."

"So how is school?" Her mom's voice sounded far away.

"Fine."

"Classes are okay?" The words were muted and fleeting.

"Yeah."

Bridget hardly noticed the dripping dishes she took from the dish rack, hardly remembered swiping her towel over them before stacking them on the counter.

"Bridget?"

Bridget blinked. "What?"

"I said, I heard you're going to the Winter Formal."

Her mom smiled; less of an "oh, isn't it sweet my baby girl's going to a school dance" smile and more of an "it's about friggin' time, I was beginning to think she was anti-social" kind of smile.

"How did you know?" It was a stupid question. There could be only one answer.

"Well, Matt was so excited. When he said you'd invited him, he could hardly—"

"Wait, Matt said *I* invited *him*?"

Her mom tilted her head. "Didn't you?"

"Hell no!"

"Watch your mouth, Bridget Liu."

"Sorry." Bridget was thankful her mom didn't hear half the colorful pirate talk that came out of her mouth on a daily basis.

Her mom lifted the slow cooker into the sink, added a squirt of liquid soap, and filled it with water. "It's your school dance. If you didn't invite him, then how are you two going together?"

That was the million dollar question, now wasn't it? "Um, it's a long story."

"It's this Saturday, right?"

"I guess." Bridget wasn't even sure.

"Did you want to ask me something? About being grounded?"

Bridget smiled as a wonderful realization dawned on her: She couldn't possibly go the Winter Formal because she was still grounded.

Her mom winked. "It's okay. You can go to the dance."

Bridget's jaw dropped. "What?"

"Well, of course you can, Bridget." Her mom was clearly confused by Bridget's lack of enthusiasm. "As long as you're going with Matt Quinn."

"Oh." Great, perfect. Typical that Bridget got the mom who actually *wanted* her daughter to go to the dance even though she was grounded, not the hardass who kept Bridget home to "make a point."

Bridget would have preferred the hardass.

Her mom shut the water off with unnecessary force. "Bridget, what is going on with you?"

Uh-oh. "Nothing."

"Nothing? Please, do you think I'm completely stupid?"

"Um . . ." Loaded question.

"You've been drifting through life for the past few weeks," her mom said. "Lost in your thoughts, barely paying attention. It's not like you at all."

The stress that had been building up in Bridget's world snapped. "Not like me?" she said, tossing the dishrag onto the counter. "How would you even know what I'm like?"

"Excuse me?"

"You heard me. You have no idea what's going on with me. I could be growing weed in the basement and you wouldn't even notice."

Her mom narrowed her eyes. "I'd notice if you were growing drugs in the house, Bridget."

"Oh, yeah? When you're not at work you're coddling Sammy like he's still attached at the umbilical cord."

"Sammy needs—"

"Sammy's fine, Mom. He's eight and he's way more independent than you think, okay?"

Her mom's face clouded over. "Don't tell me what Sammy is or isn't."

Bridget clamped her mouth closed. She'd gone too far. "Well, even when you're home, you're not here. You're with one of *them*."

Her mom's freckled Irish skin flushed pink. "With whom?"

"Oh, come off it, Mom. Dad hasn't even been dead a year, and you're already splitting your free time between Mr. Darlington and Sergeant Quinn?" She threw up her hands. "It's messed up."

Her mom clenched her fists. "Don't you dare." There was a quiver in her voice, but Bridget was over it.

"Did you even ask where Monsignor Renault wants to take me after school tomorrow?"

A wave of horror washed over her mom's face.

Bridget held her hand up in front of her. "Oh, God, it's not that. I could handle *that*, Mom."

"I figured you'd tell me if you wanted."

"Right. 'Cause us teenagers, we're so big on sharing."

Her mom sighed. "All right, Bridget. Where are you going with Monsignor Renault after school tomorrow?"

Bridget rolled her eyes. Yeah, like now was the time to bring that up. "It doesn't matter. Just don't pretend like we're buddy-buddy, okay? Because we're not."

"Bridget—"

Bridget turned on her heel and stomped out of the kitchen. "Go call one of your boyfriends," she said over her shoulder. "I'm sure they'll have wonderful advice on how to deal with me."

Bridget slammed her bedroom door as hard as she could. Her dad had removed the lock when she was a kid, but Bridget was relatively sure that her mom would leave her alone. It was easier to "give Bridget her space" than to confront the demon of her temper head-on.

Demon. Crappy choice of words. This whole exorcism business had seeped into the core of her soul, affecting every thought she had, every aspect of her life. A cat she couldn't see, the empty stare in Peter's eyes, demonic possessions around every corner. And then there were Father Santos's theory and his obsession with her bracelet.

Bridget slumped to the floor and rested her head against the bed. There was a logical explanation for all of it. There had to be.

She held up her right arm and watched as the dangling square cross on her bracelet twisted back and forth. The once-sharp edges were dulled with wear and the raised scroll-work was not quite as defined as it had been when she first put it on. But the lettering, as Father Santos had shown, was clearly legible. Two bars crossed in the middle, with the letters C S P B in each of its quadrants, all encompassed by a circle of letters that had never made any sense.

What had Father Santos read? She peered at the charm and read the letters out loud, clockwise. "V R S N S M V."

Beneath her fingers, the charm jumped.

That damn charm! Bridget pulled her laptop out from under her bed and fired it up. It had to be connected to what was happening to her. Either that, or her body had suddenly gone magnetic. She strummed her fingers impatiently on her leg as she waited for the internet portal to load, then typed each of the letters from the charm in order.

V R S N S M V—S M Q L I V B

Google didn't fail her. Bridget had an answer within seconds.

"The St. Benedict medal?" she read from an encyclopedia entry. "A Catholic emblem dating back to the fifteenth century, used by laypeople to protect against spirits, witchcraft, and other diabolical influences." She scanned the entry and found an illustration of a typical St. Benedict medal: on the front, the image of the saint in question holding a cross in one hand and a book in the other; on the back, the same lettering Bridget had on her charm.

Huh. How come her charm only had one side?

She continued to read. "The lettering remained a mystery until a manuscript was discovered at Metten Abbey in Bavaria in 1647. The letters were found to correspond to the *Vade retro satana* prayer."

As if to punctuate that statement, her charm shuddered.

Vade retro satana. Again? It was a prayer?

> *Vade retro satana*
> *Numquam suade mihi vana*
> *Sunt mala quae libas*
> *Ipse venana bibas.*

The passage was helpfully translated:

Step back, Satan
Never tempt me with vain things
What you offer me is evil
You drink the poison yourself.

So her father had given her an exorcist's good-luck charm when she was seven, a charm that had caught Father Santos so off guard he'd promptly lost his cool, a charm that moved by itself when its prayer was read out loud.

Coincidence? Could it have been a weird twist of fate that this charm just happened to catch her dad's eye in a store window? No. That was too ridiculous for even Bridget to buy. But the alternative was even more disturbing: Her dad had known exactly what that medal meant when he gave it to her.

How?

She snapped her laptop closed and shoved it back under the bed. Nothing but questions that had no answers. That was her life now: one giant question mark.

Why her? Why was all of this happening to her? She felt like a baton getting passed along in a relay race, completely devoid of any control over her own destiny. She hadn't asked for this power, and now she was expected to "help" people like it was her nine-to-five job.

What if she didn't want to? What if she didn't go with Monsignor tomorrow? The world wouldn't end. He'd be disappointed, sure, but he'd do the banishment himself, as he'd done hundreds and hundreds of times before. It wouldn't be a big deal.

That was it. She was taking control. She wasn't going to be anybody's pawn. If she didn't want to do the banishment tomorrow, then that was that.

Bridget's temples throbbed. The stress of the last few days was taking its toll. Matt was right; she needed someone to confide in.

Her dad would have understood. He would have listened to her, calmly and without judgment. He'd always been like that. Where her mom was emotional with a wicked temper, her dad had been quiet, serene, unflappable. He had always understood Bridget, always seemed to know what his Pumpkin Bunny was thinking and feeling, even when she didn't understand it herself.

Pumpkin Bunny. Bridget's eyes drifted to the bookshelf where her favorite childhood toy sat propped up in the corner. It had been a gift from her dad from before she could remember, a soft, fluffy stuffed bunny popping out of a pumpkin like a stripper from a birthday cake. She and Pumpkin Bunny had been inseparable. She had dragged that thing with her everywhere she went, since before she could walk until she was old enough to think that stuffed animals were lame. Its once-white fur was now yellowish gray, and its head had undergone so many surgeries, the multicolored threads from her mom's sewing kit made it look more Frankenbunny than Pumpkin Bunny. But even when the toy had been relegated to a spot on her bookshelf, the nickname stuck. To her dad, Bridget was always Pumpkin Bunny.

Bridget rested her forehead against her knees, closed her eyes, and listened to the sound of her breath: inhale one . . . two, exhale one . . . two, inhale one . . . two, exhale one . . . two.

"I miss you, Dad," she said out loud. "I wish you were here."

Something brushed past her leg. Something small, fuzzy, and moving quickly. Bridget's eyes flew open. Not only was she hearing a phantom cat, now she was feeling one too?

From deep inside her closet, Bridget again heard the faint scratching of a cat's claws.

THIRTEEN

"WHAT DO YOU MEAN YOU'RE not coming?" Monsignor said, holding open the door of his navy blue Crown Vic.

Bridget glanced from Monsignor to Father Santos and back, then shrugged. "I'm not going. I don't want to do this anymore."

"Bridget, I don't understand." Monsignor frowned and shot Father Santos an accusatory look, before turning back to her. "I thought we understood one another."

She couldn't look him in the eye. "I don't want to be like this."

"Like what?"

A weapon? "A freak."

"Bridget, you have a gift, a gift many people would kill to possess."

Kill to possess? Was he crazy? Maybe kill to get rid of. Or maybe just kill.

Monsignor knelt in front of her, his bushy white eyebrows pinched together above his nose. Bridget wasn't sure if he was about to give her a pep talk or a proposal.

"Bridget, think about what you're saying." He leaned an arm on his knee in what Bridget suspected was an attempt to look casual. She had to bite her lip to keep from laughing. "Think of the people you've helped already. The Fergusons and Mrs. Long."

It was true, Bridget couldn't deny it. Who knew what would have happened that night to Danny and Manny if she hadn't been there?

Or maybe it was true that the demons were there *because* she had been babysitting at the Fergusons'. Possessions seemed to be following her around.

Father Santos stepped between them. "We can't force Bridget to go," he said lightly. "I doubt her gift is as effective if she's using it against her will."

Monsignor's eyes flashed toward Father Santos with a look of what Bridget could only describe as disgust. "This is none of your business, Father."

"If she doesn't want to go," Father Santos continued with a smile, "she doesn't have to." He looked utterly pleased with the turn of events.

Monsignor bolted to his feet. "I'm sorry, Father Santos. I did not realize that you were in charge of exorcisms for this archdiocese. I did not realize that you were the only senior exorcist in the United States."

Father Santos had to tilt his head back to look Monsignor in the face. The older priest towered above him, hands clenched at his sides, looming over Father Santos like a wave about to break on the lowly shore.

"Er," Father Santos stuttered. "Well, no, of course. I mean, the Vatican has, well . . . I mean."

Bridget almost felt sorry for Father Santos. It was like watching a rabbit go up against a grizzly bear. Slaughterfest.

"Exactly." Monsignor narrowed his eyes. "And if you think for one second that you have enough experience, enough faith, enough knowledge of this girl and what she is capable of, then by all means, I shall step aside and let you proceed with today's banishment."

"M-M-Monsignor Renault," Father Santos managed to spit out. "I—I'm only saying that Bridget, well, she—she should decide for herself."

"Really?" Monsignor swung around and addressed Bridget in his booming, official exorcist's voice. "Bridget, what have we trained for? What have we spent all this time working on together?"

Oh, so *this* is what Catholic guilt felt like.

"Well?"

"I, uh . . ." It was a silly question. Monsignor was right:

He'd spent so much time training her, teaching her, believing in her. Was she really going to give all that up because she freaked out at the feeling she got when she banished a demon? Was she really that selfish?

"Hey, Bridge!" Matt Quinn ran across the parking lot. Flail. "Bridge, wait up."

"Matt," Bridget said, trying to sound casual. "What are you doing here?"

"Hey, I thought maybe you'd want a ride home," he said as he jogged up to the car. "I saw Hector out front and he said he hadn't seen you after school so I came looking for you."

Bridget closed her eyes. Sweet cartwheeling Jesus! God forbid she do anything without Matt and her mom sticking their noses in it.

"Bridget has some official parish business to attend to this afternoon," Monsignor said.

"I'm sorry, sir," Matt said to Monsignor with a nod of his head. Such a good Catholic boy. "I didn't realize—"

"You are Sergeant Stephen Quinn's son, are you not?" Monsignor asked.

"Yes, sir."

"I see."

"Matt," Bridget started, "I need to go."

"Oh." Matt looked at her sidelong. "You okay, Bridget?"

"Yeah." She didn't want to get into it with him; he'd be on the phone to her mom five seconds after the words "I'm going to an exorcism" hit the air.

Matt's eyes flicked between the two priests, then landed on her face with a look of confusion. "Do you need me to come with you?"

Bridget, Monsignor, and Father Santos all answered in unison. "No!"

Matt's brows drew together, and Bridget recognized that familiar look of concern and, barf, responsibility. His face pleaded with her silently for some sort of explanation. She didn't know why, but she thought it was kind of sweet. "I'm fine," she said, reaching for the car door. "I'll talk to you later, okay?"

He grasped her hand, intertwining his fingers loosely in hers. "Promise?"

Bridget's heart thumped in her chest. What was wrong with her? "Yeah," she said, trying to keep her voice steady. "Yeah, I promise."

Far from appeased, Matt's brows lowered over his eyes. He bent his head close to hers. Bridget held her breath. "We're still on for Saturday night, right?"

"The Winter Formal?" Father Santos asked. He sounded surprised.

Matt straightened up and withdrew his hand from hers. Bridget wasn't sure if she wanted to thank Father Santos or murder him.

"Yeah," Matt said. "Bridget and I are going."

Father Santos's jaw dropped. "You're going to the Winter Formal? Together?"

"Yes, we are," Matt said. "Is there a problem?"

"N-no. I just, I just thought—"

"BRIDGE!" A shriek pealed across the parking lot. Bridget spun around to find Peter Kim sprinting to the car.

Really? *Really?* First Matt, now Peter? She'd managed to avoid him all day and now he found her? Was she being punished for something?

"Interesting timing," Father Santos muttered.

"Bridge," Peter panted as he trotted up to her, all red faced and sweaty from his brief outburst of physical activity. He brushed past Matt without a glance in his direction. "Bridge, I've . . . I've come to take you home."

Bridget snorted. "I can get myself home, Peter."

"But I can protect you."

Was he serious? "Protect me from—"

"If anyone's taking Bridget home," Matt interrupted. "It's me."

Oh, great. A pissing contest. "Guys, seriously? I don't need either of you to—"

Peter turned to face his rival. The pointy ends of his spastic hair barely reached Matt's shoulders. "I've known her longer."

Matt took a step forward. "No, you haven't."

"Bridget's my responsibility."

She freaking hated that word. "Guys, I'm right here."

"I think Bridget can decide for herself," Matt said, ignoring her. "Who she wants to take her home."

This was ridiculous. "Yes, Bridget can," she said, folding her arms across her chest. "And she chooses neither."

They turned to her at the same time. "Huh?"

"Yeah. Parish business, remember? I need to go."

Peter grabbed her arm. "But—"

"Boys," Monsignor barked. His patience was maxed out. "We're on a bit of a schedule. So if you don't mind?" He draped an arm around each of them and aimed them back toward the school.

Peter stumbled, resisting the strong arm of Monsignor. He kept trying to wiggle free, like he was going to run back and sweep Bridget away before anyone could stop him. But Matt allowed himself to be led away, glancing back at Bridget as Monsignor shepherded him across the courtyard. There was a piece of Bridget that wanted to run after him, to tell him everything that had been happening with her, in case he was somehow able to shield her from the darkness that had overshadowed her life. But she couldn't. She couldn't let her guard down, show her weakness. She was tough, and she wasn't about to let Matt Quinn take care of her.

Monsignor ushered the boys into the school building, then strode purposefully back to the car. "Well, Bridget? What will it be?"

Oh, that. With a sigh, Bridget opened the door and ducked into the car. She knew Monsignor was right; she had to do this.

"Excellent." Monsignor dashed to the driver's side with unexpected spryness.

Father Santos stuck his chubby face through the car door before Bridget could pull it closed. "Are you sure?"

"Yeah, why not?" For some reason, his concern annoyed her.

He stared at her for a moment, then shrugged. "Never mind."

Bridget used her boot to push open the back door of the Crown Vic. She always got vaguely carsick riding in the backseat and that afternoon was no exception. It wasn't the twisting and turning so much as the painful stop-and-go motion, the Monsignor's braking technique pitching the heavy old lady car forward at every stop sign, traffic light, and crosswalk from St. Michael's Prep to the Marina.

Thankfully it was a silent ride, so Bridget could focus all of her attention on not blowing chunks in the backseat of Monsignor Renault's car. Not that anyone would have noticed. Monsignor and Father Santos were too preoccupied with ignoring each other to pay any attention to their captive.

Captive. Okay, maybe she was being a little dramatic. After all, it had been her choice. But then why did she feel like she was there against her will?

"Um, are you sure you're okay, Bridget?" Father Santos said from the sidewalk.

"Yeah, why wouldn't I be?"

"Because you've been sitting in the car for five minutes."

"Oh. Right." She scooted across the seat and slid out onto the street.

For the first time Bridget noticed where they were: a store on a side street off the busy Marina shopping district. It was one of the newer buildings, constructed after the Loma Prieta earthquake destroyed huge parts of the neighborhood. There were three stories of apartments stacked above the main floor, all with the traditional paneled bay windows that marked even the new additions to San Francisco architecture, and there was some sort of shop below, its façade of floor-to-ceiling windows painted with garish bubble-gum pink Victorian lettering.

Bridget had banished the demons in the twins' bedroom. She'd liberated old Mrs. Long. But she'd never faced—

"Mrs. Pickleman's Tiny Princess Doll Shoppe?" she said. "Please tell me we're going to an apartment upstairs."

Monsignor Renault gripped her shoulder as if he thought she might make a break for it. "No, this is it."

"A doll shop?"

Oh, shit.

Oh, shit, oh, shit, oh, shit.

There was nothing creepier in the whole wide world than dolls. Even as a kid Bridget couldn't handle the porcelain-faced little freaks her grandma sent her. She'd stuff them into the bottom of her toy chest, where the moonlight couldn't reflect off their beady glass eyes while she slept—eyes that seemed to follow her around the room, just waiting for her to turn her back before the dolls leaped off the shelf to throttle her with their wee cold hands.

Monsignor gave Bridget a nudge, and she stumbled forward. Why couldn't she have said no and meant it?

He pushed open the glass door, tripping an old-fashioned bell that hung overhead. Its high-pitched tinkling was like a death knell.

Bridget froze just inside the doorway. Facing her was a display case populated by old, withered dolls. They were bald, sort of, hair painted on their freaky little wooden skulls. They wore varieties of period clothes—some kind of Old West-y, some more turn of the century—all with a similar look on their faces: painted eyes staring straight ahead, lips puckered and slightly flared like they were cooing. Most of them were chipped, the flesh-colored paint flaking off their faces, and they sat at odd angles, leaning on one another for support like an infant leper colony.

Right in the middle of the case sat the largest doll, a *Little House on the Prairie*-ish thing whose wooden face looked like it had been mauled by a dog. Bridget glanced away from the doll, then froze. She could have sworn the thing moved. Her heart pounded as she tentatively stepped back in front of the case and bent down so her face was level with the doll. This time there was no mistake.

The doll winked at her.

In a panic, Bridget spun around for the door but found

herself staring at a wall of dolls. To her left, to her right, all four walls were lined with similar glass cases, packed to the brim with round-faced dolls. Plastic, porcelain, swaddled like infants, dressed like fairy queens and Disney princesses. Caucasian, black, Hispanic, Asian—a United Nations of horror.

Bridget shivered. Of course this place was infested with demons. Of course it was. This was Hell.

"Monsignor, I'm so glad you're here." A woman rushed forward. She had wavy black hair and wore a black turtleneck, skirt, and tights, with painfully red lipstick smeared across her mouth. She looked more late-nineties goth than fussy doll shop owner.

"Of course, Ms. Laveau."

"Papa said if anyone could help, it would be you."

"We'll see what we can do."

"The noises have gotten more . . ." Ms. Laveau passed a hand over her hair. "Violent."

Monsignor nodded. "I see. Still only at night?"

Ms. Laveau nodded. "I'm sorry you couldn't witness it yourself when you were here last week, but I noted the times like you suggested." She handed him a piece of notepaper.

"Hmm. Sunset and three o'clock in the morning?" Monsignor asked with raised eyebrows.

Father Santos whistled.

"Is that bad?" Ms. Laveau asked. Her voice was breathless.

Monsignor placed a hand on her arm and turned her away

from the younger priest. "Not at all, Emily. It will be fine."

Ms. Laveau caught sight of Bridget huddling near the door. The red lips bent into a frown. "I'm sorry, the store is closed."

"Bridget is with us," Monsignor said with a nod.

Yes, I'm with them, Bridget thought. Aren't I just the luckiest girl in the world?

Ms. Laveau glanced at Monsignor, who nodded in a reassuring manner. "Never fear, Ms. Laveau. Bridget's done this kind of thing before."

Bridget swallowed hard and forced a smile in an attempt to look like she wasn't about to pee in her pants.

"Oh." Ms. Laveau sounded disappointed. "I guess . . . whatever you suggest, Monsignor."

Monsignor inclined his head. "Thank you."

Ms. Laveau watched with wide eyes as Father Santos began to assemble the candles and sacramentals on the main counter. "What shall I do?"

"I recommend you go and get a cup of coffee," Monsignor said. "Or maybe dinner with a friend?"

Ms. Laveau's face fell. "I don't get to stay?"

Great. One of those amateur ghost hunter chicks. She probably had at least one set of tarot cards and a Ouija board stashed in her apartment.

"I'm afraid you might complicate the situation." Monsignor led Ms. Laveau expertly toward the door. "For a successful, er, blessing, we need to have only professionals present."

Ms. Laveau was about to protest, but with a tinkling of the bell, Monsignor had maneuvered her out the door. "I'll give you a call when we're finished."

Bridget couldn't help but smile at how Monsignor handled Ms. Laveau. Too easy.

Now if only the doll shop was the same.

FOURTEEN

FATHER SANTOS HAD ALREADY PREPARED the room. White candles blazed on the counter next to the cash register; their orange-and-yellow flames reflected in the endless glass display cases, making the entire shop look like it was ablaze. Decanters of holy water and oil stood valiantly side by side, and a stripe of salt lay across the back entrance, with a small pile in each corner of the shop.

"We're ready," he said.

Monsignor didn't even look at him. "Did you sanctify the front entrance? I do not see any salt across the threshold."

He was right. No salt across the front door. After what had happened at Mrs. Long's, it was a careless blunder.

"Yes, yes," Father Santos said. He grabbed the bowl of

salt and ran to the door. "S-s-sorry."

"Hmm." Monsignor waited until the salt was poured and Father Santos had returned the bowl to the counter before he turned to Bridget. "Now we are ready."

Bridget took a deep breath. Showtime.

But something was off. With the painful exception of a hundred soulless faces staring every direction, the shop felt . . . normal. The air wasn't charged with malevolence, not cold, not sharp. There was no telltale sense of dizziness, no room pitching back and forth like the deck of a ship. No popping in her ears as the air condensed around her. At the Fergusons', at Mrs. Long's, Bridget had felt like someone was watching her, not from behind, but from everywhere at once, as if the house itself had grown a million pairs of eyes. Now here she was in the creepiest place on earth, surrounded literally by a million pairs of eyes, and what did she feel?

Nothing.

"Are you sure there's something here?" she asked, peeling off her bomber jacket. Far from being cold, the shop was pleasantly warm.

"Yes," Monsignor said patiently.

Bridget ran her fingers across the wall of the shop. No voices, no grunts, no howls, no screams. "I just don't hear anything."

Monsignor removed his stole from Father Santos's bag. "Rule Number Four."

"Do not let your guard down," Bridget said diligently.

"Precisely." Monsignor kissed the embroidered cross before draping the purple stole over his neck. "Watch." He took his crucifix out of the bag and placed it on the counter.

The mood changed in an instant. Pressure built in Bridget's ears. She tensed her jaw, and her ears popped. The new energy continued to build, centered on the cross. The atmosphere turned bad, foul, and Bridget caught a whiff of that familiar tangy metallic scent.

Out of the corner of her eye, Bridget saw a doll's head spin.

"Dammit," she said under her breath.

"Focus."

Another movement from her left sent her heart racing. This time she thought she saw a whole shelf of dolls tilt their heads toward her. They were staring at her now, a wall of dead glass eyes. She was pretty sure they hadn't been a second ago.

"Did you see that?" she whispered.

"See what?" Father Santos asked. Seriously, did he need glasses?

"Do not engage," Monsignor said calmly, invoking Rule Number Three.

Don't engage the creepy dolls possessed by Satan who are now all staring at you. Just pretend they aren't there.

Bridget closed her eyes. Please don't let a Chucky doll lunge at me with a freaking butcher's knife. Please, please, please.

What happened next was almost worse.

"We have heard about you," squeaked a chorus of high-pitched voices.

Bridget's eyes flew open, and her heart leaped to her throat. Every doll in the shop was staring right at her.

"We know who you are. We know who you are. We know who you are," the dolls sang. Like, all of them. Like, the entire freaking shop full of dolls in singsong unison.

"Christ on a cross." Don't panic. Don't panic. Don't panic.

"Bridget?" Father Santos sounded worried. "What is it?"

"You don't hear that?" she asked. So not good.

"What?" Monsignor asked. "What do you hear, Bridget?"

"A Watcher is here. What fun! What fun!"

A Watcher? Where had she heard that before?

"We defeated you. We defeated you," the dolls taunted. *"The Master is strong."*

Bridget spun around. The whole shop was alive, hundreds of dolls jittering and squirming behind their glass cases. She was so terrified, her brain was starting to shut down. She had to force herself to concentrate on what the dolls were saying. "Defeated me before?"

A childlike giggling rippled through the room. *"Defeated the Watchers."* The dolls laughed. *"Defeated the traitors."*

"Traitors?" Bridget asked. "What traitors?"

Monsignor's voice sounded small. "Bridget, are you all right? What is happening?"

"What are they saying?" Father Santos added.

The giggling crescendoed, then abruptly cut off. *"TRAI-TOR! TRAITOR! TRAITOR!"* the dolls shrieked from the silence. *"ONE OF US! ONE OF US! YOU ARE ONE OF US!"*

Bridget clamped her hands over her ears. One of them? How could she be one of them, something evil and twisted, something that wasn't even a part of her world? "I'm not! I'm not one of you."

"LIAR! LIAR! THE TRAITOR LIES!"

Bridget felt like she was drowning under the voices. They swelled in volume and crashed over her in waves. Her legs buckled and her body sank to the floor. Why wasn't her power working?

"WE WILL DESTROY YOU!"

As if to remind her, the St. Benedict medal vibrated violently, flapping back and forth against her wrist.

"WE WILL DESTROY THE WATCHER!"

That's right. The charm had a motto. *"Vade retro satana,"* Bridget murmured. She was barely aware she spoke the words out loud. *"Vade retro satana."*

"LIAR! LIAR!"

"Vade retro satana. Vade retro satana." Feet and hands tingled.

"TRAITOR AND A LIAR!"

"Shut up!" she screamed. Bridget pushed with her legs like she was power lifting a heavy weight. With a withering effort, she lurched upward, shoving the voices away. "SHUT UP!"

Silence.

Bridget slumped forward, hands on her knees, trying to catch her breath.

"What did they say?" Father Santos stood behind the counter, his ever-present notebook and pencil at the ready. "Do you remember?"

Yeah, I'm fine. Thanks for asking.

A heavy arm reached around her shoulders, bracing her while she panted. "Are you all right, Bridget?" Monsignor asked.

Bridget nodded and straightened. "I think so."

"Good."

"Now if you can remember"—he shot a hard look at Father Santos—"tell us what the entities said."

"They said," Bridget panted, "they said they knew who I am. That I was one of them."

"Interesting."

"What do they mean?" she asked. The dolls' words had her worried.

Monsignor frowned. "I'm not entirely sure."

"Why doesn't she ask them?" Father Santos said. He didn't look up from his notebook, just continued to write.

"Rule Number Three," Monsignor said. His voice was steely. "Do not engage. It is never a good idea to actively address an entity unless you are trying to discover its name."

Father Santos shrugged. "If we want to know what they're talking about, Bridget should ask them."

As Father Santos uttered her name, a murmur echoed

through the room, pinging from corner to corner like a demonic game of telephone. *"Bridget. Bridget. Bridget,"* the dolls echoed.

Monsignor put his hand on her shoulder. "What do you think, Bridget? Would you like to try?"

Try talking to a shop full of demonic dolls? Not really. "Okay."

He patted her shoulder, then took several steps away.

She could do this. She had a great power, didn't she? And they were just dolls, anyhow. "That's right," she said, pivoting in place to face each wall in turn. "I'm Bridget. Do you know me?"

"We know who you are," giggled one wall of dolls.

"Shh, don't tell her," replied the opposite side.

"She cannot harm us. We are strong. We are many."

Bridget laid her hand on the nearest display case. "Tell me what you know," she said. "Or I will banish you."

The instant the word left her mouth, chaos erupted in Mrs. Pickleman's Tiny Princess Doll Shoppe. Hundreds of dolls leaped to their feet and began to twitch and lurch in their display cases. Bridget felt like she was going to be sick.

"Holy shit," Father Santos said under his breath.

"The Master is strong! The Watcher cannot banish!" the dolls screamed.

"I—I can and I will," Bridget said, trying to stay calm.

"The Watcher is a fool. The Master's spies are many! He will break you."

The sound of tiny plastic and porcelain bodies crashing into glass thundered through the shop as the dolls launched themselves against their glass prisons. Faces and arms, bodies and legs smashed and shattered. The entire shop vibrated, whole display cases lurching and tottering away from the wall. The shelf on which Bridget rested her hand gave a sickening crack as the glass splintered. A Little Red Riding Hood doll's face jutted through the glass like Jack Nicholson in *The Shining*.

"I will banish you," Bridget said again. Her voice wavered.

Then it got really weird.

The dolls began to chant nonsensical verses as they stomped their feet in unison. It was no longer a child's squeak, but a hundred booming voices rumbling through the shop.

"Pothered tints strut."

"Spins truth tottered."

"Amazing," Monsignor said.

"What does it mean?" Father Santos asked.

Bridget turned to them. "You can hear that?"

Father Santos scribbled at a frantic pace. "Absolutely."

"Thunder totters spit."

"Potent dither trusts."

From amid the roar of incessant chanting, Bridget caught a distinct voice calling her name. Her full name, just like her mom did when Bridget was in a metric ton of trouble.

"Bridget Yueling Liu."

Bridget spun around and found herself facing the display

case of historic dolls. Her stomach sank as she watched the *Little House on the Prairie* doll—the one that had winked at her—stand up and place its wooden hands against the glass.

"Bridget Yueling Liu," the doll repeated.

"How did you know my name?"

The doll inclined its head. *"He told me."*

"Who? Your master?"

The doll shuddered but didn't answer.

"Okay." Not the talkative type, this one. "Not your master?"

"I have a message," the doll said.

It was the first time Bridget had heard a demon refer to itself in the singular. This entity felt different from the rest, kind of like the last demon who inhabited Mrs. Long—the one who had given her a cryptic warning. This demon had a distinct voice and personality, separate from the collective.

"Who are you?" she asked. "What is your name?"

Again, the doll was silent. Not that it mattered. The name was already forming in Bridget's mind.

"Penemuel," Bridget said hesitantly.

The doll didn't even pause. *"I have a message for Bridget Yueling Liu."*

"Fine. What is it?"

"The messenger was sent. His warning was not delivered. You must find the messenger."

That was a new one. "Messenger?"

"You must find the messenger."

"I don't understand."

With a shrill cry, the doll thrust its wooden arm into the case, cracking the glass door. *"YOU MUST FIND THE MESSENGER!"*

All right, all right. Don't argue with the possessed doll, Bridge. She fought back her confusion and her fear and tried to concentrate on what Penemuel was saying. "Okay, find the messenger. How?"

The voice turned rigid and struggled to get the next word out. *"Me-yer. Un-der. Un-der. Me-yer."*

Bridget froze. Milton Undermeyer.

The man who had killed her father.

"Un-der. Me-yer."

"Who told you this?" she asked, panic welling up. "Who sent you?"

"Bridget Yueling Liu. He calls you Pumpkin Bunny. He says you will know."

"No!" she screamed. Impossible. How could her dad be sending messages through a demon? That would mean . . . She felt sick to her stomach. That would mean he was where they were. That would mean he was in Hell. No, no, no! She refused to believe it.

The chanting in the shop rose to a fever pitch as the dolls continued to launch themselves against their cases. From around the room, Bridget heard the smashing of glass and a series of bloodcurdling screams as, one by one, the dolls hurled themselves at Bridget and the priests.

Bridget shielded her face with her arm as a Madame Alexander princess and two American Girls went flying past her head. "How did you know that? Who told you?"

"Pothered tints strut."

"Spins truth tottered."

"Thunder totters spit."

"Find the messenger." With a fierce jab, Penemuel sent its tiny arm through the display case, lodging it in the splintered glass.

"Potent dither trusts."

"Where is my father?" Bridget screamed.

Penemuel lifted its head to Heaven. *"My penance is done."*

Bridget slapped her hands to the glass case against the wooden nub of Penemuel's hand. "Tell me where he is!"

"I am released!"

The doll lifted up off its shelf, shuddered once as Mrs. Long had done, then crumpled, lifeless.

"Bridget, what is going on? What are you doing?" Monsignor's voice swirled through the chaos of the shop where piles of broken, mangled dolls lay twitching on the floor. "You need to finish the banishment."

Bridget didn't care, not about the demons or Monsignor or the carnage that was Ms. Laveau's creepy little store. She only cared about what Penemuel had told her. A message from her dad to find Milton Undermeyer. She felt like she'd been kicked in the gut with her own steel-toed boots.

"Bridget!" She could barely hear Monsignor. The clamor

had escalated, and the roar of voices encircled the room like a tornado. She needed to focus. *Vade retro satana.*

"I banish you," she said halfheartedly.

The demons screeched in pain as the familiar tingle raced up Bridget's arms and legs, strengthening her voice.

"I banish you from these dolls, from this shop, from this world."

"No! No! Have mercy, little girl. Mercy!"

"Get out," she repeated. The energy intensified in her stomach and her voice was a frightening roar. "Get out!"

"The Emim will release us. You will feel our wrath. You cannot keep us out forever!"

Bridget held her hands in front of her. They were hot, searing, the warmth shooting up through her wrists and arms. "Maybe." She laughed drily. "But I can try."

She felt the weight of them as she threw her hands forward, concentrating on the demons themselves. *"Vade retro satana!* I banish you."

There was a final shriek, then Bridget watched with satisfaction as a hundred dolls collapsed into silence.

FIFTEEN

"**S**O ARE YOU GOING TO tell me what's going on or am I going to have to start making stuff up?"

Bridget froze midbite into her grilled cheese sandwich and slowly looked across the table at Hector. His diet snack bar and celery sticks lay untouched on top of his lunch bag. His arms were folded across his chest, and his left eyebrow kinked at a sharp angle. Uh-oh. Hector meant business.

"I don't know what you're talking about."

"Really?"

Flail. Peter must have spilled about her "official parish business" after school yesterday. How was she going to explain it?

"You were going to tell me *when* that you asked hunky

Matt Quinn to the Winter Formal?"

Bridget's whole body relaxed. Oh, that. "It just sort of—"

"Look, if we're going to be friends, you have to text me epic life events like this immediately. Like, within twenty seconds of the occurrence immediately. Get it? I have a reputation to maintain, and how would it look if I'm getting my information from—" He dropped his voice. "Peter?"

Bridget winced. "You heard it from Peter?"

"Heard it?" Hector snorted. "More like I got dragged into the insanity. He's really freaking out."

"Yeah." Bridget remembered the wild look in Peter's eyes when he confronted her in the hallway, the angry line of his jaw when he challenged Matt in the parking lot. "I know."

"He cornered me in English this morning. Kept asking if I knew anything about it, rambling on and on about how you lied to him. Dude, seriously scary."

"Yeah," Bridget repeated, sinking her head into her hands. "I know."

"I mean, not that I blame you. I'd ask Mr. Sexy Eyes Baseball Player to the dance myself if I thought I had a chance. But did you have to go and do it after you turned Peter down . . . what was it, three times?"

Bridget groaned. "Five."

"Five? Daaaaaaamn."

Bridget snapped her head up. "Okay, but what was I supposed to do? Go with Peter? And besides, it's not like I asked Matt to go with me."

Hector pursed his lips. "Really? Then how did it happen?"

"Um . . ." Why was everyone so intent on knowing how Matt ended up as her date to the Winter Formal? It just happened, people. Get over it.

Hector's eyes flicked off Bridget's face to something behind her. He pulled his hand to his mouth. "Peter," he said through a fake cough, a second before Peter Kim dropped his lunch tray down next to Bridget.

"Hey, Peter," she said, trying to sound casual. Pretty much anything out of his mouth at this point was going to be a disaster. She held her breath and waited for the worst.

"Hector," Peter said through clenched teeth.

"Uh . . ." Hector's eyes darted from Peter to Bridget, then back. "Hey, man."

Peter slowly unwrapped his spork-napkin packet. "How did you do on the algebra test today?"

Oh, so that was it? Peter was going to ignore her? Bridget's shoulders relaxed. Finally something was going her way for a freaking change.

"Okay, I guess," Hector said.

Peter stabbed at his fruit compote. "Good."

Silence descended upon their corner of the table. Bridget amused herself by switching between Hector's uncomfortable fidgeting and Peter's metered eating as he slowly lifted bits of his lunch into his mouth, chewed five times, and swallowed. He was like a robot, not even registering whether he was ingesting a piece of bean-and-cheese burrito or a wilted lettuce leaf. Peter just continued to lift the spork from plate to mouth while his eyes remained fixed on the table. It was mesmerizing and horrifying at the same time.

"Why so quiet?" Brad slid his tray down the table and climbed a gangly leg over the bench. "You guys have a fight or something?"

"Beats the hell out of me," Hector murmured.

"Hello, Brad," Peter said with the same mechanical *Stepford Wives* voice. "How are you today?"

"Dude," Brad asked. "Are you okay?"

"Perfectly well, thank you."

Brad looked to Hector, who just shook his head, and then to Bridget. "Liu, what's going on with him?"

"I'm sorry," Peter said, dropping his spork to his tray. He turned his head from side to side, looking straight through Bridget as if he didn't see her at all. "To whom are you speaking?"

Brad pulled his head back. "Are you serious?"

"Oh, come on, Peter!" Hector threw his hands in the air.

Peter turned his cold stare on Hector, as if threatening him as next on the ignore list. "I don't know what you're talking—"

"Would you knock it off?" Hector barked. "You're creeping me out. We all know you're pissed at Bridge, but get over it, okay?"

"He's pissed at Liu?" Brad asked.

She so did not want this topic of conversation resurrected. Bridget bolted to her feet and whisked her tray with its half-eaten sandwich off the table. "Guys, I've . . . um . . . got to go check on my . . . er . . . choir music for rehearsal."

"Huh?" Hector said.

"Yeah." She shoved the contents of her tray into the nearby trash can and grabbed her backpack. "See you later."

Bridget dodged small packs of students eating in the hallway as she hurried away from the cafeteria. Freshmen, mostly. They sat huddled together on the floor, laughing and joking without a care in the world. Bastards.

Her excuse to bail on lunch was total crap, but with fifteen minutes left before the warning bell, she needed something to do with her time. Going over her music for the upcoming show choir winter concert was as good an excuse as any, and maybe it would keep her mind off . . . everything. Bridget turned a corner, thankful the hall was free from giggling freshmen, grabbed her music notebook from her backpack, and plopped down on the floor to study.

She only made it a page into Mozart's "Ave verum corpus" before a shadow passed in front of the light. Bridget glanced up to find the deep green eyes and snarling smile of Alexa Darlington towering above her.

"Well, if it isn't Bridget Liu."

Bridget leaned her head back against the row of lockers. She so wasn't in the mood. "What do you want, Alexa?"

"With you?" Alexa sneered. "Nothing."

Bridget casually returned to her music notebook. "Then piss off, okay? I've got work to do."

"I just think it's interesting that you're picking up my hand-me-downs now. That's all."

"What?"

Alexa took a step back and folded her arms across her chest. "You asked Matt Quinn to the Winter Formal, didn't you?"

"I didn't *ask*—"

"So I think it's funny." Alexa barreled on. "I mean, I always knew you were jealous of me. Just didn't think you'd go so far as to steal my—"

Okay. That's it. Bridget shot to her feet. "Jealous of you? Are you kidding me?"

Alexa laughed, light and airy. "Duh. Ever since you assaulted me back in the sixth grade. Sister Ursula said you hit me because you were jealous."

Bridget hated Sister Ursula, their old principal at St. Cecilia's, almost as much as she hated Alexa.

"You should thank me, really," Alexa said with a thin smile.

"Thank you?"

"Sister Ursula wanted to expel you, but I told my father that I forgave you so they let you stay."

Getting expelled from St. Cecilia's would have been the single greatest day of Bridget's life. "I'm supposed to thank you for that?"

Alexa ignored her. "And now I guess I'm returning the favor."

"Huh?"

"I should thank *you* for getting Matt Quinn out of my hair."

"Out of your hair?"

Alexa shook her crown of red ringlets as if to emphasize her point. "Matt's just never gotten over our breakup. He can't seem to let me go."

All right. Time to stop the crazy train. "Really? Because from what I saw, he totally ditched you after school the other day to take me home."

"Is that what you think happened?"

Bridget took a step toward Alexa. "That's what I *know* happened. And in front of your little posse of sycophants. That must have sucked for you."

"I don't know what you're—"

"*Sy-co-phants.* I know, big words are hard for you. Sound it out and maybe Daddy will tell you what it means later."

Bridget felt the momentum swing her way, but Alexa wasn't about to back down.

"I guess it makes sense that you'd want to date Matt," Alexa said, jutting out her chin. "I mean, since his dad is at your house, like, every night of the week."

Bridget smiled. "Still not as often as your dad."

Alexa reared back her hand as if she was going to slap Bridget across the face. Bridget tensed, but just as Alexa started the down swing, she froze. Her eyes dropped, and instead of a bitch slap, Alexa ran her hand over ringlet curls.

"As least *my* dad didn't get *yours* murdered," Alexa said coolly.

Bridget flinched. "Bitch."

Alexa hitched her purse up on her shoulder and straightened her neck. "I see your anger-management counseling didn't do much good."

Bridget clenched her fists. She wanted to smash one into the side of Alexa's face, erasing that smug smile. She bit down hard on her lower lip instead. Alexa was intentionally baiting her, maybe to try and get her suspended before the Winter Formal so she couldn't go. She needed to resist temptation.

They stared at each other, Alexa's green eyes sparkling with her plastic smile while Bridget took deep, slow breaths, trying to cool her temper. After a minute, Alexa sighed, broke her eyes away, and sauntered down the hallway.

"You and Matt probably won't last very long anyway," Alexa said, glancing back over her shoulder. "The way people around you end up dead, who knows what might happen?"

SIXTEEN

"HALLELUJAH! HALLELUJAH!

"Hallelujah! Hallelujah! Hal-le-e-lujah!"

At a vigorous nod from Ms. Templeton, Bridget leaned forward and flipped the top edge of the score; the pianist's nimble fingers didn't miss a single orchestrally transcribed note. Handel's famous chorus ticked along under Mr. Vincent's baton. The choirmaster bounced on his toes as he conducted, his baton pattern square and regular as a military band.

"For the Lord God Omnipotent reigneth.

Hallelujah! Hallelujah!"

Bridget yawned. She couldn't concentrate. Her mind kept drifting to the state mental institution in Sonoma County where Milton Undermeyer was confined. Why would her dad

want her to see the man who killed him?

Rule Number Five: They lie. Yeah, yeah, she'd seen plenty of that. But the demonic presence of Penemuel was different, somehow. It was flying solo, clearly not a part of the chaotic infestation she'd been brought there to cleanse. *"He calls you Pumpkin Bunny. He says you will know."* Of course it was possible that a demon would know her dad's nickname for her; Monsignor had warned her that demons gain power over their victims by promising them visions of the future and knowledge of the unknown. But Penemuel was not like any demon she'd encountered before.

It had a message for her, and when the message had been delivered, Bridget could have sworn the painted features of the doll had changed, morphed into an expression of euphoria. *"My penance is done. I am released!"*

"Bridget!" Ms. Templeton hissed.

Bridget jumped up and turned the page. "Sorry."

> *"The kingdom of this world,*
> *Is become the kingdom of our Lord."*

With the exception of Hector's bright tenor, the sparse male sections mumbled their words and missed the majority of their cues. The sopranos were flat and the altos sang the soprano part because they couldn't remember their own, but Mr. Vincent flailed his baton like he was James Levine at the Met, cuing singers who weren't even paying attention. Handel's finest had proved a bit beyond the St. Michael's show choir.

Another nod from Ms. Templeton brought another page turn from Bridget, and inside she cringed. Page seven was where Mr. Vincent's own creation took off.

Mr. Vincent's baton took a dramatic pause, and on the next downbeat the entire musical mood changed. Ms. Templeton's accompaniment was no longer Handel's jaunty composition, but an asymmetric pop track. From the front row of the choir, four sopranos spot-turned away from the risers, beginning a routine straight out of the last episode of *So You Think You Can Dance*. The rest of the singers parted down the middle, and Hector strutted between them onto the altar, picking up a hand mic from Mr. Vincent's music stand, and Christina Aguilera'd his way into "Hip-Hop-Elujah," arranged by Blair Vincent, based on source material by G. F. Handel.

> *"King of kings and lord of lords.*
> *And He shall reign forever and ever."*

The choir kicked in as Hector crooned his way through the lead vocals, the show choir dancers pirouetting and gyrating around him.

Bridget was pretty sure Handel had just rolled over in his grave.

Disgusting as the entire display was, Bridget had to admit that Hector was a star. He exuded confidence, like he didn't care what anyone thought. Bridget envied him for that. She always felt at odds—with her mom, with her brother, with school. Even the piano, her refuge from everything in the world that bugged her, had become a burden after she'd been roped into this gig as second accompanist for the show choir. She felt like little pieces of her soul were dying while classical masterpieces were being turned into *American Idol* reject fodder and there was nothing she could . . .

"Bridget!"

Ms. Templeton turned the page so violently the whole score slipped out of the music holder and came crashing down on the Yamaha baby grand, producing one dissonant train wreck of a chord.

Bridget closed her eyes and scrunched up her face. How many page turns had she missed? She had no idea. Her brain was oatmeal.

Mr. Vincent's nasal voice cut through the silence. "Ms. Templeton, is there a problem?"

"Technical issue," she said, shooting a glance at Bridget. "With the page turning."

"It is the job of the second accompanist to be following along at all times." Mr. Vincent glared down her. "I must have your full attention, Bridget, as if you were playing the music yourself. Otherwise, I could have"—he waved his baton around his head—"anyone sitting there turning pages."

"I'm really sorry."

"Mr. Vincent?" Alexa's sickeningly sweet voice made Bridget's skin crawl. "If the second accompanist is having issues concentrating, I'd be more than happy to turn pages."

Mr. Vincent smiled. "That's very kind of you, Alexa, but

I need your voice in the soprano section. There's no one else who can carry the obbligato in the chorus."

A murmur of agreement rippled through the choir. Alexa batted her long auburn lashes at Mr. Vincent and feigned a blush. "Of course. Whatever you need, Mr. Vincent."

Bitch.

Mr. Vincent sighed and turned back to Bridget. "Bridget, why don't you take a break before you play the second half of rehearsal today? I need your head in the game, with the winter concert a week away."

Bridget rolled her eyes as she stepped off the altar and down to the floor of the church. A "break" was hardly going to help her focus. She meandered down the aisle as Mr. Vincent tapped his baton to regain his choir's attention.

"We'll take it from measure two-fifty-eight, Ms. Templeton. And a one, two, three, four."

The click of Bridget's boots against the hard marble died under the booming acoustics of piano and choir. The Church of St. Michael wasn't nearly as shiny and ornate as her parish church at St. Cecilia's. It was half the size, older, dingier. Horrifying in a European kind of way, with dark stained glass windows depicting martyrs and saints enduring acts of brutality—stoned, shot full of arrows, burned at the stake—while angels looked on. Not the cherubic, benevolent angels with rosy cheeks and curly blond hair you'd find at other churches, but dark, ominous angels, their skin tinged with a pallor of gray, their expressions hard and completely devoid of compassion. Oh, and they each held a sword, some tipped with bright red blood. Not exactly a touchy-feely kind of church.

Her dad had taken the family to Mass there every year on September 29, the Feast of St. Michael, and Bridget had dreaded the day every year. Once, when she was a kid, she could have sworn the angels were looking at her. So. Not. Cool.

Ironic that Bridget ended up in school there, though as far as Catholic schools went, she could have gotten stuck at Mercy, the all-girls school. That would have been hell.

Bridget paused near the back of the sanctuary by an old confessional that had been transformed into an alcove to display the jewel of St. Michael's: mounted on the wall, in a Plexiglas display case, was a giant sword.

The Sword of St. Michael, a relic of the archangel, supposedly created from secret Vatican schematics of the angel's actual sword. Bridget had heard its history at least a dozen times in religion class, and each time she rolled her eyes. Secret Vatican sword blueprints? Ooooo. Was she really supposed to believe that crap?

The sword was the treasure of the Church of St. Michael, and special venerations were held in the sanctuary throughout the year. Bridget found the sword vaguely disturbing like the rest of the church. The golden blade was two feet long, thin with patches of tarnish, and marred as if it had actually been used at some point. The hilt was also gold and ornately carved with symbols and swirls she couldn't decipher.

Beneath the sword was perhaps the most disturbing thing of all—a plaque that read:

Sword of St. Michael, Archangel
Replica
Donated by the Darlington Family at the dedication
of the Church of St. Michael, 1922
"To Destroy the Evil That Lies Within"

"Too bad you can't destroy this evil," Bridget said, nodding her head toward the choir as she leaned against the smooth stone of the church wall.

"Does she not think so?" a voice whispered.

Bridget spun around. Was someone else in the church?

Behind her lay an empty expanse of uniform wooden pews.

"The humans are fools. This we know, Koras."

No, not here. There couldn't be demons here. This was a church.

"You are wise, Mecadriel." The second voice was right on top of her, clearly discernible above the music.

"But have you heard?" the second voice continued. *"There is a Watcher now."*

Bridget froze. A Watcher? That's what the dolls had called her: a Watcher and a traitor.

"Hallelujah! Hallelujah!"

"The Master's servants will take care of the Watcher, as they have done for centuries."

"Yes, Mecadriel. Yes. There will be much enjoyment."

Bridget ran down the aisle, scanning pews to the very back of the church to make sure there was no one hiding. Then she threw open the doors of the rear confessional—first the two penitents' doors, then she cracked the priest's door, just to make sure it was empty. There had to be someone here messing with her. Had to.

"Bridget Liu!"

She slammed the confessional door. From the altar, Mr. Vincent, Ms. Templeton, and the entire show choir were staring at her.

"What are you doing?"

"Um, nothing?"

"Well, if you've finished exploring back there, could you please take your place for the carols medley?"

Bridget felt the heat rise from her chest as she trotted back up to the piano. Ms. Templeton had already packed away her binders, leaving Bridget's sheet music on the piano.

Maybe she was imagining it. Maybe she was sleep deprived. She pushed the invisible voices from her mind and flipped through her pages, making sure they were all in order, then prepped and looked expectantly at Mr. Vincent.

At his downbeat Bridget launched into the relatively simple accompaniment for "Angels We Have Heard on High." She focused on the music. This was a church, after all, a place of God. They couldn't be here. They couldn't, they couldn't, they couldn't.

The whispers exploded overhead, singing along to the carol in a cacophony of shrieks.

"Gloria in excelsis Luciferi."

"No!" Bridget pushed away from the keyboard, toppled off the bench, and cracked her head against the hard marble of the altar floor.

The voices stopped.

Hector's hand was on her shoulder, helping her to her feet. "Bridget? What's wrong?"

"I'm sorry. I—I have to . . ." She stumbled backward, her eyes darting about the altar. They were here. How could they be here?

"You have to what?" Mr. Vincent said.

Everyone stared at her, of course, like she'd just grown a second head. But she didn't care. There was something evil in the church, something that shouldn't, by the laws of Heaven and Hell, be there.

The dark interior of the sanctuary began to spin before her, the walls skewing and stretching from vertical. As she staggered away from the piano, the angels in the stained glass windows above the altar turned to her with cold grins.

"Bridge?" Hector's voice broke through her malaise, bringing the choir back into focus. His face was pale, his eyes lacked their usual sparkle. "Are you okay?"

Her hands were clammy, and she could feel droplets of

sweat cascade down her back. "I'm not . . . I don't . . ."

"You look pale. Maybe you should go to the nurse's office?"

A flick of dense auburn curls from the back row of the choir caught Bridget's attention, and she found a pair of deep green eyes, narrow as a cat's, fixed on her. Then Alexa tilted her head ever so slightly, her lovely fringe of lashes obscuring her eyes altogether.

"Heard us. Heard us. The dark one heard us."

"Impossible, the Master says he knows all who hear."

"Look at her! She knows. She knows!"

With a sharp intake of breath, those piercing eyes flew open.

Alexa heard the voices too.

"I gotta go." Bridget grabbed her backpack and ran.

SEVENTEEN

BRIDGET SPRINTED OUT THE SIDE door of the church, down the granite stairs into the school courtyard. Demons in the church? That was impossible, right? *Right?*

She stopped running and gulped deep breaths of crisp, damp air. Alexa had heard the voices too. She was sure of it. How could she and Alexa possibly be connected by those . . . *things*?

She wanted to confront Alexa, but what was she going to do—march back into choir practice and demand to know why Alexa was hearing disembodied voices in a church? Yeah, that was a one-way ticket to the loony bin.

No, she needed answers. Now.

Bridget whirled around and made for the rectory, throwing

the door open with such force that the crucifix in the entryway thumped against the wall in protest. She took the stairs two at a time and barged straight into Monsignor's office.

"Monsignor, I need to talk to—"

Father Santos was crouched behind Monsignor's desk. He shot to his feet as Bridget barreled through the door, his face bright red. "Bridget! W-what are you d-doing here?"

Bridget arched an eyebrow. "Me?"

"Yes, well. Yes, of course." Father Santos stepped out from behind Monsignor's desk. "I was just, er, retrieving a book. Yes, a book I lent Monsignor Renault."

"A book." There was no book in his hand, just a screwdriver he was trying desperately to shimmy up the sleeve of his jacket.

Father Santos cocked his head. "Are you all right?"

"Fine," she lied.

"D-did you need to speak with Monsignor? I believe he's with Ms. Laveau today, down at the doll shop."

Why was no one around when she needed them?

"Perhaps—perhaps I could be of some help?"

"Oh." Bridget stopped, taken aback. She hadn't thought to ask Father Santos, mostly because the last time they had a one-on-one, he had assaulted her. They'd just been having a normal conversation when he'd caught sight of her bracelet and lost his mind. A normal but totally weird conversation about the hand of God and . . . Whoa! That's where she'd heard about the Watchers first. Father Santos.

"Who are the Watchers?" she blurted out.

Father Santos's beady black eyes grew wide. "Has Monsignor mentioned them to you?"

"No."

"But someone has?"

"Yes."

Father Santos scratched his neck and scrunched up his face. "At the doll shop?"

Bridget nodded.

"How much time until your next class?"

Bridget glanced at the clock on the wall. "Fifteen minutes."

Father Santos nodded. "All right, then."

He walked straight out the door and across the hall. Not a word, not a gesture requesting her to follow. When he reached his office, he turned back and noticed she wasn't behind him.

"Well?" he asked with a sigh. "Do you want to know about the Watchers or not?"

Bridget cast a glance at Monsignor's desk. There was no doubt in her mind that Father Santos had been trying to get into the locked drawer, but why? The two priests didn't like each other, but what could Monsignor possibly have that would reduce Father Santos to breaking and entering?

He disappeared into his office. He could tell her what she needed to know, but did she really want to lock herself up in his office again? Or should she just wait for Monsignor?

Nope. This couldn't wait. She'd have to brave the multiple personalities of Father Santos.

Bridget heaved her backpack higher on her shoulder and followed the priest into his office.

"I'm going to tell you a story," Father Santos said when he was comfortably seated behind his desk.

Bridget rolled her eyes. Oh, wouldn't this be fun.

Father Santos held up a hand. "I know what you're thinking, but bear with me."

"Fine." Bridget slumped back in her chair and wondered if coming to him had been a mistake.

Father Santos swung his chair around to an antique cupboard against the wall. Bridget was pretty sure it hadn't been there during her last visit. He unlocked the cupboard with a tiny key and extracted a box: flat and wooden with a smooth, polished lid and a little brass latch on the side. Father Santos laid the box reverentially on his desk. He whipped out a pair of white cloth gloves, which he pulled on with great care, like a doctor about to go into surgery. Once he was sure the gloves were spotless, he opened the box and removed a plastic sleeve in which rested a collection of papers.

Father Santos slid the worn, yellowed pages from the plastic cover, and Bridget saw that their edges were jagged and frayed, as if they had been torn from a book, and they were written in a highly ornate, embellished scroll in what appeared to be Latin.

"Eighth century," Father Santos said, tracing the intricate border work with a gloved finger. "All that remains of the Skellig Manuscript, transcribed by the Augustinian monks of

County Kerry. The Vatican obtained these after they were smuggled out of Ireland during Cromwell's invasion, and they have remained in the archives ever since."

"They just let you take this from the Vatican?" That didn't sound like the Catholic Church she knew.

Father Santos cleared his throat. "I, um, have special privileges."

"Right." Of the five-fingered discount variety. Great: he was weird, schizophrenic, *and* a klepto.

"As I was saying," Father Santos said quickly. "The Skellig Manuscript tells a very unique version of how a group of angels fell from grace, a version that had never been told before, and never since."

Bridget arched an eyebrow. "Hello, Catholic school? I've heard this about a bazillion times."

"Do you want me to tell you about the Watchers or not?"

"Fine."

"Good. Now there was the first fall, when Satan led a rebellion against God and was defeated by the Archangel Michael. That's the one you learned about in school, no doubt. But there was another fall from grace, a second fall. The angel Semyaza led two hundred angels to Earth, where they had, um, *relations* with human women."

"Ew."

Father Santos laughed nervously. "Yes, well, Semyaza and his angels were banished for all eternity, where they became Satan's kings of Hell."

Bridget had to stifle a yawn. Her head was starting to spin with all the biblical nerdery. "Okay, sure." Why not?

He smiled in understanding. "Don't worry, this is where it gets interesting."

Bridget sure hoped so.

"According to the apocryphal books of the Bible, Semyaza and his followers were known as the Watchers."

Bridget sat upright in her chair. That was not what she'd been expecting. "No way."

"Way. And their human mistresses bore a race of half angel–half human giants known as the Nephilim."

"But why would the demons in the doll shop accuse me of being a fallen angel? It doesn't make any sense."

"I'm getting there. The Nephilim were evil, and they spread their corruption throughout the world of man. Eventually, God sent a great flood to rid the Earth of the Nephilim, but . . ." Father Santos carefully turned over the first loose page of the Skellig Manuscript and pointed to a line on the next page. "According to this, the Nephilim survived and remained loyal to their banished forefathers. To this day, they await the opportunity to summon the kings of Hell to Earth and take revenge upon God for their banishment."

Bridget was getting a little lost. "And that's bad, right?"

Father Santos cocked his head to one side. "Yes, that would be bad."

"Oh. Okay, got it."

"Here is where you come in."

Bridget grimaced. "If you tell me I'm in that book, I'm going to throw up on this desk right now."

"Heh." Again Father Santos carefully flipped another page of the manuscript. "Some of the Watchers," he continued, "showed repentance for their lust and wished to make amends to God. But an angel, once fallen from grace, cannot repent his sins. Instead, God took pity on their offspring. He separated the Nephilim into two groups: the Emim, descendants of the unrepentant fallen angels, and the Watchers, the children of the penitent angels tasked to succeed where their fathers had failed. God granted certain powers—the touch of God—to the Watchers, which allowed them to hold dominion over the Emim. It was their job to prevent the Emim from summoning their demon forefathers from Hell."

It all sounded so ridiculous. Bridget laughed out loud.

Father Santos looked hurt. "What's so funny?"

"You're trying to tell me that I'm part angel? Is that it?"

Father Santos laced his chubby fingers together. "That's exactly what I'm saying."

"That's the stupidest thing I've ever heard in my life."

"How do you figure?"

"Look, that's a cool story and all, but I don't believe I'm the latest in a line of biblical demon slayers. That's a little too Buffy for me, okay?"

"Then how do you explain what has been happening to you?"

Hormones. Depression. Maybe she was crazy? Any of those

options made more sense than Father Santos's story.

"You can't explain it, can you?"

Bridget threw up her hands. "But it doesn't even make sense! This is like a fairy tale, a bedtime story." She pointed at the Skellig Manuscript. "Things like this don't happen."

Father Santos pursed his lips and flipped to another page in the manuscript. "Oh, really? Then how do you explain this?"

Bridget followed his white-clad finger to the next page of the manuscript. It was a map, supposedly of Europe, Asia, and Africa, as best she could tell, though the topography was all wrong. Several of the land masses were labeled with titles Bridget didn't recognize, with arrows coming from the area around the Holy Land and sweeping north, south, and east.

"This is an eighth-century map of the known world, showing emigration patterns out of the Holy Land. The Emim did not care to be held in check by their cousins. Though they could not physically touch or harm the Watchers, they could use their influence over men against them. The Emim raised human armies that slaughtered hundreds of Watchers. The surviving Watchers fled, scattering themselves throughout the barely habitable regions of the world, forgetting much of who and what they were in the process. Nordic Europe, the barren deserts of Africa, the northern plains of China."

"China?" Bridget gaped.

"Yes," Father Santos said, flipping to the last of the manuscript pages. "The line of Watchers, listed here by their clan names. How's your Latin?"

Bridget cringed.

"Then I'll translate." Father Santos didn't even look at the page; he apparently had the manuscript memorized. "A tribe of Watchers moved to the east, to the kingdom known as Han, to the protection of the ruler of the Han, Emperor Gaozu, also known as Liu Bang."

Liu? "But that would mean my dad . . ." Her voice faltered.

Memories flooded her mind: her dad asking if she ever heard monsters in her room at night, reminding her if she ever had anything she needed to talk about, something she didn't understand, that she could always come to him. And her bracelet. That damned charm bracelet, which was, apparently, an amulet of exorcists going back a couple hundred years. Had he known what she was? Had he known because he had the same power?

"He would have told me," she said at last.

"Not necessarily. You only discovered your talents in the face of a demonic infestation, which is rare, to say the least. It's difficult to estimate how many Watchers never have an experience like that. Also, we aren't entirely sure whether the powers exist in each generation or only manifest randomly throughout a family line."

Bridget gripped the arm of the chair. Her hands trembled.

"He was k-killed last year," Father Santos said gently. "Wasn't he?"

"Killed" was an insult. "Murdered."

"Er, yes. By the man who broke into the sanctuary here at St. Michael's?"

Milton Undermeyer. Bridget nodded.

"Your father h-h-had seen Mr. Undermeyer on several occasions, and was in the process of diagnosing his mental capacities, correct?"

Father Santos knew way too much about the Undermeyer case for someone who had just shown up from the Vatican. It made her nervous.

"What's your point?" she said.

Father Santos stared at her with his small, dark eyes. "Schizophrenia is a common misdiagnosis for demonic possession. If your father was a, well . . . was like yourself, don't you think it rather odd that his death should coincide with such a case?"

"But—"

"Have you ever wondered why Milton Undermeyer, the school janitor, would have had to break into the church? He had a key to every door at St. Michael's."

"He was crazy."

"Or maybe he was possessed. And he knew something, something he never told anyone else. Something that made him break into the church that night."

Penemuel's words flooded her mind. *The messenger was sent. His warning was not delivered. You must find the messenger.* A message from her dad. A message from a Watcher.

Bridget closed her eyes. Could she really deny it? Could she really keep pretending that this wasn't happening?

"They called me a traitor," she said.

"Who did?"

"The demons at the doll shop. This is what they meant." She felt trapped. "I'm a traitor because I'm one of them. I'm a demon too."

"That's not true."

Bridget jumped to her feet. "Isn't it? If you're right, then we come from the same source, those demons and me."

Father Santos yanked at his collar. "Well . . ."

"So this thing I can do? This ability that you and Monsignor seem to think is so great? It's a big hot mess for me. Do you get that?"

"Bridget, let's not jump to conclusions."

"Monsignor said that demons are evil. Pure evil. Like, they have no other goal than spreading that evil through our world. How am I not a part of that?"

Father Santos sighed. "Honestly? I don't know." He leaned back in his chair and drew a hand over his brow. "But since you have the ability to banish evil from our world, it would make sense that you're not a part of it."

Like any of this made sense.

"Bridget, I know this is all very difficult, but you have to remember: You make your own choices, your own destiny. If you work against evil, against the powers of darkness in our world, it doesn't matter much who your ancestors were."

Easy for him to say. She seriously doubted that Mr. and Mrs. Santos had a demonic great-grandfather in the family tree.

"Speaking of which," Father Santos said. He reached into

his drawer and pulled out a Xeroxed piece of paper. "Maybe you can help me with this."

Bridget cast her eyes over the page. Handwriting, all caps, small and neat.

"It's what the dolls were chanting in the shop," he said. "What I could catch of it before they started launching themselves at my head."

"It's just gibberish."

"Demons rarely speak gibberish."

Bridget leaned forward and squinted at the words. "*'Potent dither trusts.'* Yeah, reads just like Shakespeare."

"Take it home. Read it over. Maybe something you heard will shed some light on this. I have a feeling it's important."

"Sure." Wasn't it always?

The bell rang and Bridget slowly rose to her feet, absently shoving the paper into her backpack. Once again, Father Santos was trying to get information out of her. Information she didn't have. Whatever. None of it mattered. Watchers, demons, lost tribes, Father Santos's demonic transcriptions. They could all take a flying leap as far as she was concerned.

"Bridget?"

"I said I'd look at it, okay?"

"I'm s-sorry," Father Santos stuttered.

Yeah, Bridget thought as she trudged back to the school building. Everybody was sorry. Sorry was easy. Sorry was for suckers.

EIGHTEEN

BRIDGET SIFTED THROUGH A SALE rack of dresses. "I can't believe I'm doing this." It was so not how she wanted to be spending her Saturday.

"I can't believe you waited until the last minute to pick out something to wear." Hector held up a lime green strapless dress with a bedazzled bodice. "Too much?"

Bridget snorted. "Not for you."

"Too bad *I* don't have a date for Winter Formal."

Bridget grimaced. "Sorry about the concert. I forgot they were the same night."

"Doesn't matter. You're grounded until the end of time anyway."

"True."

"Except where Mr. Dreamy Hazel Eyes is concerned."

"Barf."

Hector sauntered to the other side of the rack and dramatically flipped hangers back and forth. "No worries. Besides, I already have a date."

Bridget's jaw dropped. "What?"

"Don't look so surprised, beyotch."

"Let me guess, the barista from Grinds?"

Hector smiled and looked coy. "Maybe."

"Awesome." Bridget beamed from ear to ear. It was the first date Hector'd had since she'd known him. Maybe this would help him get over his hopeless crush on Brad. "I'm so happy for you."

"Wait till after the concert, then you can help me pick out engagement rings, okay?"

"Fine." Bridget moved to another rack. "Well, at least one of us will be having fun tonight."

"Oh, please, Bridge."

"What?"

Hector brought his fists to his eyes and wiggled them back and forth like a crying baby. "Wah, wah, wah. I'm Bridget and I have to go to Winter Formal with the hottest guy in town. Poor me."

"He's not the hottest guy in town," Bridget said, turning her back on him. "And even if he was, he still bugs me."

"Sure he does."

She whirled on him. "He does!"

Hector planted his hand on his chubby waist. "What you say: 'I hate him, I hate him, I hate him.' What I hear: 'I want to stick my tongue down his throat.'"

Bridget wrinkled her nose. "I think I just threw up in my mouth a little bit."

"Sure you did," Hector said, returning to the clothes rack.

She moved to the last rack, praying she found something decent for this stupid dance. Winter Formal. Blech. Was she supposed to get him a flower thingie for his jacket? Or was that only for prom? Was he going to show up with a corsage she'd have to wear, flapping around on her wrist all night? Would there be, like, official photos at the dance? Bridget's hands went cold. Sweet cartwheeling Jesus! Why was this so complicated? Why couldn't they just go for coffee for a first date or something?

Bridget froze.

First date. Try as she might to pretend otherwise, the truth of it was she and Matt were going on a date. But did he think of it that way? Or was Matt just doing what he thought he was supposed to: keeping an eye on her. Bridget shook her head. That had to be it. The only way a guy like Matt Quinn would invite himself to her Winter Formal was because *his* dad and *her* mom had told him to keep an eye on her.

Bridget sighed. Stop thinking it's something it's not, Bridge. Matt wouldn't want to date a spaz like you. He's not your boyfriend, he's your babysitter.

Somehow that was even more pathetic.

Bridget pulled a plum-colored dress off the rack and held it up in front of her before the mirror. It was simple—just an empire bodice with spaghetti straps and a flow-y skirt to the knee—but the shimmery, purple fabric made her normally blue eyes look a deep shade of aquamarine that was kind of cool.

"That's it," Hector said, coming up behind her. "That's the one."

"You think?"

"Look at your eyes," Hector said, rolling his. "They're, like, all magical."

She gave him a light elbow to the gut. "Don't be stupid."

"Whatever. Just try the damn thing on so we can get the hell out of here, okay? Girl departments make me feel . . ."

"Jealous?" Bridget smirked.

Hector narrowed his eyes. "Nauseous."

Bridget headed for the dressing room while Hector wandered around, checking out the accessories wall in the teen department. She stood before the mirror in her little changing cubicle and stared. That pinched look about her temples was still there, making her narrow Asian eyes droop at the corners. She didn't used to have it. It made her look sad and old.

Bridget lowered herself onto the little bench seat and sank her head in her hands. What was she going to do? Fallen angels, warring demons—this wasn't her life. It was like a comic book. If she hadn't heard the voices in the walls, experienced the old lady's possession, witnessed the dolls in the shop, she wouldn't have believed it herself.

Bad enough she was a freak, but having no one other than two priests to talk to about it was really starting to grate on her nerves. She thought of Hector digging through teen-girl belts outside the dressing room. She'd known him since they were in the seventh grade, when Mr. and Mrs. Gutierrez had yanked their only son out of public school. It had royally sucked for Hector, since he knew even then that (a) he was gay and (b) his parents wouldn't be accepting.

But he'd dealt with it, hadn't he? Not having anyone to talk to about what was going on? He'd opened up to Bridget. They'd bonded over a love of old nineties mod music like the Smiths and the Cure, and eventually he felt comfortable enough to tell her he had a crush on a boy in their class. He'd trusted Bridget with his secret. Maybe she could do the same?

"Bridget!" Hector whined from the dressing room doorway. "Hurry up. I'm hungry."

Bridget rolled her eyes. He was always hungry. "Coming!"

She left her jeans on and just pulled the dress up. Fit her hips? Check. Zippered up past her boobs? Check. Under fifty bucks? It looked like she had found her Winter Formal dress.

She hurried back into her Union Jack T-shirt and bomber jacket, paid for the dress, and collected Hector.

"Panda?" she asked as they exited the department store into the mall.

"You're the only Asian person I know who likes crappy Chinese food."

"It's the Irish half that craves it," she said, linking her arm through his. "Come on. My treat."

As much as Hector might bitch about it, Bridget knew he fostered a secret, eternal longing for Panda's orange chicken, which he proceeded to order two servings of before they found a quiet table near the back window of the food court.

"I want to talk to—" they said at the same time.

"Heh." Bridget laughed. It was so like them to have the same thoughts at the same time. "You first."

Hector laid his chopsticks on his napkin. "Is everything okay?"

Bridget dropped her eyes to her spring rolls. "Yeah, you know. Yeah."

"You seem a little . . ."

Bridget stole a glance at him. Hector shrugged and stabbed at a random piece of chicken.

"What?" she asked.

"I don't know. Off."

"Off like different than how I've been off for the last year?"

Hector traced a cascading water droplet down the side of his soda cup with his finger. "Well, yeah."

Bridget bit her lip. This was what she wanted, right? To confide in someone about all the weirdness that had started happening in her life? Here was her opportunity, wrapped up with a pretty little bow and delivered into her lap. All she had to do was say the words and make Hector believe them. Just say it. Just tell him.

Buzzzzz.

Hector and Bridget reached for their cell phones at the same time.

"Mine," Bridget said. She flipped open her phone and groaned out loud. "From Peter."

"Uh-oh."

Bridget read Peter's text. "'Where are you? Who are you with?'" She closed her eyes and shook her head. Bizarro Peter was back.

"Whoa." Hector pulled her hand over so he could see the text. "That's pretty desperate sounding. Even for Peter."

"Yeah." She remembered his face in the hallway, the haunted, obsessed look in his eyes.

Buzzzzz.

This time it was Hector's phone. "Oh, look, it's Peter," he said drily. "'Where are you? Are you with Bridge?' Wow, you've really turned that boy into a grade-A stalker."

"I have that effect on people."

"It's your kind and sweet nature."

Bridget snorted. "Thanks."

They fell silent. Bridget didn't know what to say about Peter's recent, disturbing behavior, and Hector seemed lost in thought. Maybe he'd comment on Peter and then she could transition the conversation to what she really wanted to talk about? That would seem totally natural. Maybe

Hector would even believe her this time.

Hector lifted a piece of orange chicken to his mouth and chewed really slowly, like he was buying time, trying to decide whether or not he wanted to say something. Bridget held her breath.

"I think you'll look freaking fantastic in that dress," he said at last.

Bridget felt deflated. "Thanks." The moment was gone. Did she really regret it? Telling someone about what had been going on with her would have been such a relief, but was Hector really the person who could handle it?

She wasn't sure. The only thing she knew was that, once again, she was on her own.

NINETEEN

RULE NUMBER FIVE: THEY LIE.

It was about the millionth time she'd reminded herself in the past week. Still, the message delivered by Penemuel haunted her, creeping up at odd moments of the day. She tried to fight it back, to remind herself that you couldn't trust the demons, but it didn't matter. Again and again she heard Penemuel's words in her mind:

Me-yer. Un-der. Un-der. Me-yer.

Again and again, over and over until she thought she would lose it. And every time her mind would drift to a mental hospital in Sonoma County, where an insane killer was locked away for the murder of Dr. David Liu.

With a heavy sigh, she leaned closer to the bathroom

mirror and ran a wand of liquid eyeliner over her lid, ending with a tiny swoop at the corner. The freckles on her nose and cheeks still peeped through the layers of foundation, powder, and blush, but there wasn't much she could do about them. She was already wearing more makeup than she'd applied since her mom let her quit Irish step dancing, and short of spackle, those annoying freckles would just have to stay. This was definitely the most effort she'd put into her appearance since before her dad died.

Bridget squeezed her eyes shut, so tight she thought her eyeballs might pop out the back of her head. She'd done a relatively good job of forcing the memories of the trial from her mind, but in the last few days they'd come rushing back with renewed force. Undermeyer at the defense table, twitchy and erratic. The insanity plea and the parade of mental health professionals who attested to a level of paranoid schizophrenia heretofore unseen in a patient. And, of course, Sergeant Quinn's testimony. How he'd brought Milton Undermeyer to see Dr. Liu for a series of psychiatric evaluations after his arrest. How two men had gone into Dr. Liu's office that day. How an hour later Undermeyer was found in the office alone, the body of Dr. Liu lying in a massive pool of his own blood, his throat sliced from ear to ear.

She'd never seen the crime scene photos of her dad's murder, but she didn't need to. The image of her dad's mangled body was burned into her brain forever. Her imagination was way worse than reality. Panic swept over her. Her heart raced and her chest broke out in a damp sweat. She gripped the St. Benedict's medal on her bracelet and held her breath.

She forced her eyes open and stared at herself in the mirror. "Breathe, Bridge," she said out loud. "Breathe."

She locked eyes with herself and practically willed her body into submission. Calm. Calm. Her breaths came slower; her heart rate receded to normal, nonfrantic levels.

Nothing made sense anymore. If Penemuel was lying to her, trying to lead her astray, why tell her to go talk to her dad's killer? It wasn't logical.

With a sigh, Bridget picked up a creased piece of white paper and reread Father Santos's Xeroxed notes.

Spins truth tottered.

Thunder totters spit.

Potent dither trusts.

Nonsense. The only thing she'd been able to figure out was that each line had the exact same letters, which she'd scribbled below.

D E E H I N O P R R S S T T T T T U

Anagrams. She was crappy at them. She even put the letters into an online anagram generator but only got more of the same weird gibberish. She laid the page back on the counter and grabbed her lip gloss. Maybe it didn't mean anything, just crazy demon talk? Why was Father Santos so convinced it was important?

A sharp knock at the bathroom door jarred Bridget just as she was about to apply a layer of gloss.

"What?"

"Bridge," Sammy whined. "I need to use the bathroom."

"Use Mom's."

"Nooooo," he whined.

"Why not?"

"I don't like it."

"Okay, okay. Hold on." Bridget took one last look in the mirror. Her curly brown hair was piled up on her head, her makeup was as good as she could possibly make it, and surprise surprise, she didn't look nearly as heinous in the dress as she thought she would. This was as good as it got.

Woo. Hoo.

"All yours, Sammy," she said, opening the door.

Her mom hustled down the hallway, camera in hand. "You look beautiful."

Bridget translated: You look so nice when you make an effort and don't wear that damn jacket and those boy boots. "Thanks, Mom." Better to let her have this moment, this fantasy of a normal daughter going to a dance with a normal boy. No harm in it.

"Your dad . . ." Her mom's voice quavered. "He would have been so proud."

Heavy tears overflowed from her mom's eyes and cascaded down her ruddy cheeks. There had been such a gap between them the last few months, with Bridget's new drama and her mom's friendships with Sergeant Quinn and Mr. Darlington. But suddenly none of it mattered.

Bridget threw her arms around her mom's neck and kissed her lightly on the cheek. "I love you, Mom."

She felt her mom's chest heave, but neither of them said another word.

"Ew," Sammy said, pushing past them. "Lame."

Her mom laughed and brushed a hand over each cheek. Then she grabbed Sammy from behind and pulled him to her in a tight embrace.

"Stop it, Mom. I'm not a baby."

"You'll always be my baby."

The doorbell saved Sammy from further embarrassment. He wiggled free of his mom's embrace and sprinted down the hall to answer the door. Bridget tripped after him, slow and a little awkward in her heels. She prayed she wouldn't fall on her ass in the middle of the St. Michael's gym and make herself the laughingstock of San Francisco high school lore for decades to come.

Matt stood in the entryway. She'd expected to find him in a boxy black suit with a foul-looking corsage in a Tupperware container. What she saw caught her off guard. Matt wore dark gray slacks and a matching five-button vest over a light gray shirt. It was a funky, retro look, topped off with a short-brimmed fedora in matching gray. No boxy jacket, and not a Tupperware container in sight.

"Hi," he said, removing his hat. "You look beautiful."

Bridget's eye went to the plum-colored tie around his neck that almost perfectly matched her dress. She was about to ask how he knew, but the answer hit her before the words escaped her mouth.

"Hector?"

Matt grinned.

"That traitor."

"I can be quite charming. When I need to."

They stood there on the landing and smiled at each other while her mom snapped random pictures behind them. Bridget tried to reconcile this funky version of Matt with the varsity jacket clad, overly protective, annoyingly perfect guy she knew.

"Come on, you two," her mom said, patience gone. "Stand together so I can get a good photo."

Bridget swallowed hard as Matt slid in next to her. He smelled really good, sort of musky and orange, and she couldn't help but close her eyes and take a deep whiff of it, letting the scent fill her nostrils. She wished she'd put perfume on. Or, um, had perfume to put on.

With her eyes still closed, Bridget felt Matt slip a tentative hand around her waist. Her eyes flew open, and Matt held his breath, waiting—she guessed—for a quick elbow in the ribs.

"Smile!" Bridget's mom said, and snapped off a half dozen photos.

After a second or two with no violent reaction, Matt's grip on her waist strengthened, and he pulled her into his body while her mom continued to snap away.

Bridget's heart raced, and she fought the urge to lean into

him. What the hell was wrong with her?

"Ew," Sammy said, and wrinkled his nose.

"Go to your room, Sammy," her mom said. Instead he plopped down on the floor with a pencil and a folded piece of paper and started working on one of his puzzles.

"We should go," Matt said, heading for the door.

Panic set in. She was going to a dance, a lame-ass school dance. And other than Matt, she wasn't going to know anyone there.

"Bridget," he said when she hadn't moved an inch. "Are you ready?"

"Uh, yeah," Bridget pulled a sweater from the coat rack. Oh, dear God, I'm really going to do this? "I guess."

"Home by midnight," her mom said from the door as Bridget picked her way down the stairs in her ridiculous silver heels.

Bridget was just stepping into Matt's truck when Sammy came tearing down the stairs after her.

"I solved it, Bridge. I solved it."

Bridget was confused. "Solved what, Sammy?"

Sammy waved the piece of paper he'd been fiddling with upstairs. "Your puzzle. The one you left me in the bathroom."

Bridget plucked the paper from his outstretched hand. She immediately recognized Father Santos's handwriting and the nonsensical demonic phrases. "Oh, no."

"Sammy, get inside," their mom called from the doorway. "Now!"

Sammy did a little pirouette, he was so pleased with himself, then pranced up the stairs.

"Everything okay?" Matt asked as he put the truck in gear.

"Yeah, totally," Bridget lied. "Sorry about that."

"It's okay. I like that little dude." Matt smiled and backed out of the driveway. As they drove away, Bridget glanced down at the paper of anagrams still clasped in her hand. At the very bottom, in a deliberate all-caps scrawl, was Sammy's solution:

DON'T TRUST THE PRIEST.

TWENTY

WHATEVER VAGUE HOPE BRIDGET HAD of concentrating on the St. Michael's Winter Formal disappeared in an instant. Don't trust the priest. Really? She went to a bloody Catholic school and was literally surrounded by priests every moment of every day. How in the hell was she supposed to know which one *not* to trust?

Rule Number Five: They lie. They lie. The demons at the doll shop were attempting to confuse her, fill her with questions and distrust. According to Monsignor Renault, that's what they did. You had to be strong. You had to ignore them.

"You okay?" Matt asked, glancing in her direction.

"Fine, yeah." Bridget shoved the scribbled bit of notepaper into her clutch. Perfectly totally fine except for the fact that I don't want to be here and I hate my life. Oh, wait . . .

"You seem kind of quiet."

Bridget snorted. "How long have you known me?"

"All right, calm down." Matt slowed for a light and flashed his winning, all-American smile. "That temper of yours is something else. I don't know whether I want to high-five you or slip you a Xanax."

Bridget pursed her lips. "Thanks."

"I just thought you might be nervous. About the dance."

What was she, twelve? Bridget was about to set him straight when she realized that it was probably safer for Matt to think she *was* nervous about the stupid dance rather than it was to explain what was really going on.

"Er, yeah. Yeah, I guess I am," she said.

"I'm sorry," Matt said quickly. "I know I kind of conned you into coming. I just thought you might—"

A loud buzz came from Bridget's bag. She pulled out her cell phone and saw she had a text. From Peter Kim.

Are you really going to Winter Formal?

"Anything important?" Matt asked.

"Nope." Just this stalker I seem to have picked up.

Another buzz.

You are, aren't you? Going with Matt Quinn?

"I just thought you might enjoy the dance. Have a little fun. Smile."

It was equal parts sweet and pathetic. "I smile, thank you very much."

"Yeah." Matt glanced in her direction. "But you should do it more. It's cute."

Did Matt Quinn just call her cute?

Buzz.

How could you, Bridge? How could you?

Peter was starting to creep her out. Bridget needed something to distract her.

"You won't get in trouble with your coach?" she said, hoping this would be a topic Matt could prattle on about. "Staying out so late?"

Matt's shoulders relaxed. "No. Practice isn't till noon tomorrow, and it's optional."

Buzz.

He's no good for you.

Buzz.

AND his dad practically killed your dad.

Buzz.

ANSWER ME, BRIDGET!

Bridget shoved her phone into her bag. What the hell was wrong with everyone tonight?

"How long have you played baseball?" she asked mechanically.

"Since I moved in with my mom," Matt said. His voice sounded enthusiastic. Finally, something he wanted to talk about that wasn't the dance or her dad.

"Oh, yeah?"

"She needed something to keep me busy. Little League,

pitching coaches, then Riordan."

Buzz. Buzz. Buzz. Buzz.

"I've been scouted," he continued. "Couple of colleges plus the big leagues. Could be really good for me."

"That's awesome."

Buzz. Buzz. Buzz.

Matt shrugged. "Maybe. If I stay healthy. I could blow out my arm tomorrow and it would all go away. You never know."

Buzz. Buzz. Buzz.

"I guess not."

Matt pulled into the parking lot at St. Michael's. Couples in sparkly dresses and ill-fitting suits trekked to the gym, and Bridget was suddenly horrified. She was at a school dance, something she'd sworn she'd never do. It was a sign of the Apocalypse.

Matt cut the engine, then laid a hand on Bridget's arm as she started to open her door. "Wait."

He slipped out of the driver's side and walked around to open her door. The perfect gentleman. As he made his way around, Bridget flipped open her phone to read the messages she'd ignored. All from Peter.

Why would you do this?

This is all your fault.

Bridge, just give me a chance.

I'd make you happier than he could.

I'll die without you.

Maybe you didn't go after all? Bridge?

Perfect. She'd managed to turn Peter Kim into a complete psychopath. The night just got better and better.

Matt pulled the door open and offered her his hand. "Ready?"

Bridget took an apprehensive glance at the couples lined up outside the gym, and part of her wanted to run screaming home, crawl under the covers, and hide.

She caught Matt's eye and he smiled. "You'll have fun. I promise."

Her phone buzzed, but this time she didn't even look at the text. She hit the mute button, shoved it in her purse, and took Matt's outstretched hand. "Okay, but if I don't, I'm going to kick your ass."

Bridget trotted beside Matt, who strode confidently across the parking lot, holding her hand firmly in his. His confidence was almost annoying, considering this wasn't even his school, but at the same time she felt a sense of protection in it. At the very least no one would hassle her as long as she was with Matt Quinn.

"Matt!" Bridget turned to see a vaguely familiar-looking senior. He was tall with a shaved head and goatee. Class president maybe? She had no clue.

"Hey, Chris," Matt said. They did the patented brosive handshake—chest bump combo. "What's up?"

Chris's date wore the littlest little black dress Bridget had ever seen. If she dropped her purse and had to pick it up there'd be a Britney getting out of the limo moment. She pawed at Chris's arm in a nauseatingly territorial display like she was afraid he was going to ditch her.

"This is Chelsea," Chris said. "She goes to Mercy."

Otherwise known as the Sluts on the Slope. Bridget was pretty sure she saw Chris wink at Matt. Ew.

Matt ignored it. "Nice to meet you. And this is Bridget. Bridget, Chris and Chelsea."

Chris nodded at Bridget while Chelsea ignored her. That was about right.

"So what are you doing here, man?" Chris asked.

"I'm pretty sure there's a dance tonight."

"A St. Michael's dance. You crashing?"

Matt looked sidelong at Bridget. "Dude, Bridget goes to school here."

Chris looked at Bridget again, squinting, trying to place her. "Oh," he said at last, still not convinced. "Oh, yeah. Cool!"

"Liu, is that you?" Brad bounded up and slapped her on the back like she was a teammate. "I didn't know you were coming to the dance."

"Oh, I guess I forgot to mention it." More like avoided mentioning it in front of Peter. Like death.

"Hey," Matt said. Again with the handshake–chest bump. "Bridge, you didn't tell me you knew Brad."

"Yeah, man," Brad said. "We totally hang out."

A look of confusion flashed across Matt's face. Hang out. Right. She prayed he wouldn't ask her about Brad later.

How was she supposed to explain that gay men flocked to her like she was wearing a freaking disco ball as a hat without totally and completely outing Brad who, to be honest, might or might not be gay?

Thankfully, Brad was unfazed. He turned and waved to a group of dudes—some with dates, some without—standing by an SUV in the parking lot. "Guys, look! Matt Quinn!"

Then there was a dude-alanche as the entire St. Michael's JV and varsity baseball teams piled on Matt. He chest- and/or fist-bumped his way through them with a chorus of "Wussup?" and "Hey, man" until he had completed the gauntlet. Then Bridget found herself being introduced to a blur of people.

"You're in my fourth-period shop class," said a freckled redhead baseball player.

Um, no.

"Hey, I think we had religion together freshman year," said one of their dates.

The girl was a senior, so Bridget doubted it.

Bridget smiled and tried to remember names and faces, but it was totally hopeless. She wasn't used to this new social thing, and she wasn't sure she ever would be.

"See you inside, guys." Matt placed a hand on Bridget's back and guided her toward the line of students outside the gym. Could he tell she was reaching social overload?

"I think you know more people at my school than I do," Bridget said. She wasn't sure if she was amused or horrified.

"You think?"

Bridget scowled. "Your sarcasm is not appreciated."

Matt's smile was playful. "Come on. You only hang out with, like, two people." He glanced back at Brad. "Three, I guess. And you do it on purpose, so don't throw that poor-me crap."

"Maybe I just don't find them that interesting."

"Maybe," he teased, "you're afraid they might not find *you* that interesting."

Ouch. That hurt.

They made it to the front of the line and were searched by a security guard. The school secretary, a frazzled woman who Bridget thought was named Mrs. Freeny, asked for Bridget's ID and checked her off a list. Then her eyes rested on Matt.

"Matthew Quinn!" she cried. Her whole face lit up. "It's so good to see you."

"Hi, Mrs. Freely." Freely, not Freeny. Oops. "How's Jacob's swing?"

Mrs. Freely stamped Bridget's hand without looking at her. "So much better since you worked with him. He still talks about you all the time. Are you coaching summer camp again this year?"

"Yeah, I think so. Tell Jacob I say hi."

Mrs. Freely beamed at Matt while they walked to the bag check table. There was another round of "Hey, Matt" as they walked inside, accompanied by confused looks in Bridget's direction.

Matt literally knew half the people in the gym. At *her* school. Bridget stared at the floor. It was more than a little embarrassing.

He slipped his hand around her waist. "You okay?"

"Fine," Bridget lied.

He checked her purse, tucking the ticket inside his vest pocket, all while keeping one hand on her waist. Her gut instinct was to flinch away, but his hand was strong and confident resting there above her hip. It felt . . . nice?

Matt guided her to the edge of the dance floor and glanced down at her feet. "No combat boots? But you promised."

"I threatened."

"Do you fight all the time with everyone you know, or is it just me?"

Bridget's witty comeback was interrupted by a hoarse laugh from behind. "Hello, Matt."

Bridget spun around to find Alexa Darlington's green eyes staring through her. She was wearing the most gorgeous dress Bridget had ever seen: a kind of wispy tiered skirt with a sweetheart fitted bodice, all in icy blue with a hint of sparkle. Her deep auburn hair was piled up in a complicated twist, with tendrils of her signature corkscrew curls framing her neck and face.

"Doing charity dates now, are we?" she said without even trying to hide her disgust.

Matt drew Bridget behind him, as if to protect her from Alexa's venom. "Are you kidding? I was lucky Bridget agreed to go with me."

"Like anyone here knows who she is."

Matt took a step forward. "At least when you get to know Bridget, you still like what you see."

Bridget stepped out from behind Matt to get a full look at him. His eyes were narrow, his cheeks pinched. Whatever had happened between them, he pretty much hated Alexa as much as Bridget did. Point to Matt Quinn.

"Aw, that's cute. Playing the big man in front of your little date."

Bridget bristled. She didn't need anyone sticking up for her. "Hey, Alexa, don't you have an entire football team to make out with? You know, now that you've worked your way through the spring sports?"

"Bitch!" Alexa spat the word out; her eyes glowed with anger.

"Come on, Bridge," Matt said, taking her hand. "Let's dance."

Bridget was painfully aware that everyone in the gym was staring at them as Matt half dragged her out onto the dance floor. Great, now she had to stress about an audience witnessing her total lack of dancing ability. Last thing she needed to do was embarrass herself further.

Thankfully, sort of, the DJ morphed into a slow song, and instead of some half-assed attempt at hip-hop, Bridget found herself swaying awkwardly with her arms around Matt's neck.

"Can I ask you something?" Bridget said.

"Sure."

"Why did you date her?"

She felt Matt's body stiffen and realized she'd probably overstepped her bounds. What were they to each other anyway? This wasn't a real date, just some prolonged babysitting on his part.

"I—I don't know," Matt said. His voice sounded far away.

Bridget had no idea how to respond to that. "Okay."

"I met her last spring, right after your dad's funeral."

Now it was Bridget's turn to stiffen.

"She came up to me after a game I pitched against St. Michael's. And then, I don't know. We were dating. I don't really even remember asking her out, I just remember those deep green eyes . . ." Matt gave a shake of his head and looked down at her. "Can we not talk about Alexa?"

"Gladly."

Matt pulled her close and rested his head against her shoulder. Bridget's heart nearly leaped up her throat. She'd never danced with a guy before, but now she found herself wrapping her arms tightly around Matt's neck. It felt good to be that close to him, the orangey scent of his cologne dulling her senses.

It should have been awkward, uncomfortable, the worst moment of her life. But it wasn't. She felt protected, like for once she could let her guard down. She was so proud of being strong, tough, someone who could stand by herself without anyone's help. But it was exhausting. It felt nice, for once, to give in.

Matt lifted his head from her shoulder, grazing his cheek against hers. His clean-shaven face was soft, and Bridget couldn't ignore the chill that rocketed down her spine. Matt slipped his arms farther around her waist, wrapping them one over the other as he held her body firmly against his own, gazing into her eyes. Bridget's breaths were short and her brain was fuzzy. Suddenly she didn't care if the entire gym was staring at her, she only cared that Matt was holding her, protecting her. And it felt good.

He rested his forehead against hers and closed his eyes. Bridget wasn't even sure if they were moving to the music anymore. She had a desperate urge to feel Matt's lips against her own. She stood on her tiptoes, arching her face up to his. . . .

That's when she heard it.

"Yesssss."

TWENTY-ONE

BRIDGET BROKE AWAY. "DID YOU say something?"

"No."

"Oh." Dammit. Not now. Not here.

Matt pulled her face close to his; the warmth of his breath on her face calmed her. "Are you okay, Bridge?"

"I'm fine," she said hesitantly. "I just thought I heard something."

Matt put his arms back around her, and they continued to dance. But Bridget felt stiff, on edge, like she was tensing up in expectation of a punch to the gut. That lovely sensation of abandon had vanished.

"*Yesssss,*" the voice hissed again. "*It is the hour. We are ready.*"

This time Bridget pushed Matt away, her eyes scanning

the room, waiting for any sign of the telltale vertigo that usually announced a demonic presence.

The DJ started a bass-thumping Ke$ha remix that set the whole dance floor screaming with glee. Students rushed forward in a dizzying blur of dark and light that made Bridget stagger. Matt caught her arm. "You want to get something to drink?"

"Yeah, thanks."

They headed to the refreshment table, where Matt ordered them two glasses of sparkling apple cider. Bridget downed hers in one gulp, wishing there was booze in it. If ever she needed a drink, it was now. First the church, now the gym. Demons. Why were they here?

"We are ready!" There were several voices this time, all speaking in unison. Bridget could feel the demons gathering in strength—like the rhythm of a collective breath heaving in and out—but the atmosphere of the gym hadn't changed. The temperature hadn't dropped and the air didn't have that dense, meaty feeling as if it were thickening with every passing moment. The demons were somewhere close by, but not in the gym.

"Bridget, do you need to sit down?" Matt was staring at Bridget's hands; they were shaking. "You look like you're going to be sick."

"No, it's just . . ." It's just what? I can hear demons in the walls and I'm having a tough time ignoring them, even with your cute, boyish smile?

"Just what?"

"We are ready for the Master! Ready for the Master!" The voices were shrieking now. A nasty, bone-chilling howl that shook her to the core. *"Slit his throat! Spill his blood for the Master!"*

"No!" Bridget yelled out loud.

"Bridge?"

Bridget spun wildly around the gym, a kaleidoscope of streamers and swirling lights, flailing arms and spinning bodies. Another murder. There was about to be another murder, and only she could stop it. All she had to do was figure out where the voices were coming from.

Bridget ran for the back door of the gym into the south courtyard of St. Michael's Prep. The whole courtyard was awash in strange, dancing lights—blues and greens, reds and purples. Bridget looked up and saw that the stained glass windows of the church looked alive as light flickered and lapped at their panes.

Matt trotted up behind her. "Bridget, what the hell is going on?"

She held up a hand. "Shh!"

"Don't shush me. Look, I told you I didn't hear anything."

"You wouldn't." God what was he going to think of her? A complete loony? Shake it off, Bridget. It doesn't matter. She had to find where the voices were coming from.

"Blood! Blood! Blood! The Master demands blood!"

The church.

She ran for the side door of the church, but Matt grabbed

her arm. "Where are you going?"

"The church. Matt, please, you have to let me go. Something terrible is going to happen."

"In the church?"

"I think someone's about to be murdered."

"Murdered?"

"I know you think I'm crazy, but you have to believe me."

Matt forced a laugh. "Bridge, come on. How could you possibly know—"

A bloodcurdling scream pierced the courtyard.

Without a word Matt and Bridget sprinted toward the church. Matt reached the door first and twisted the handle, but the door was locked. Bridget veered right and made for the door to the sacristy. She yanked it open and ran through the priests' dressing area, out onto the altar.

"Not enough! Not enough! Not enough hatred! Not enough pain for the Master!" the voices wailed in agony.

The atmosphere inside the church was heavy and thick. There were hundreds of candles lit, standing all around the altar, like she'd interrupted some kind of ritual. Footsteps echoed through the church, and somewhere near the front entrance, a door opened, sending a gust of wind racing through the sanctuary. It snuffed out the candles and plummeted the church into darkness.

"You have failed. You have failed the Master!" The demons were losing power, their numbers dwindling with the wispy smoke of the extinguished candles, their voices fading into

the darkness. *"Failed, failed, failed, failed, failed."*

The oppressive energy in the church evaporated. The entities were gone, but what had they been talking about? Slit his throat? Spill his blood? Bridget's eyes had not yet adjusted to the dark, but there had to be someone here, someone in danger. She stepped forward cautiously, arms reaching out in front of her in the blackness. She barely made it three steps before her silver heels slipped in something on the slick marble floor.

A moonbeam streamed through the stained glass window, illuminating a figure on the ground just blow the tabernacle. Lying in a pool of dark, shiny liquid—his throat slit from ear to ear and a twisted look of horror on his face—was Peter Kim.

The next hour was a blur. Bridget felt like she was swimming through a pool of Jell-O. Her limbs were heavy: Simply lifting an arm or putting one foot in front of the other took three times as much strength as usual.

The world slowed down. There had been another scream, that she knew for sure. She was pretty sure the strangled cry came from her own throat, though honestly she couldn't be sure. She remembered someone's arm around her waist, pulling her away from the blood-soaked body of her friend. Matt's arm, probably, though again she was only vaguely aware of it.

Then there had been more people, more screams, more

noise. She wasn't sure how, but Bridget found herself outside in the damp, cold air. The fog had rolled in again, a dense, gooey bank of the stuff that muted the lights of the school, the murmur of voices, the dull thud of feet running to and fro, and the eventual wail of sirens. The fog was appropriate, somehow. The buildings came and went from view with the varying gusts and billows. People seemed to appear from nowhere, then disappear once more. Nothing felt solid, nothing real. Maybe it had all been a dream. Maybe she'd never gone to the dance at all. Maybe.

Arms. She remembered a pair of strong arms around her, keeping everyone at bay, the occasional sharp word to someone who wanted to ask her a question. Then soothing words. "It's okay, Bridge. It's okay. It's not your fault."

Did she think it was her fault? Maybe. Those text messages on her phone. She should have answered him, told him to calm down, told him she wasn't going on a date, lied to him. How had Peter ended up at the Church of St. Michael? Had he come to spy on her? To confront her and Matt? That anger and rage she'd seen recently—that wasn't the Peter Kim she knew. What had come over him?

"Shh. It's not your fault, Bridge. It's not."

"Yes, it is," a voice sobbed. Her voice. "You don't know. You don't understand."

The police arrived, a whole army of them. They scurried through the courtyard, in and out of the church, the gym, and the school like ants on a feeding frenzy. Sergeant Quinn was there. He trembled when he hugged her.

She wanted to sink down onto the ground, curl up in a ball, and cry, but there were detectives who wanted to ask her questions, and Bridget was the only one who could help. Answers to *their* questions, at least, were easy.

"You found the body?"

"Yes."

"Did you know the victim?"

"Yes.

"His name?"

"Peter Kim."

"Why did you go into the church?"

"Heard a scream."

"Did you see anyone else?"

"No."

"Are you sure?"

"Yes."

Matt had been pulled away for questioning of his own. And Bridget felt naked without his arm around her waist. Still the questions came. Still her voice answered. But she was tired. So tired.

Someone patted her shoulder, and then there was a hand on her arm. Not Matt this time, but it was comforting all the same. Someone had come to rescue her.

"This way, Bridget," Monsignor Renault said. "Let's get you out of here."

TWENTY-TWO

BRIDGET SHIVERED UNCONTROLLABLY. HER TEETH chattered and her palms were damp. Beneath the thin, shimmery fabric of her dress, her skin was covered in goose pimples. Only she wasn't cold. Quite the opposite. As she sat next to Father Santos in Monsignor Renault's office, she felt as if she were running a fever.

"This is a very serious situation," Monsignor was saying. Bridget could barely hear him over the chattering of her own teeth. "Very serious."

Bridget nodded. Her brain couldn't form a word to save her life.

"The police will conduct a thorough investigation?" Father Santos said.

"Quite," Monsignor replied.

"They'll see the pattern, won't they? This murder and that of Dr. Liu?"

A shock went through Bridget's body. She thought of Sergeant Quinn as he gripped her by the shoulders and looked her dead in the eye. He'd thought the same thing.

"A copycat killer, in all likelihood," Monsignor Renault said.

"I doubt they'll find anything," Father Santos continued. "Just like last time. No murder weapon, no evidence. Just a corpse."

Monsignor glanced at Bridget. "Hmm. Um, Father Santos . . ."

"And there will be days of questions. The boy's body was—"

"Peter," Bridget said, her voice raspy and coarse. "His name was Peter."

Father Santos leaned forward in his chair to look Bridget in the face. She didn't even glance his way, just continued to stare at the Pietà paperweight on Monsignor's desk.

"I'm sorry," Father Santos said, leaning back again. "Peter's body, found in that condition and with the symbols drawn in a circle around his body. There are bound to be questions about the religious implications of such a death."

"Murder," Bridget corrected him. They might as well call it what it was.

"Murder," Father Santos repeated.

"Yes, questions." Monsignor rested his elbows on his desk and twirled the silver ring absently around his finger. "They won't find what they are looking for that way."

"And, of course, Bridget will be their focus."

Monsignor tilted his head. "I'm sorry?"

"The police. They'll want to talk to Bridget again. After all, she's the link between these two murders."

Bridget stared straight ahead. She was a link between the murders. Of course. Alexa had said it; now Father Santos too. Just like possessions, death followed her.

Monsignor slammed his fist down on the desk. "Father Santos. Bridget is not responsible for these murders, do you understand? And I will not sit here and listen to any suggestion to the contrary."

"O-o-o-oh, yes. Of . . . of course." Father Santos wrung his hands in his lap. "I just wanted . . . I mean . . ."

"Bridget," Monsignor said softly. "Let's discuss what you saw tonight. If you're okay to talk about it again."

It was kind of him to change the subject, and she was eager to tell him what he wanted to know. "Yeah. I'm fine."

"Aside from what you told the police, was there anything else you remember?"

"Um . . . ," she started.

Father Santos shifted in his chair to face Bridget. "Was there anything you heard in the sanctuary? Voices? Sounds? Something familiar, perhaps? Or something that happened before that you might see in a new light now?"

Bridget opened her mouth, then snapped it shut. She was about to tell them about Penemuel when the warning message of the demon dolls popped into her head. *Don't trust the priest.* She glanced at Monsignor. She wanted to confide in him, but not here. Not in front of Father Santos.

"I know it was quite a shock," Father Santos continued. He seemed intent on getting some sort of answer out of her. "If you aren't sure, maybe we should go back and check again? Maybe something in the church will trigger a memory?"

Why was he questioning her?

"I'm sure Bridget would tell us if she heard anything relevant."

"Yes," Father Santos said quietly. "I'm sure."

"Let us recap then, shall we?" Monsignor said. "Bridget must be exhausted, and I'm sure she would prefer to be home with her family."

Bridget smiled at Monsignor. That was exactly what she wanted.

"We've had three instances of demonic infestation in just over a month, and now this murder with apparent satanic overtones. We believe these events are related?"

"Most definitely," Father Santos said.

Monsignor nodded. "I agree. But we also know that these demons have no physicality unless they are attached to a human body, and even then, to undertake a murder of this magnitude, it would have to be the strongest, most thoroughly acquiescent case of possession I've ever seen."

"True," Father Santos said.

"So we are left with the reality that a human such as you"—he pointed to Father Santos—"or I has perpetrated this crime."

"Yes," Father Santos said quickly. "But it would have to be someone with an intimate knowledge of the benefits of such a murder."

Bridget turned on him. "Benefits? What's the benefit of murdering a fifteen-year-old science whiz? What were they going to do, harvest his brain?"

"N-no," Father Santos said. "I was thinking more of his emotions."

"What about them?"

"Er." Father Santos pulled at his collar with his index finger. "You and Peter. I mean, you two. I mean, *he* . . ."

His voice died, but Bridget wasn't going to make this easy on him. "Yes?"

"He had a very strong attachment to you," he said at last. "Correct?"

"So what if he did?"

"Ah," Monsignor said as if he'd just discovered the cure for the common cold. "Of course. The killer was harvesting Peter's rage."

Bridget thought of the thirty-seven text messages sitting unanswered on her phone. "His rage?"

"Yes, his anger and jealousy." Father Santos spoke quickly with obvious excitement. "In some of the medieval grimoires, the process of conjuring a demon and creating a dominance over one involves a great deal of raw emotion. A talented conjuror could summon a lesser demon and hold it prisoner for a short length of time, using raw emotion such as anger or jealousy as a means of controlling the demon."

Anger and jealousy. The demons in the church had said as much. *"Not enough hatred for the Master."* Judging by the text messages on her phone, Peter was chock full of enough anger and jealousy to conjure a whole fleet of demons. Was that it? The killer was trying to use Peter's emotions in some sort of ceremony?

Monsignor rose from his chair and came around to the front of his desk. "I think we have missed something. Some clue as to who our killer is and what he wants."

Clue? This wasn't exactly Colonel Mustard in the conservatory with the revolver.

"Bridget, is there anything you overheard, anything you didn't tell us?"

Why was she hiding anything from Monsignor Renault? Wasn't he the only person she'd been able to talk to about her new abilities? Hadn't he spent his time helping her, guiding her, showing her how to banish these demons?

"Do you think," she began tentatively. "Do you think there's anyone who can hear the same things I hear?"

Monsignor looked taken aback. "What do you mean?"

"I just was wondering." Bridget thought of Alexa and how she seemed to hear those voices in the church during choir practice. "I thought, maybe, someone else might have heard what I did."

Monsignor raised his left eyebrow. "Really? Who?"

Bridget swallowed hard. "Alexa Darlington."

"No," Monsignor shook his head. "That's impossible."

Was he serious? "It's impossible for her but not for me?"

"Bridget, the Darlingtons are one of the oldest families in this parish. I've known Alexa since she was born. If there was anything out of the ordinary about Alexa, I would have noticed it by now."

"Oh." Bridget sighed. Of course he would have noticed. Maybe she'd just been imagining things?

Silence. Monsignor didn't move, and Bridget felt both his and Father Santos's eyes on her. They were waiting for her to say something else, but Bridget bit her lips closed. *Don't trust the priest.* She had nothing to say. Not to them.

"Very well," Monsignor said.

Bridget slid forward in her chair, sensing that the interview was coming to an end. Her body ached, and as the adrenaline wore off, a chill had settled over her. The goose pimples and chattering were for real now.

"Go home, Bridget," Monsignor said. "Go home and spend time with your mom and your little brother."

Sammy. God, how was she going to explain Peter's death to Sammy? "Yeah."

"Good." Monsignor patted her hand. "If you think of anything, remember anything, let me know. Promise?"

Bridget met his eye. She wanted to cry at the thought of keeping a secret from him, but somehow she knew that she needed to tackle Milton Undermeyer on her own.

"Promise," she lied.

Bridget was numb as she got out of her chair and shuffled toward the door. Her feet hurt from those stupid heels, and her body felt like she'd been hit by a truck. But she barely registered her pain, she was so focused on what she needed to do next. Milton Undermeyer. It was time to talk.

"Bridget!"

Matt was waiting for her, sitting on the rectory steps with Bridget's clutch purse in his lap. As soon as she came through the door, he scrambled to his feet and rushed toward her.

"Are you okay?"

Matt's clothes were wrinkled. His sandy blond hair stuck straight up from his head as if he'd been running his hands through it incessantly for the better part of an hour. His tie hung limp and loose on either side of his neck, and his vest flapped open, completely unbuttoned.

"Yeah," she said, lying for the second time in as many minutes.

They stood for a moment staring at each other. Then Matt's eyes drifted to her bare, goosefleshy arms. His hands flew to his chest before he remembered that he wasn't wearing a jacket.

He took her hand and pulled her across the courtyard. "Come on."

Bridget was too tired to argue. She allowed him to tow her through the damp, frigid courtyard and out to the front of the school. There were three squad cars and a coroner's van parked out front.

"Hey, Officer Terry," Matt said, flashing a smile.

"Matt," Office Terry said. "What are you—" His eyes drifted to Bridget. "The dance?"

"Yeah. Hey, do you have an extra jacket in the squad car?"

"Sure, man." Officer Terry reached through the open passenger side window and pulled a heavy black jacket off the floor of the squad car. "Anything for a Quinn."

Matt smiled. "Thanks. I'll have my dad bring it back tomorrow."

Officer Terry winked and strode back toward the crime scene. Bridget didn't watch him go, trying hard to keep the image of Peter's mangled body out of her mind.

"Better?" Matt said, draping the coat around her shoulders. The thing practically reached her knees and it reeked of stale cigarettes, but it was warm.

"Yeah, thanks."

"Bridget," Matt started. She could tell by the sound of his voice—all deep and parental—that something weighed on his mind. "Bridget, what's going on?"

"How would I know?" Wow, who knew lying could be so easy once you got the hang of it?

"I don't . . . I mean." He took a deep breath and ran his fingers through his hair. The long bits in the front hung vertical for a moment, then flopped over his forehead. "Look, I'm sorry about your friend and all, but how did you know? How did you know there'd be a murder?"

Bridget dropped her eyes to the ground. How was she supposed to explain this?

"I heard you with Detective Paulson. You didn't tell her about the voices you heard."

Bridget tried to look like she had no idea what he was talking about.

"Please, I saw you. In the gym, in the courtyard. You heard . . . something."

"Something" didn't even begin to cover it.

"And then you got hauled into Monsignor's office with that other priest. Those were the ones you were with after school on Thursday, right?"

Bridget nodded. She was so tired of keeping secrets. She felt hopeless and powerless against the misery around her. Her dad was dead. Peter was dead. Bridget was the link between them, and Matt was slowly putting the pieces together. There was just no point in denying any of it.

"Well?" he asked.

"Well, what?"

"Well, it's . . . weird."

Bridget pulled the police jacket up over her ears. Weird was an understatement.

Matt waited, no doubt hoping Bridget would chime in and save him from whatever bizarre ideas were running through his mind, but she just didn't have the energy to do it. He reached out and found her fingertips with his own, grazing against them lightly before pulling his hand away.

"I guess what I'm trying to say is that, well, I know you don't like me very much, but if you want to talk or you need anything . . . anything at all."

Need anything? There was one thing she needed desperately.

"Take me to Geyserville tomorrow," she blurted out.

"Huh?"

"You said what do I need? I need to go to Geyserville."

Matt cocked his head. "Why?"

She needed to say it, to trust someone, anyone with her secret. He might not have been her first choice, but at that moment Bridget needed to trust Matt Quinn.

"I need you to take me to Sonoma State Hospital. To see Milton Undermeyer."

Matt's eyes grew wide as he realized exactly what she was asking. It wasn't just a quaint Sunday drive into the wine country; she was asking him to take her to see the man who had killed her dad.

"Please," she said softly.

Matt looked her straight in the eye as if he were searching for some reason to say yes. He must have found it. "I'll pick you up at ten."

TWENTY-THREE

MATT IDLED THE TRUCK WHILE Bridget plodded up the stairs to her front door. Her legs felt like they were made of cement. The staircase was interminable—she might as well have been climbing Everest—and just when she thought she was going to sink down onto a step and crawl her way to the top, her feet met the soft cushy doormat. Phew.

She half turned and waved a lank good-bye at Matt as she fumbled for her keys. She had been dreading this moment, dreading the idea of having to tell her family what had happened in the church that night, dreading the memories of her dad's murder that would inevitably bubble to the surface.

The door swung open before Bridget got her key in the lock. Her mother stood in the entryway, her eyes red and puffy. Bridget realized she wouldn't have to explain anything.

"Bridget!"

"Mom."

Mrs. Liu pulled Bridget to her with a force so desperate in its need, so violent in its panic that it knocked the breath right out of her. "My baby girl. I'm sorry. I'm so sorry."

Bridget let her body sag into the embrace. Once again the release felt so good. She wanted to tell her mom everything, to relinquish control of her life, to let someone else make all her decisions. It would feel so wonderful. . . .

"Annie?" Hugh Darlington's voice made Bridget's stomach drop. "Is she all right?"

Her mom broke away. "Yes. Yes, Hugh." Bridget's guard was instantly back in place. "She's just fine."

"Wonderful." Hugh Darlington moved languidly out of the darkened living room into the light of the entryway. "We were worried about you, Bridget."

"Hugh came over to tell me what happened."

Bridget wanted to hate the big douchebag who always seemed to be in her house at the most inopportune moments, but she couldn't. One look at her mom's face told Bridget that the news of Peter's murder, and the memories of her dad's, had been broken to her kindly, thoughtfully. There had been tears, but they were gone. Bridget had been spared the worst of it and for that, she was thankful.

"Monsignor Renault called to let me know what happened at St. Michael's tonight." Mr. Darlington stood behind her mom and placed a hand on her shoulder. "I came right over. I wanted Annie to hear the news from a friend."

Mr. Darlington gave Bridget a small smile, and Bridget surprised herself by smiling back. Monsignor must have called before he came and rescued her from the police questioning, which was really very sweet. He was looking out for her, just like Mr. Darlington—as much as she might not always like it—was looking out for her mom. It was a comforting thought, and Bridget felt a twinge of guilt about keeping the secret of Penemuel's message from her mentor. She was being silly, influenced by the horror of Peter's murder, and she vowed to call Monsignor in the morning and tell him everything.

Mr. Darlington nodded. "I'll leave you two alone, then."

Bridget stuck her hand out to Mr. Darlington. "Thank you. For coming over and all."

He looked at her outstretched hand for half a second but didn't take it. Instead he leaned in and gave Mrs. Liu a kiss on the cheek. "Good night, Annie."

That was rude. Did he hold a grudge because she'd punched his daughter in the face a few years ago?

Mrs. Liu escorted Mr. Darlington to the door. "I appreciate tonight more than you know, Hugh."

He squeezed her mom's hand. "I'm always here, whenever you need me." His eyes shifted to Bridget, and he smiled. "Always."

Bridget was wide awake when Sammy tapped on her bedroom door.

"Bridge?" He popped his head into her room. "Are you asleep?"

"Yes."

Apparently Sammy hadn't gotten the memo. He padded over to the edge of her bed. When Bridget made no move to pull the covers back for him, he yanked the duvet half off the bed.

"Not tonight, Sammy. Please?"

He started to climb in. "Nightmare."

She couldn't deal with him tonight. "Can't you go see Mom?"

"Bridge?" His voice cracked.

"Go back to bed." Bridget rolled onto her side and pulled the covers up over her head.

But she couldn't block out the sound of Sammy's sobs as he fled back to his room.

Bridget squeezed her eyes shut until the little flecks of pink-and-blue lights stopped floating around the dark background of her eyelids and faded almost to nothingness. She shouldn't feel guilty. She wasn't going to feel guilty. There was no reason for her to feel guilty.

Dammit.

Bridget slid out of bed and grabbed a sweatshirt off the floor, pulling it on against the chill of the house as she tiptoed down the hall to Sammy's room.

She didn't knock, just eased the door open and slipped inside. Even in the darkness of the room, she could see Sammy hitch his Transformers comforter up over his head as she entered.

"Sammy?" she said softly. "Are you asleep?"

He took a breath, then paused. She could picture him trying to figure out this change in their pattern. "No," he said at last.

"Good."

As she crossed to his bed, Sammy pulled the comforter down and flattened his body against the wall to make room for her in his twin bed. She climbed in, careful not to touch him, then waited until she felt his toes gently press against the back of her legs.

"I had a nightmare," she started. Sammy giggled. "Elephants again."

"No."

"Not elephants?" Please, please, please don't say it was the phantom cat.

"Mr. Moppet."

Kill me.

"Not a nightmare," Sammy said adamantly. "Not a dream."

"Of course it was a dream."

"He's here."

Bridget turned halfway around. "You saw him?"

Sammy shook his head. "But he's here."

"It was just a dream," Bridget said as she settled back into the mattress. "Go to sleep."

Sammy snuggled into his comforter. Suddenly Bridget wanted to wrap her arms tightly around her brother and protect him from the world. It had been building slowly, but with Peter's death, Bridget couldn't help but worry about Sammy. Alexa and Father Santos were right: Death followed her around. Could this new power of hers be somehow to blame? And if Father Santos's theory about her dad was right, could Sammy have inherited the same curse? He could hear the phantom cat, how long before he was hearing voices in the walls too?

She couldn't let him face that. Her determination to visit Milton Undermeyer doubled. If there was something she could learn that would save Sammy from her fate, she'd find it.

Sammy yawned and rolled onto his stomach. "Mr. Moppet was here, Bridge," he said. "He was."

"Okay, Sammy," she said, trying to appease him. "Whatever you say."

"He was," Sammy said through another yawn. "And he wants something in your closet."

TWENTY-FOUR

IT WAS A GLORIOUS MORNING. The November sky was unusually blue, and a layer of thin, wispy clouds streaked across the heavens, so high only the space shuttle would be able to see them up close. The pea-soup fog that had been parked over San Francisco for the better part of two weeks had miraculously evaporated.

As they emerged from a tunnel, Bridget sucked in her breath. The orange-red spires of the Golden Gate Bridge towered above them, silhouetted against a perfect sky. In the almost sixteen years Bridget had lived in San Francisco, she could count on one hand the number of unblemished, picturesque days she'd seen. This one topped them all.

Matt snaked his truck onto the Golden Gate Bridge.

Once onto the span, he pulled to the far right lane and slowed down so that the joggers were almost passing them. At that speed Bridget soaked in the view. A navy of white sailboats had invaded the bay, filling the empty spaces on either side of Alcatraz Island. Ferries shuttled tourists around the "must-see" sights of the bay while cargo tankers slowly maneuvered into port. She could even make out a hiker's neon yellow jacket amid the wilds of Angel Island.

Beyond the bay, the silver-and-glass high-rises of the financial district glittered in the morning sun. They huddled together on their itty-bitty strip of land, reckless and defiant, jutting out into the bay like they were built directly on the water. The Bay Bridge soared out of their heights with no beginning and no end as it stretched toward Treasure Island.

It was just like a postcard.

"Cool, yeah?" Matt said. They were the first words he'd spoken since he picked her up, and she noticed how forced and strange they sounded.

"Yeah." Good answer. The awkwardness in the truck swamped her. She paused a second, wondering what else she should say to him before the obvious popped into her head. "So it was okay? I mean with baseball practice and all?"

"No worries," Matt said, moving back into the fast lane as they began to climb the hill on the north side of the bridge. "Sunday's a pick-up practice. Optional. I usually go, so I figured it would be no big deal to ditch."

"Thanks."

They fell into silence again, and Bridget was grateful that Matt didn't force conversation on her.

She'd only seen Milton Undermeyer once, on the last day of his trial. Her mom had kept her and Sammy away from the proceedings, but Bridget had insisted that she be present when the verdict came down. At that point, the assistant D.A. had prepared her mom for the worst: Undermeyer's insanity defense would probably be successful.

Even though they'd been warned, Bridget's mom shook like a leaf when the words "not guilty by reason of insanity" rang out from the jury foreman's lips. Not that anyone doubted it. The man was clearly a fruit loop. Bridget had followed reports of the trial online, where the daily accounts of Undermeyer's behavior included speaking in tongues, spitting at the public defender, pulling out chunks of his own hair, banging his head against the defense table after he'd been restrained in a straitjacket, and general prophesies of doom and destruction.

Not that it made much of a difference to Bridget. He had murdered her dad. She didn't care if he threw himself out of the courthouse window so long as he suffered an agonizing death in the process, and she'd hoped that confinement in the loony bin up in Sonoma would be worse than prison, worse than hell, worse than the gaping, empty hole he'd left her with when he ripped her dad from her life.

The scenery outside changed as Highway 101 wove through the northernmost suburbs of San Francisco. Gas stations and minimalls gave way to rolling hillsides blanketed with the empty, hibernating grapevines of the California wine industry. It was supposed to be one of the most beautiful places in the state, but all Bridget could think was that with every twist in the road she was coming closer to an answer.

"You must find the messenger," Penemuel had told her. *"Me-yer. Un-der. Un-der. Me-yer."* Could it be true? Could her dad have really told her to seek out his murderer?

Bridget's heart thumped in her chest as the truck slowed down and Matt turned off the highway. The town of Geyserville looked so serene and peaceful, all nineteenth-century storefronts and single-story ranch houses. Then the vineyards, sandwiched between country roads like a patchwork quilt creeping slowly toward the hills to the east. And hidden behind the greenery of the hillside, the glimmering steel-and-stone edifice of the Sonoma State Mental Hospital.

Matt pulled up to the security gate. "We don't have to do this. I can just take you home."

Bridget shook her head. She had to go through with it.

A security guard approached the driver's side window. "You have an appointment?"

"Yes, I should be on the list. Matt Quinn."

The guard sifted through some papers on his clipboard. "Appointment made by Sergeant Stephen Quinn?"

"Yes, sir."

Bridget's jaw dropped. "You told your dad?"

"ID, sir?"

Matt pulled his wallet out of his back pocket and handed his license to the guard, then reached for Bridget's. The guard walked back into his security hut. "How did you think we were going to get in here? It's not like visiting hours at S.F. General."

She hadn't thought of that. But still the last thing she needed was for Sergeant Quinn to tell her mom where they'd gone.

"He promised he wouldn't say anything," Matt said, reading her mind.

Bridget rolled her eyes. "And you believed that?"

"I trust my dad. He asked why you wanted to go, and I told him I didn't know." Matt paused as if he expected Bridget to jump in with her reason. She didn't. "Then I asked him not to say anything to your mom, and he said he wouldn't."

"Whatever."

"He's not going to say anything," Matt repeated. "Why would he?"

The words "Because your dad's in love with my mom" were on the tip of her tongue, but the look on Matt's face was so completely innocent and confused that Bridget realized he had no idea about his dad's feelings for Annie Liu. Boys. Typically clueless.

The guard came back to the window with their IDs. "Straight through the gate, up the road to the right. Visitor parking's in front and there'll be someone waiting to escort you. Good luck."

As they rounded the bend from the security gate, Sonoma

State Mental Hospital loomed above them. With its gleaming steel and glass, it was out of place, an anachronism, a state-of-the-art, high-security prison in the midst of lazy, rolling hillsides and a quaint old town. From the front entrance, you'd never even know that multimillion-dollar vineyards lay just yards from the main gate. All she could see was the paved parking lot, the sleek façade of the hospital, and the twenty-foot stone walls topped with coils of barbed wire.

A guard waited for them at the front door, and he ushered them to yet another security checkpoint. Again, they showed their IDs, and their names were located on a computer file.

"So you're the ones here to see Undermeyer?" A beefy nurse-looking guy in light blue scrubs sauntered down a long hallway.

"That's us," Matt said. He was trying to sound light and casual but failed utterly.

The nurse shifted his gaze from Matt to Bridget, then shrugged and headed back the way he came. "Follow me."

Bridget's boots clunked against brilliantly polished tiles, punctuated by the occasional squeak from Matt's Converses. She had to hustle to keep up with the nurse, though he seemed to move at an almost leisurely pace.

"You guys look kinda young," the nurse said. He paused at an elevator and hit the button. "To be visiting one of our inmates." His eyes kept drifting to Bridget, which made her think he was either a super perv or he had some idea who she was.

"Weird that you'd be seeing Undermeyer too," the nurse continued when neither Matt nor Bridget responded to his nonquestion. But this time Bridget was interested.

"Why?"

The door slid open and the nurse gestured for her and Matt to enter. "Well, he doesn't get many visitors, is all. And by 'many,' I mean 'none.'"

From what she'd seen, Bridget wasn't surprised. "Oh."

The nurse hit the button for the fourth floor and the elevator crept upward. "I should warn you guys, though. Whatever you want to talk to Undermeyer about, you probably won't get very far."

Bridget crinkled her brow. "Why not?"

The elevator dinged for the fourth floor and the nurse turned to her with a big, cheeky grin. "Oh, you'll see."

Bridget shook her head as she followed the nurse out onto the fourth floor. What was she doing? If Undermeyer was even half as crazy as he'd been at his trial, this whole trip was pointless.

Another security door awaited them at the end of the hall, and the nurse pulled a badge from his belt on a little zip line to scan them through. They entered some kind of recreation area for the inmates: tables with checkers and chess, a television showing *Seinfeld* reruns, a few magazines strewn on tables. Only four inmates occupied the room, identifiable by their dark blue jumpsuits. All four sat at solitary tables; all four did nothing but stare off into space. Fun times.

The nurse and/or security guard ratio in the rec room was two to one, and as Matt and Bridget followed their guide across the room and through yet another security door, Bridget couldn't help but notice the whispers that went up among the staff. Everyone must have known she and Matt were there to see Milton Undermeyer. It was the big thrill of the day.

Bridget was glad when their burly nurse ushered them into what could only be described as the crying room in the back of a church. There were a couple of plastic chairs lined up to face a huge window that opened onto an adjacent room. There, swaddled in a straitjacket and flanked by linebacker-sized orderlies at each shoulder, sat Milton Undermeyer.

It had only been a couple of months since Bridget had last seen him in the courtroom, but Undermeyer had aged twenty years. His hair, which had been a wavy black mane, was now heavily lined with streaks of white. Not gray, but stark white. Deep ravines crisscrossed his face, marring his forehead, his chin, and the sides of his mouth with heavy shadows. The violet bands beneath his eyes extended halfway down his cheeks, and his lips were dry and cracked like a man left to die in the desert.

Undermeyer sat perfectly still in his chair, feet planted firmly on the floor in front of him, his head lowered so he could look out at her from beneath unkempt brows. The eyes were the only part about him that was wholly familiar. Utterly black.

"Mrs. Long," she whispered.

"What?" the nurse asked.

Bridget shook her head. "Nothing." But it wasn't nothing. Those black eyes were the same as the ones Bridget had seen in Mrs. Long. Father Santos was right: Milton Undermeyer was a demoniac.

She felt a hand on her back and turned to see Matt at her side. "Are you okay?" he asked for the bazillionth time.

For the first time since she'd known him, Bridget was glad Matt was an overprotective worrywart.

"I'm good," she said. And she was. She wasn't sure how she'd react when she saw Undermeyer again, and her calmness almost surprised her. "I can't go in there?" she asked the nurse.

"Hell no," he said.

"Even with the guards?"

"Girlie, seriously. You're not going in there. Even with the guards."

Bridget narrowed her eyes. Girlie? Really?

"Can she talk to him?" Matt asked quickly.

"Yep, and he can hear you. But this is as close as you get."

"Fine," Bridget said, turning a cold eye on the nurse. "A little privacy, please?"

The nurse looked disappointed. Clearly he'd wanted a firsthand account of their conversation. Too bad, so sad. He lumbered from the room, though Bridget guessed he probably had his ear to the door outside. Whatever. Not like he'd understand a word of what he'd hear.

For a half second she thought about asking Matt to leave as well. The conversation she was about to have would probably scare the hell out of him. Still, there was something comforting in having him there, and after what he'd seen last night, he might as well get the whole freaky picture.

Bridget closed her eyes and took a deep breath to center herself. She reached across her body and gripped the St. Benedict medal tightly in her hand. She needed her dad with her.

It's now or never, Bridget. She focused her mind on the man on the other side of the glass, just as Monsignor Renault had taught her. She went over the Rules one by one in her mind, reassuring herself that she was the one with the power here, with the means to banish. *Vade retro satana.*

When she opened her eyes, she was all business.

"Milton Undermeyer," she said. Her voice sounded big and boomy, and she saw Matt start. "Milton Undermeyer, I was sent by Penemuel to speak to you. I know you are the messenger and I demand you give your message to me."

TWENTY-FIVE

At Penemuel's name, Undermeyer pushed his feet against the ground, launching his chair back several inches. The guards had their hands on him almost immediately, dragging him back to his chair.

"Liar!" he screamed. His voice flooded the room through a loudspeaker. "Who are you? It's a girl. Don't trust her. Why not? She lies!"

Several voices were all speaking through him at once, but Bridget noticed immediately that the room in which she stood felt pretty normal. No dizziness, no vertigo. The demons inside Milton Undermeyer were more like Penemuel and the entity who had given her the warning through Mrs. Long. She was beginning to learn the difference. Interesting.

"I know what you are," she said. "I need you to tell me what you know."

Undermeyer became more agitated. He tried to wiggle away from the guards' grasp, and his feet stomped against the floor erratically. "Maybe we listen? Shut up, you. She isn't the one we were sent for. We cannot trust her."

The one they were sent for. Bridget swallowed hard. That had to be her dad. "You came with a message for David Liu."

Undermeyer froze. His eyes grew wide, not with recognition but with fear.

"Penemuel told me you had a message for David Liu."

"How does she know of this?" Undermeyer hissed.

"David Liu was my father."

"Maybe, maybe, maybe," he chanted, bouncing slightly in his chair. "Maybe, maybe not."

"I am," she said, taking a step closer to the glass. "And I need to know what you were sent to tell him."

Undermeyer threw his head back and laughed, a harsh, frantic sound that came from both the speaker and up from the very floor at the same time.

"Bridget," Matt said. His voice shook. "I don't think this is a good idea."

"You have no power over us." Undermeyer laughed. "The Emim have no power here."

The Emim? Father Santos had mentioned them: the Nephilim who remained loyal to the kings of Hell.

"I am not the Emim," she said, trying to sound like she

knew what she was talking about.

This time, Undermeyer's laugh dissolved into a giggle. "She wouldn't say she is, would she? Do they think we are fools? Not fools! We will not be fooled."

She needed to convince the demons inside Undermeyer that she was on their side. "Penemuel was here," she said, grasping at straws.

Undermeyer stopped giggling and muttered unintelligibly under his breath.

"He told me to find you, that you'd been sent to my father with a message."

"Penemuel?" he said. "Penemuel follow us? Penemuel with us?"

"Yes," she said. This seemed to be working.

"Then . . ." Undermeyer launched to his feet. "THEN SHOW PENEMUEL TO US!"

"I—I can't. He's gone."

"Gone," Undermeyer mocked as the guards slapped him back into his chair. "Gone, gone, gone."

What had Penemuel said right at the end? "His penance was done," Bridget said, quoting the demon's words. "He was released."

There was a moment of agonizing silence while Undermeyer's eyes darted around the room. His lips didn't move, but she could hear the voices in his head as clearly as if they were speaking through him still. *Released? Penemuel released? Can we trust? Do we dare? We cannot be released until we deliver the message. We cannot. We cannot.*"

Released. Penemuel had sounded joyous when he said that word. Maybe these demons were the same?

"I can release you," she lied. Was it like banishing? She had no clue, but it seemed to be working. "I released Penemuel after he told me to find you. I know how."

Undermeyer's face went slack with longing, like a man dying of thirst when he catches a glimpse of an oasis. *"You?"*

"Yes."

The voices started again, babbling rapidly in the same language Bridget couldn't understand, arguing among themselves, trying to come to a decision.

"Please," she said.

"Bridget, who are you talking to?" Matt asked. He was freaked out, only hearing one side of this conversation.

But she couldn't stop to explain. She was so close.

"Yes," the voices said in unison. *"Yes."*

Undermeyer closed his eyes; his body stilled. Then the voices filled the room again.

"We did not kill David Liu, David Liu of the Nephilim, David Liu, the Watcher."

Somehow she knew this was coming. "If you didn't, then who did?"

"Emim. Emim. An agent of the Emim." The voice broke into gibberish, harsh and biting. Then the voices stilled. *"We have a message."*

A message. That was their purpose, their penance, their

price for release from the legions of Hell. But she wasn't going to let them off that easy. There was something she needed to know first.

"If Undermeyer didn't kill my dad, then who did?"

"Bridget!" Matt grabbed her arm. "What the hell are you talking about?"

She shook him off, focusing on the demon voices. It was just more gibberish, heated and loud.

"I promise I can release you," she said. "Only I need to know this first."

"Find the tapes," a voice said.

"Tapes?" Her dad kept tape recordings of all his sessions, but according to the police they were all accounted for in evidence. "We have the tapes."

"More," said a voice.

"Hidden," said another.

"Don't tell her!" a third hissed.

"The truth," said the first. *"The Watcher demands it."*

More. Hidden. "There are missing tapes from Undermeyer's sessions?" Bridget asked.

But the demons' patience had run out. They had a message to deliver, and they were done being distracted from it by Bridget's question.

"We have a message for David Liu of the Nephilim, David Liu the Watcher," they said, back to their script. *"The Emim are rising, called forth from their exile by the King of the West, the wielder of the silver ring, the prince of Hell. Amaymon calls his servants to arms!"*

Undermeyer shivered in his chair and slumped forward. The interview was draining him.

"*Hurry!*" a voice said before launching into unison again. "*The priest is their minion, he serves the Emim. You must stop the conjuring. If Amaymon takes form in this world, all will be lost.*"

"Why are you telling me this?" Bridget said. Even if they felt different to her, these were demons, after all. Why would they warn her about one of their own?

"*To warn David Liu, to warn David Liu, to warn a Watcher of the threat.*"

"Bridget . . ." Matt's hand was on her shoulder. "What is—"

"*It is our penance. Amaymon wishes power, to control the other kings of Hell. Must not let him. Must not let him. Must not let him. Must not let him.*"

"Okay!" Bridget yelled to cut off the chant. "How?"

"*Stop the priest. The Emim cannot summon Amaymon without him. They need the priest. The priest wields the sword.*"

"The priest is working for the Emim?"

"*Yes.*"

The priest? Yeah, that narrowed it down. "Which priest?"

But that was it. The demons had reached the end of their message.

"*We tell David Liu, we tell the Watcher. Our penance is done.*"

"Release us!" Undermeyer screamed. He launched himself out of the chair. "We are done. Release us!"

"Um, okay," Bridget said. What was she supposed to do

now? "I release you?"

The guards were on him in a second. The first grabbed him in a choke hold from behind, while the second removed a syringe from his pocket and approached Undermeyer from the front. But demoniacs weren't subdued that easily, a fact Bridget had witnessed firsthand.

Undermeyer leaned back, pulling both feet off the floor, and landed a ferocious kick to the chest of the approaching guard. Then he threw his body forward, rolling the other guard over his back. Dazed from the speed of the attack, the guard couldn't recover fast enough. Undermeyer kneed him in the jaw with a crack so loud Bridget could hear it through the staticky speakers.

Undermeyer threw himself against the double-paned window. "Release us! Release us!" Again and again, as if he was trying to puncture the glass with his skull. Gashes appeared on his head, blood poured down his face. "Release us! Release us!"

Bridget flattened her hand against the glass. She could feel their desperation, their longing to be released. But how? What did she need to do?

She remembered the doll possessed by Penemuel, its hand stuck through the glass trying to reach her. Reach her! That's what happened. She had touched the doll. That was the release.

"I need to get in there."

"What?" Matt grabbed her arm.

"Let me go!" Bridget shook him loose and yanked open the door. The nurse loitering outside didn't have time to react before she pulled open the door of Undermeyer's room.

"What the hell are you doing?" the nurse roared.

At the sound of the door opening, Undermeyer stopped throwing himself against the window. "Yes," he hissed.

He lurched toward her, but the guard who still lay on the ground nearby had regained consciousness. He lunged at Undermeyer's feet and tripped him.

"Please!" Undermeyer begged.

Bridget tried to reach him, but a dozen hands were on her at once.

"What the hell?" a guard yelled. He had an arm around her waist.

"Stop!" Bridget screamed. "Let me go!" She had to release the demons trapped inside Milton Undermeyer. That was their pact, the deal they had made to deliver the message to her father. She had to fulfill it.

"Release us!" Undermeyer cried.

Bridget stretched out her arm, desperate to touch Milton Undermeyer, but it was too late. The nurse had gotten the syringe into Undermeyer's leg, and he was already falling into unconsciousness. As the guards hauled her away, the last image she saw was the black, pleading eyes of Milton Undermeyer as they fluttered closed.

TWENTY-SIX

"**B**RIDGET, WHAT WERE YOU THINKING back there?" Matt's face was red as he backed her up against the side of his truck.

"I don't . . ."

"I don't know" was what she meant to say, but she did know. She knew exactly what she was doing, but how could she explain it to him?

"You were hearing things that weren't there. Just like last night."

Bridget laughed. She couldn't help herself. "Oh, they were there."

Matt grabbed her by her shoulders, his eyes wild. "You had a conversation with something no one else could hear.

And you sounded weird, like it wasn't really you."

"Yeah?" He was right, sort of. In the presence of the demons she felt different. "What did I sound like?"

Matt straightened up, his brows low over his hazel eyes as he tried to put it into words. "Your voice was deep and booming, like someone else was speaking through you. It scared the hell out of me, actually."

Bridget smiled. That was kind of sweet.

"Stop laughing, Bridget!"

"I wasn't laughing. I just, well . . . no one's mentioned that before."

"This has happened *before*?"

"Um . . ." Bridget swallowed hard. Of course it had happened before. Each time she encountered the demons, the feeling of power grew stronger, more tangible. And worse— Bridget found she was enjoying it.

Matt took a step back and ran a hand through his hair. "What's going on?" he repeated.

She hadn't told anyone other than Monsignor Renault, and that was only because he confronted her. Maybe it was time to share what had been going on. After all that Matt had already seen, he was the perfect confidant.

"Can we get something to eat?" Bridget said.

"Huh?"

Bridget pantomimed putting something into her mouth and chewing. "Food. There was a diner back in town, right?"

"Then you'll tell me?"

Bridget sighed. "Then I'll tell you."

Matt nodded and they got into the truck. Bridget noticed that his hand shook as he started the ignition.

The diner was mostly empty on a Sunday afternoon, just an elderly couple in a booth and two trucker types at the counter. Matt made a beeline for a booth tucked into the far corner.

The waitress was on them almost immediately, with a big, sunny smile that felt so out of place with their mood that Bridget almost laughed out loud.

"Can I get you kids something to drink?"

"Diet 7Up," Bridget said.

"We got Sprite."

"Whatever." Then, without even opening the menu, Bridget ordered her favorite. "And a grilled cheese on sourdough with fries."

"All righty then," the waitress said, turning to Matt. "I like a lady who knows what she wants. And you?"

"Same." Matt didn't even look at her, just fidgeted with the fork at his place setting, thumping it up and down on the laminate table.

Matt waited until the waitress had disappeared behind the counter. "Okay, spill it."

"Um . . ." Where the hell did she start? With Monsignor Renault it had been easy; he asked questions, and she answered them. But Matt didn't know exactly the world of hurt he was about to step into, and for a moment, Bridget was tongue-tied.

"Yeah?"

"So here's the thing," Bridget said. "This is all going to sound really, really weird. I mean, a level of weird that's not going to be easy for you to understand, okay?"

Matt tilted his head to one side. "Weirder than watching you talk to a crazy man like you were reading the thoughts in his head? Weirder than finding your friend murdered in the church last night?"

The boy made a good point. "Okay, fine. But just remember, you asked."

Her story flowed easier than she expected it to: the events at the Fergusons' house, her first meeting with Monsignor Renault, Mrs. Long, the doll shop, even her brother solving the anagram telling her not to trust the priest. It all came easily, quickly, like she couldn't wait to get the whole story out into the world.

Matt listened in silence. When she was done, she glanced up at him, hoping for an encouraging smile or a softness in his eye, something to indicate that he didn't think she was completely bat shit. But he just continued to stare at the napkin dispenser without saying a word.

Perfect. He thought she was crazy, delusional, or both. So much for honesty.

"So Undermeyer," Matt said hesitantly. "He's possessed by . . . by . . ."

"Demons. Yep." No reason to beat around the bush at this point.

"And you can communicate with them? Read their minds or something?"

"Something like that."

"Does that make you one of them?"

Good question. "I have no idea."

"How do you do it?"

Another good question, but at least one she had some semblance of an answer to. "Father Santos—"

"Was he the chubby little priest from last night?"

"Heh. Yeah." Bridget snorted.

The waitress plopped a pair of grilled cheese sandwiches and Diet Sprites on the table. "Here you go. Can I get you anything else?"

"No," Matt and Bridget said in unison.

The waitress pulled back like she'd been slapped. "Okay then. I'll just leave you two alone." Bridget heard her whistle low and long as she walked back to the kitchen.

"So Father Santos showed me this old manuscript from the Vatican," Bridget continued. "He said it was the only one of its kind and it tells the story of the Emim and the Watchers."

"Sounds like a comic book."

"Nerd."

"Crazy." Matt smiled at her. It wasn't his patented sparkly smile—just a hint of grin around the corners of his mouth— but it gave Bridget a warm, homey feeling inside.

"I don't remember all of it, but basically a bunch of angels fell from Heaven to have sex with mortal women and then got banished to Hell. Some of those angels repented, and God granted their half-mortal offspring special powers to control the offspring of the nonrepenting angels. The Watchers and the Emim."

Matt's eyes grew wide as Bridget took a huge bite of her sandwich, trailing a long strand of melted cheese away from her mouth. "Which one are you?"

"Watcher. I think we're supposed to be the good guys."

"Supposed to be?"

Bridget dropped her sandwich on her plate. "Look, I don't know. All I've got is two priests who, according to a demon messenger, I'm not supposed to trust. It's not like this thing came with an instruction manual. Page one—You're the Good Guy! I mean, until a month ago I didn't believe any of this was real."

Matt dropped his eyes. "Sorry."

"S'okay." Bridget crammed some fries into her mouth and washed them down with a long sip of her soda. She was suddenly ravenous, like she hadn't eaten in weeks.

"So you're one of them?" Matt asked.

"One of who?"

"One of *them*. A demon."

Bridget winced. She was instantly nauseous at the idea that she was part supernatural anything. "Do I look like a demon?" she asked by way of an evasion.

"Yeah, like I know." Matt finally picked up his untouched

food. "What are they like? The demons, I mean?"

Bridget hadn't really thought about it before. "Kind of like nasty little kids. They like to scare you, slam doors, and show up as ominous shadows. They're not really dangerous until they get their hooks into a human."

"Oh, yeah?"

"Yeah. They can make you do things, give you extra strength, make you levitate. All kinds of crazy stuff."

"Like with Milton Undermeyer?"

Bridget smiled. The boy was quick. "Yeah."

"And that can happen to just anyone?"

"I don't think so." Bridget took a contemplative bite of french fry. What had Monsignor told her? "You have to invite them in somehow. Let them into your house and then once you engage with them, it's game on."

Matt pondered Bridget's words before he launched into his next question. "So, it sounds like real cases of possession are pretty rare, huh?"

"I think so, yeah."

"Then how come you've had four of them in the last few weeks?"

It was a good point, one that had been bothering Bridget. The Vatican seemed to agree with Matt and had sent Father Santos to investigate the swell in demonic activity in the area. But Monsignor seemed more excited by it than anything, because it gave him a chance to test Bridget's abilities. Meanwhile, the more Bridget contemplated the eerie events of the last few weeks, the more she was determined to get to the bottom of things.

They fell silent as they finished lunch, but after the waitress brought the check, Matt had one last question.

"What did they tell you?"

"Who?"

"The demons inside Milton Undermeyer. You kept ordering them to tell you something."

"Oh, right." He was in it up to his neck at this point, might as well finish the job. "They said that the Emim are attempting to summon a demon, Amaymon, who's a king of Hell, and that they are using a priest to do so. I'm supposed to stop the priest."

"That narrows it down," Matt snorted.

"Yeah."

"Do you think it's Father Santos or Monsignor?"

Bridget bit her lip.

"I hope not," she said. "But the only thing I know for sure is that Milton Undermeyer did not kill my dad. Maybe if we find the real killer, it'll lead to the priest?"

"All right," Matt said, scooting out of the booth. "Let's go, then."

"Go where?"

Matt took her hand as she climbed to her feet. "Let's go find your priest."

TWENTY-SEVEN

A MIDDLE-AGED OFFICER WITH A steel gray topknot and horn-rimmed glasses circa 1973 pushed the door open with her ample rump and deposited a heavy file box on the table.

"Is that all?" Bridget asked.

The officer leaned against the table to catch her breath. "Yes, that's *all*, honey."

Bridget eyed the box. All the evidence from the Undermeyer case shoved into a single two-by-three-foot box.

"Thanks, Agnes," Matt said. Bridget saw him flash the officer his winning, toothy smile.

Agnes melted. "Don't mention it. Anything for you and your dad, Mattie."

"Does that work on everyone?" Bridget said after

Agnes waddled from the room.

"What?"

Bridget did her best imitation of Matt's smile and puppy-dog-eye combo. "Thanks, Agnes."

Matt drew his face close to hers. "Not on everyone."

Bridget turned her head and hoped Matt didn't notice the faint pink blush rising from her chest to her neck. "Well, apparently it worked on Alexa Darlington."

Matt's mood changed as soon as he heard Alexa's name. His smile vanished, and he reached over to the box and took out a stack of CDs burned from the audio recordings of her dad's sessions with Undermeyer. "I'll start with these."

"Um, okay." Bridget bit the inside of her cheek as she grabbed Undermeyer's patient file from the box.

She'd been half joking, bringing up Alexa, but only half. The rest of her still wondered how a guy like Matt, cute and popular and clearly not a total douchebag, would go for a bitch like Alexa Darlington. Sure she was hot and dripping with money, but was that what he was looking for?

She stole a glance at Matt while he pushed a CD into his MacBook and pulled a set of headphones over his ears. He'd sounded so weird last night when he talked about Alexa, like he'd tried to forget those months of his life. And the look on his face when she spoke to him, like he was biting through nails. Maybe he'd really loved her and she'd broken his heart? The thought made Bridget want to hurl.

Bridget sighed and turned to the stack of file folders. As

she opened the first file, she grimaced. What exactly was she looking for? She knew her dad's record keeping pretty well: audio recordings of each session, which he would burn onto a CD; notes on topics and comments of interest during the session; postsession impressions of each client, along with medications prescribed and suggestions for the next session. All completely, one hundred percent straightforward. No codes, no gimmicks, no secret shorthand. There was no reason to believe she'd find anything that had been missed the first bazillion times these notes had been examined.

Still, this was her dad, and after her mom, Bridget knew him best. Maybe she'd see something everyone else missed.

Undermeyer's file started out normal enough. The first session was mainly for initial reactions, stating that the patient arrived heavily sedated, and that acute schizophrenia and possible multiple personality disorder were the most likely culprits for his condition. Not a word, not a hint of anything out of the ordinary.

But there wouldn't have been, right? Her dad couldn't very well have said, "Undermeyer is possessed by several demonic entities that only I can communicate with." It wouldn't exactly fly with Sergeant Quinn and the assistant district attorney. The session ended with the request that he see Undermeyer again, this time without any drugs in his system.

The next session was a week later and was, apparently, a complete disaster. At the end of the session Dr. Liu had to call in the accompanying officers from the other room and have

Undermeyer restrained after he attempted to throw himself through the fourth-story window of Dr. Liu's office. Not much there, other than that her dad requested another interview.

This was a bust. They weren't going to find anything here that the police missed. She'd hit a dead end.

Matt sat bolt upright in his chair. "Whoa."

"What?"

He held up a hand. "Hold on. Let me check something." Matt scrolled the recording ahead two, three times, then cupped his hands over his ears, listening acutely. After a few seconds his hand flew to the space bar and he paused the recording. "Whoa."

"*What?*"

"I think I found something."

Bridget sucked in a breath. "Really?"

"Yeah." Matt moved quickly. He reset the recording back near the beginning and handed the headphones to Bridget. "So that CD has Undermeyer's first and second sessions with your dad. They're each thirty minutes long, and pretty much what you'd expect. But this CD, with the third and fourth sessions, they're shorter. The third session is only twenty-two minutes, the fourth only fifteen."

Bridget felt a ripple of excitement race through her body. "That doesn't sound like my dad."

"Right? So I went through them again and . . . well, listen for yourself."

Bridget slipped the headphones on while Matt started the recording.

"And have you been taking your medication, Mr. Under-meyer?" Dr. Liu asked.

A lump welled up in Bridget's throat at her dad's voice. He sounded infinitely calm, totally professional, not an ounce of emotion reflected through the even cadence of his words. God, she missed him.

"Yes. Yes, yes, yes." It was Undermeyer's voice, with that taunting style of the demoniac that Bridget had come to know so well.

"Excellent. And do you care to tell me why you broke into the Church of St. Michael?"

"No. No, no, no." Bridget could almost see the taunting grin on Undermeyer's face.

"I see."

Matt held up a finger. On the recording, Bridget heard a faint click.

Dr. Liu's voice picked up almost immediately with a heavy thumping sound in the background, like chair legs bouncing on the floor. "Well, then, Mr. Undermeyer, I will see you next week."

"Not safe!" Undermeyer shrieked. "Not safe here! Not safe! Not safe here!"

Another click, and the session was over.

Matt paused the recording. "Did you hear the click, right before your dad told Undermeyer he'd see him next week?"

"Yeah."

"Same as the click at the end of the recording."

Bridget gasped. "He turned it off. My dad didn't want something to be on the official session recording."

"Exactly. And it happened again, exactly the same way, in session four." Matt slumped back into his chair. "Which means something is missing."

The missing tapes, just like Undermeyer said. Bridget leaned her elbows on the table and rested her chin in her hands. "My dad kept recordings of every second of every patient session. If he turned off the official police recording, he must have had a second recorder going. For his personal files."

"But where? My dad went through both of Dr. Liu's offices with tweezers and a magnifying glass. There's no way he missed anything."

"Nothing that he was meant to find."

Matt tilted his head. "What do you mean?"

"Well, it's just this. If my dad was a Watcher, he wasn't exactly going to advertise that fact, right? I mean, it's not something you brag about at the office Christmas party."

"It might make the Christmas party more interesting."

Bridget rolled her eyes. "Focus."

"Sorry."

"My point is, what if what's missing here—the audio, maybe even some notes—what if they were never here?"

"You mean he hid them?"

Bridget shrugged. "That's what I'd do. Especially if I thought the Emim were on to me."

Matt ran his fingers absentmindedly through his hair.

"And my dad wouldn't have missed it. He wouldn't have realized there was anything wrong with what he found in Dr. Liu's office." He sounded relieved.

"I wasn't blaming your dad. I never thought he screwed this up."

"Oh, I know. It's just . . ." Matt shifted in his chair so he faced her. "This is some really weird shit we're dealing with."

Bridget couldn't help herself. His serious expression and the way he described her situation, it was too perfect. She burst out laughing, head thrown back, hand slapping the table. Her cheeks ached, her stomach felt like it was going to burst right out of her body with the effort. It was the first time she'd laughed like that in months.

Matt pursed his lips and folded his arms across his chest. He clearly didn't appreciate Bridget's mood. She immediately put on a serious face.

"I wasn't trying to be funny," Matt said, once she'd quieted down.

"I know, I'm sorry," she said, wiping a tear from her eye. "Don't be mad. It was just so . . . perfect."

"So if he kept secret notes, they weren't in his office," Matt said, ignoring her apology. "My dad would have found them."

Bridget wasn't entirely sure that was true, but she decided not to press the point. Besides, she had a more likely place in mind.

She dug into the pocket of her jeans and whipped out her cell phone.

"Who are you calling?" Matt said.

Bridget held up her hand for silence while she dialed. "Mom? Hey, yeah, we're still out. Um, I was wondering what you were planning for dinner? Shepherd's pie? Cool. Yeah, I think he'd really love to stay for dinner. Perfect. We'll be there soon."

"Did you just get me invited to your house for dinner?"

"Totally."

A sly grin stole across Matt's face. "You know, it's amazing how you keep asking me on dates."

"Excuse me?"

"Your Winter Formal, dinner at your house. Really, I'm flattered."

Bridget narrowed her eyes. "You know what? Forget it. I can totally do this on my own without your help."

"Don't be so touchy." Matt reached out and grazed her hand with his fingertips. "You know I want to help."

Bridget let his touch linger, surprising herself by not pulling away. Something in the pit of her stomach shifted, like the bottom had fallen away. What was wrong with her?

"We should go," she said at last. He pulled his hand away, and Bridget was almost sorry. "My mom's expecting us."

Matt loaded the evidence back into the box. "So, shepherd's pie?"

"Every Sunday night."

"Awesome. My dad's going to be so jealous."

TWENTY-EIGHT

"**H**EY, MOM, WE'RE HERE," BRIDGET called as she and Matt came through the front door. She got no answer, just the sound of laughter—male and female—coming from the kitchen. Bridget pushed open the swinging door and found her mom holding a piece of braised carrot between her fingers while Sergeant Quinn playfully took a bite. Their bodies were almost touching, her mom laughing, happy, Sergeant Quinn's eyes fixed on her face.

"Dad?" Matt said. He sounded genuinely shocked. Time to get with the program, Matt.

"Bridget!" her mom said. She took a step away from Sergeant Quinn and straightened out her sweater. "I didn't think you'd be back so soon."

"Obviously."

"Dad, what are you doing here?"

Sergeant Quinn flushed a bright shade of fuchsia. "Well, Annie called and said you were coming for dinner, and she was kind enough to invite me over too."

"But Sunday nights you play poker with the guys from the station."

Sergeant Quinn shoved his hands deep into his pockets. "Er, well, Benny had to cancel tonight and Curtis's kid has the flu so, um . . ."

Bridget felt bad for Matt as he stood there, feet rooted to the linoleum floor, realizing for the first time that his dad had the hots for her mom. It was like watching a kid finally understand that Santa Claus doesn't exist and that your parents had been lying to you your whole life. Brutal.

"Well," her mom said, breaking the silence. "Dinner's almost ready. Bridget, why don't you take Matt to your room and then you can set the table?"

Bridget shook her head. This was seriously the only household in America where the mom *encouraged* her daughter to take a boy to her room. She turned to leave, realized Matt was still staring dumbfounded at his dad, and grabbed his arm, yanking him into the hallway. "This way."

"What the hell was that?" Matt said, dropping into the chair at Bridget's desk. "You don't even look surprised."

"Yeah, 'cause I'm not."

Realization dawned. "You knew?"

"Dude, your dad is here like two nights a week. Checking up on us."

"He was worried. Felt a sense of responsibility because . . . because . . ."

Bridget's smile was pitying. "Yeah, not so much."

Matt pointed toward the door. "They were flirting in there."

"I know. They've been doing it for, like, three months."

He fell silent, clearly internalizing what he'd just seen. Bridget felt bad for him: He really didn't have a clue.

"No wonder you were so pissed off at me," he said at last.

Bridget looked at him. His hazel eyes held a hint of sadness, and she realized that he was right. She hadn't really understood where her dislike of Matt came from. He'd been nothing but nice to her since he came back into her life, and she'd been nothing but a raging bitch in return. But suddenly it all made sense. She'd been so angry at her mom for flirting with another man less than a year after her husband's death, so angry at Sergeant Quinn, her dad's supposed friend, she never even realized that she'd totally and completely taken her anger out on Matt.

"It's okay," he said. A smile spread across his face. "I get it now. I just really thought you hated me." He walked right to her, reached out, and took her hands in his. "But you don't hate me, do you?"

"I—" Bridget's eyes locked onto Matt's, and whatever she was about to say vanished from her mind. Matt ran his thumbs gently over the backs of her hands, which trembled beneath his touch.

Did she hate him?

Not even a little.

She didn't know when it had happened, or how, but she definitely didn't hate Matt Quinn anymore.

Her face must have said what her words didn't. Matt cupped her cheek in his hand, caressing her skin with the tips of his fingers. He leaned down, hesitated to see if she'd flinch away. But Bridget had no intention of doing so. She wanted him closer.

When his lips touched hers, she was afraid to move. She'd never kissed a guy before and she was terrified that she'd do it wrong. But Matt's lips were surprisingly soft, his touch light and calm. And when he finally broke away from her, he looked nervous, as if he'd been afraid he would break her.

"Are you okay? I mean, was that okay?"

Bridget barely nodded. There was so much weirdness pulsing through her body she felt like she was going to pass out. "Yeah, thanks."

Thanks? Did she really just thank him? Bridget, you complete loser.

"Bridge?" her mom called from the kitchen with the worst possible timing in the world. "Dinner's ready."

Sunday night's shepherd pie dinner at the Liu house was the most awkward social experience of Bridget's life.

Everyone avoided everyone else. Her mom studiously avoided both Matt and Sergeant Quinn, and treated Bridget and Sammy like they were the only ones in the room. Sergeant Quinn was having difficulty keeping his eyes away from her mom, but he avoided his son's eyes like the plague. Matt stared directly at his plate, occasionally nudging Bridget with his elbow or knee to make sure she remembered he was there. As for Bridget, she didn't care if everyone in the room fell off the face of the Earth. All she could think about was the tingling on her lips where Matt had kissed her.

"Why's no one talking?" Sammy asked. He'd separated his shepherd's pie into piles of mashed potatoes, ground beef, carrot, onion, and "other" and was taking bites of them in order, progressing counterclockwise around his plate. "Are we mad?"

"No, Sammy," her mom said. "Of course we're not mad at you."

"Not mad at me," Sammy said, scooping a bit of other into his mouth. "Just mad."

Bridget worked her way through her dinner as fast as was humanly possible. She wasn't the only one. Her mom, Matt, and Sergeant Quinn were eating like they were racing to the finish line. She kept trying to remind herself that beyond her brother's eccentric eating habits, beyond the squicky flirting between her mom and Sergeant Quinn, beyond her own disturbing desire to pull Matt down on her bed and smother herself in his crisp, orangey cologne, there was a *reason* she'd brought him to her house. They needed to look for a secret stash of notes that might or might not exist. No pressure.

"How are you doing, Bridget?" Sergeant Quinn asked, breaking the silence.

Bridget had no idea what he was talking about. "Fine?"

Her mom cast a sideways glance at Sammy. "We were worried, you know." She lowered her voice. "About Peter."

Bridget dropped her fork. She'd totally and completely put Peter's murder out of her mind. What kind of a friend was she?

"Sammy," Matt said calmly. "Did you show your mom your baseball mitt? The one we broke in for you?"

Sammy's face lit up. "No!" He jumped out of his chair. "You'll love it, Mom. Matt says it's made just for me."

Bridget caught Matt's eye as her brother ran out of the room. "Thank you," she mouthed. The last thing she needed was for Sammy to overhear a conversation about Peter's death.

"Steph—" Her mom caught herself. "Sergeant Quinn told me that Peter's death was very much like . . . like . . ." Her mom's hands shook so violently she had to drop them into her lap.

"It was a completely different crime scene, Annie," Sergeant Quinn said. He reached his arm around her shoulders, then froze, casting a furtive glance at Matt and Bridget. He settled for a friendly pat on her mom's shoulder instead. "Whatever sicko killed the Kim boy, it was just a coincidence,

Annie, that it was anything like . . ." He looked at Bridget. "Like David's murder."

Bridget recalled the stricken look on Sergeant Quinn's face the night before when he arrived at St. Michael's. He knew as well as she did that the murders were exactly the same. Freakishly the same. No coincidence about it the same.

"I'm just sorry that Bridge—" She choked on her daughter's name. "That Bridget had to be the one to find him."

Bridget stiffened. Peter Kim's mangled, blood-soaked body flashed before her. His eyes wide open, staring upward, reflecting the horror of his last moments. His mouth gaping in a silent scream. The deep red gash across his throat that exposed the sinewy gore beneath.

Bridget's fingers curled around the seat of her chair, fingernails digging into the coarse underside. It was her fault, her fault that Peter was dead. Father Santos had said as much. Peter had been obsessed with her, in love with her since before she even knew what those words meant, and she'd just ignored him. She should have been kinder, more understanding. She should have texted him back last night, calmed him, told him that Matt Quinn meant nothing to her.

She felt a warmth next to her skin as Matt brushed the back of her hand, then slowly, purposefully, slipped his fingers between her palm and the chair. She gave way to the pressure and released her death grip as Matt's fingers laced between hers. Strong. He felt strong. Like someone she could finally lean on. She dropped her head as her eyes started to tear up.

"See, Mom?" Sammy had his left hand shoved into the brand-new baseball mitt. He reached his arm up like he was catching a fly ball in center field. "See? Matt says it's the same kind the pros wear."

Her mom cleared her throat. "That's lovely, Sammy. Now finish your—"

The doorbell pealed through the house.

"Who could that be?" her mom said. Bridget noticed that all the color had drained from her mom's face.

"Shall I get it?" Sergeant Quinn asked, half rising from his seat.

"No, no, Stephen. It's fine." Her mom stood up and excused herself. Beneath the table, Matt gave her hand a squeeze.

"I'm so sorry to bother you, Annie," a voice rang out from the hall. Hugh Darlington.

"Oh, no, Hugh. It's fine." This time Bridget was amused to watch Sergeant Quinn fidget in his chair.

"I was hoping you might have time to discuss the endowment I'm making in David's name."

"Actually, we're just finishing up dinner."

"I can wait in the downstairs office until you're done," Mr. Darlington said insistently.

With an audible grunt, Sergeant Quinn pushed himself to his feet and strode through the swinging door into the entryway.

"Sergeant Quinn," Mr. Darlington said. "I didn't realize you were here."

"It's a bad time, Darlington," Sergeant Quinn said. His voice sounded cold and professional. "Maybe you could come back tomorrow."

"I'm afraid," Mr. Darlington said, sounding very self-important, "that it cannot wait."

"I'm afraid," Sergeant Quinn said in a tone that made Bridget's hair stand on end, "it'll have to."

"How often is *he* here?" Matt whispered. He sounded uneasy.

"All the time," Sammy blurted out through a mouthful of mashed potatoes. "But not as much as your dad." Sammy grinned, exposing rows of potato-covered teeth, while Matt stared at his plate, aimlessly pushing bits of food around.

"I'm sorry, Hugh," her mom said. "Can we talk tomorrow?"

There was a pause, and though she couldn't see them, Bridget pictured the tall, solid frame of Sergeant Quinn and the shrewd, handsome face of Mr. Darlington, staring each other down in the entryway.

"Fine," Mr. Darlington said at last. "I'll give you a call tomorrow, Annie. Have a lovely evening." Another pause. "Good night, Stephen. I'm sure we'll talk soon." Then the door clicked shut.

It was a full two minutes before her mom and Sergeant Quinn reentered the dining room. Bridget wasn't entirely sure she wanted to know what happened during the interim.

Her mom came in first, with slightly puffy eyes. She immediately began clearing plates even though no one was done. Only Sammy complained.

"Mom," he said, snatching his plate away.

Her mom sighed.

Sammy jumped on the opportunity. "Can I watch TV while I finish?"

"Sure." Bridget's mom never gave up that easily. The confrontation between the two men in her life must have taken all the fight out of her.

"Come on." Bridget tugged on Matt's sleeve.

"Hmm?" he asked absently, like he was just coming out of a trance.

"Mom, we're going to do homework in my room, okay?"

"Homework." Her mom plopped down in a chair and stared out the back window. "Sure."

TWENTY-NINE

MATT FOLLOWED HER DOWN THE hall to her room, and it wasn't until the door clicked shut that he seemed to snap out of his stupor.

"Shutting me in?" he smirked.

"Shutting them out." Did he notice the tremor in her voice? She couldn't help it with him in her room and their parents down the hall, completely absorbed in their own drama.

They stared at each other. Matt was suddenly shy, and Bridget couldn't decide whether she wanted him to kiss her again or just go back to the way he'd been earlier in the day when they drove up to Geyserville: silent and strong.

Geyserville. That's right. There was a reason why she'd

invited Matt over in the first place. She spun around and opened her closet door, pushing the clothes aside as far as they would go.

"The closet?" Matt laughed. "Really?"

"Shut it, perv." Bridget smiled. She stretched her hand to the back of her closet, groping blindly in the dark, and eventually landed on a doorknob. "A little help, please?"

Matt gingerly stepped over her boot collection and squeezed in next to her. "Is that another door?"

"These old houses are weird. There's a room off my mom's bedroom that connects through this closet."

Matt leaned his shoulder against the door. "Why don't we just go through the door in your mom's bedroom, then?"

"Because she pushed a dresser in front of it after my dad died, smartass."

"Oh. Good reason."

Bridget twisted the doorknob and threw her weight against the hidden door. It opened a fraction of an inch, then stopped.

"Something must be in front of it," Matt said.

"Push!" Bridget ordered. Matt crouched down and put his legs into it. There was a deep groan from the other side of the door, then the obstacle beyond gave way. The door flew open, and Bridget and Matt tumbled forward into the room.

Bridget landed on top of him. "You're heavier than you look," Matt grunted.

"Bite me."

"I just might."

Bridget rolled her eyes and pushed herself up, but Matt grabbed her on either side of her waist. Before she could protest, he yanked her back down on top of him.

His kiss was stronger this time, less like he was afraid of breaking her.

She kissed him back. Deep and hungry. She wanted to feel his lips and his tongue against hers. Needed them.

She'd been afraid last time: afraid of what she might feel, afraid that she was doing it wrong. But something deep inside her ignited as Matt's hand snaked up into her curly mess of hair, his fingers twirling her strands until they felt hopelessly entangled. With a sound somewhere between a growl and a groan, she pressed her body into his, feeling every angle and crevice of his frame. The soft spots and the hard spots.

Matt slid his free hand under her T-shirt just at the small of her back, pulling her even closer. His lips moved down to her chin, then to the soft skin between her jaw and her neck. Bridget closed her eyes and moaned, a deep, aching sound that started as a dull rumbling in her belly before it escaped her lips. Her breaths came shallow and fast as she threw her head back. He took her hint and ran his lips over the sensitive flesh of her neck. It was like a million tiny explosions going off in her body all once, beginning at her lips and neck and extending downward, warming every inch of her body. Downward, until they mingled with something even more explosive deep within her.

The familiar tingling ignited in the pit of her stomach. It spread faster this time, swamping her mind with its electricity, its power. It felt exactly like . . .

Bridget rolled off Matt and scrambled to her feet. She felt like she was going to be sick.

"What's wrong?" Matt asked, his voice thick and raspy.

"We, uh, we don't have much time," Bridget said. She turned her back and pretended to straighten her shirt so he couldn't see her panic.

She heard him sit up and clear his throat. "Bridge, are you sure you're okay? I hope you're not—"

"I'm fine." She turned to him with a faint smile. "Really." Yeah, perfectly fine except apparently banishing demons and making out with you give me the same sick thrill. PERFECTLY FINE, MATT, THANK YOU!

"Oh. Okay." Matt got to his knees and looked around. "Where are we?"

"My dad's study."

"I thought his office was downstairs?"

"It is." Bridget stepped over a pile of books and hit the light switch near the other door that led into her parents' bedroom. It was a small space overshadowed by a large window looking out on the backyard. Furnishings were minimal: a leather chair like you'd see in a coffeehouse, a low table, and a wardrobe knocked askew by the closet door. And books, piles and piles of books.

"Downstairs is the office where he saw his private clients,

the ones he had before he joined Darlington's clinic. The police searched it after the murder, but no one thought about coming up here. This was his favorite room in the house, and after he died my mom couldn't handle looking at it from her bedroom."

Matt ran a finger over the coffee table and held it up, covered in a layer of dust. "So no one's been in here in months?"

Bridget nodded. "Since about two weeks after the murder."

"And if your dad was hiding something, something important—"

"This is where it would be."

"Okay then." Matt headed for the wardrobe while Bridget tackled the book piles. There were none of the professional volumes and medical journals that filled the bookcases in both of her dad's offices; these were his favorite reads. Mysteries and thrillers, a biography of Willie Mays, some pictorial histories of San Francisco.

"Seems to be mostly old stuff," Matt said. He had a leather box balanced on his knee. "Yearbooks, old letters, photos."

"Keep looking." Though for what, she wasn't sure. Would her dad have kept the missing Undermeyer files hidden or just piled among the books?

The books were a bust, so Bridget moved on to the coffee table. Old *Sports Illustrated*s and some half-finished crossword puzzles from the Sunday paper, both frozen in time to that horrible afternoon so long ago.

No, not so long. With everything that was happening, her father's death seemed close again, tangible like it was all happening anew. Only this time she didn't feel as helpless as she had before. This time she could do something so her father's death wouldn't be in vain.

"Oh my God," Matt exclaimed.

Bridget bolted to his side. "What? What did you find?"

"Is this you?" he said, holding up an old snapshot.

Bridget snatched the photo from his hands. It was a picture of a seven-year-old Bridget in a pink Sleeping Beauty princess gown, complete with tiara, plastic light-up princess shoes, and glitter wand, which she was dabbing on the head of her infant brother like she was granting him a wish. "Holy crap."

Matt was trying desperately to hold back his laughter. "I've never seen you in so much . . . pink."

"Shut it."

"Please tell me," he said with a smirk, "that you still have the dress."

Bridget shoved the photo back into the wardrobe. "I hate you. A lot."

"I know." Matt winked and he closed the wardrobe door. "There's nothing else here, though."

"Are you sure?"

"Positive. I checked and double-checked. Nothing."

Bridget sat down on the floor. Come on, think! Where

would he have hidden it?

"Bridget?" Her mom's voice drifted in through the open closet door. "Bridget, Sergeant Quinn is leaving, and I think Matt should probably go too."

"Dammit." Bridget ducked back through her closet door, Matt close behind. "Okay, Mom," she called out, trying to sound normal.

Matt pulled the door closed behind him and stepped out of the closet. "I guess that means I need to go."

Bridget cast a glance at her closet door, trying not to look disappointed. "Yeah, I guess so."

He placed a hand on her shoulder. "You'll call me? If you need anything?"

Bridget nodded.

"You'll call me even if you don't?"

Bridget tried to keep the corners of her mouth from bending up into a goofy smile, but she couldn't. What had happened to her? A few kisses and she was completely under Matt Quinn's spell. Where was badass Bridget who didn't need anyone?

Matt took a step closer. "Will you?"

Bridget melted. "Yes."

"Good." Matt leaned down and kissed her lightly, then opened the bedroom door and, with one last flash of his smile, slipped into the hall.

THIRTY

THEY SAT IN THE SAME seats—Bridget, Hector, and Brad—at the last cafeteria table on the left. Their trays held the same familiar lunches: Brad's piled high with a precarious tower of sandwiches, Bridget's grilled cheese and Diet 7Up, Hector's weight-conscious bag lunch. It was the same, and yet everything was different because of the empty seat to Bridget's left. Peter's seat.

"I can't believe he's gone," Brad said at last, breaking the silence. His sandwiches lay untouched.

Hector stared at the empty seat. "Yeah."

"I mean, I was just tutoring with him on Friday. I can't believe it."

"Um . . ." Hector fidgeted with the zipper on his hoodie.

"Brad, you know, if you still need help with algebra . . . I mean, I could totally, you know, help."

Bridget did a double take. Hector just volunteered to tutor his secret crush? That was the ballsiest thing he'd ever done.

"Yeah, man," Brad said with a smile. "That'd be awesome. Thanks."

"No problem."

Bridget was about to say something when she felt Hector's shoe nudge her under the table. She let it drop. Now wasn't the time to tease Hector about Brad.

"I just don't get what he was doing at school that night," Brad said.

"Duh," Hector said, nodding his head in Bridget's direction.

"It's not Liu's fault," Brad said.

"I'm not saying it is. But how many text messages did *you* get from Peter Saturday night?"

Bridget's eyes dashed between Brad and Hector's faces. "You too?"

"A dozen, at least," Hector said. "Before I turned my phone off."

"I got, like, eight from him," Brad said. "But I was at the dance so I didn't notice till the next day."

Hector raised his eyebrows. "Bridge?"

"Thirty-seven." Bridget pushed her tray away and sank her forehead onto crossed arms.

Hector dropped his diet shake onto the metal table. "Thirty-seven?"

"Damn," Brad said under his breath.

Bridget didn't raise her head. "Yeah, I know."

"What were they like?" Hector asked.

"Like he was going through the five stages of grief," Bridget said, sitting up. "But then near the end they got really . . ." Bridget remembered the threats Peter had texted her, the ones she didn't get until after he was dead. "Ugly."

Hector held out his hand. "Gimme."

With a sigh, Bridget handed over her cell phone. She guessed Hector and Brad deserved to see them, even though those thirty-seven text messages weren't from the Peter Kim she'd known most of her life. They were from someone else, someone whose jealousy had turned into a rage so violent it had gotten him killed.

She wasn't going to mention that part.

"Damn," Hector said as they scrolled through the texts.

Brad whistled. "I can't believe Peter wrote these."

"Believe it," Bridget said.

"I've just never heard him swear like this. Ever."

"I know."

Bridget's phone buzzed. Incoming text. "Give it."

A sly smile appeared on Hector's face. "Douchebag Quinn?" he said, reading the sender's name. "You changed his name in your phone to Douchebag Quinn?"

Ouch. She forgot she'd changed it after he got her grounded. She was going to have to fix that. "Just give it."

"'R U OK?'" Brad read aloud. "'Worried. Call me ASAP.'"

"Give it!" Bridget shot her hand across the table to grab the phone, but Brad held it out of her reach.

The phone buzzed again, and Brad leaned back on the bench to read it. "'Miss U.'"

Bridget dropped her forehead to the table with a thud. "Kill me."

"Oh. My. GOD!" Hector said. "You're dating him, aren't you?"

"Um . . ." Bridget thought of the brief make-out session on the floor of her dad's study, of Matt's sweet good-bye when he left. "We haven't really talked about—"

"You totally made out with him," Brad said, tossing her phone onto the table.

Bridget raised her head. "Um . . ."

"Oh. My. GOD!" Hector repeated, and kicked her under the table. "I can't believe you didn't tell me!"

"I, er, was a little busy this weekend."

"Yeah," Brad laughed. "Busy."

Bridget yawned. The strain of the last few days had caught up with her, and all she wanted to do was climb into bed and go to sleep.

"Bridge, maybe you should go home early," Hector said.

"Yeah, Liu. I don't think anyone's going to give you static after . . . well . . ." Brad's eyes darted to the empty seat next to Bridget. "You know."

She had history, show choir—which had been temporarily moved out of the church and into the gym—and Latin left for the day. She didn't really want to spend an hour in a classroom with Father Santos or see Alexa in show choir, and the thought of sitting through Latin was about as appealing as a *Jersey Shore* marathon.

"Maybe you're right." She grabbed her untouched lunch tray. "I'll go see Mrs. Freely. Talk to you guys later."

"Went home early," Bridget typed into her phone. "Call me l8r." She hit send, and the text to Matt Quinn sped off into the cellular unknown.

She rolled over in bed and pulled the covers up under her chin. A nap. A nap would be perfect right about now. If only she could turn her damn brain off.

Which, of course, she couldn't. There were too many elements swirling around up there to let her sleep. Peter Kim. Watchers. Alexa's eyes. Matt's lips. Gah! Matt's lips were *not* a part of the puzzle. She needed to focus. She needed to find that missing file.

There had to be something she'd overlooked, some connecting clue that her dumb, stubborn eye hadn't picked up on.

"Where is it, Dad?" she called out loud. "Where is the file?"

Pat, pat, pat, pat, pat.

Phantom paws padded across her bedroom floor. Bridget sat up in bed. Almost immediately, the scratching commenced at the door in the back of her closet.

Always the same pattern: Bridget heard the animal's paws pattering down the hall or across her room, ending with the scratching in her closet. She fell back against her pillow. If she waited long enough, maybe it would go away.

CREAK! Bridget sat up again. That was new. That was different. She crawled to the edge of her bed and peeked into her closet. A thin sliver of light shone through the darkness. The door into her dad's study was ajar.

Weird. Matt must not have closed it all the way when they rushed through, and whatever had been making the scratching noise was able to push the door open.

Bridget slipped out of bed and into her closet. Her dad's study was tiny: one open door and no place to hide. If a real animal came that way, it was trapped.

Bridget peered into the study. It was exactly how she and Matt had left it—wardrobe angled away from the door, coffee table with its grime-encrusted magazines, single bookcase, single chair. No cat—real or supernatural—anywhere to be seen.

Scratch, scratch, scratch, scratch, scratch.

Not at the door this time. From inside the room.

Scratch, scratch, scratch, scratch, scratch.

Bridget's eye caught a flurry of dust from the far corner, as if something was clawing at a spot on the floor, disturbing the layer of fine dust. It billowed upward, thousands of tiny specks illuminated in a shaft of sunlight streaming through a crack in the blinds. The scratching continued, and as the cloud of dust thickened, it began to condense, contorting itself into a definite shape. Bridget's mouth went dry. A figure formed before her eyes: bushy tail and squat legs, furry head and lopsided ears. The dust cloud looked exactly like Mr. Moppet.

She crouched in the closet, terrified of disturbing the ghost cat's frantic digging. Digging, yeah, that's what it was. Mr. Moppet's ghost was trying to dig its way into the floor of her dad's study.

What had she said just before Mr. Moppet scurried across her bedroom floor? "Where is it, Dad? Where is the file?"

Bridget sucked in a breath. It couldn't be, could it?

"Dad?"

The undulating figure of the cat stopped clawing at the floor and craned its neck around until it stared right at her. Tears welled up in Bridget's eyes. Staring back at her from the ethereal dust cloud of the phantom cat were the soft, almond-shaped eyes of her father.

Those eyes held her gaze for what felt like an eternity as heavy drops spilled uncontrollably down Bridget's cheeks.

The cat gave the floor one last scratch with his paw. Then the force holding the dust cloud together vanished in an instant, and the individual particles drifted upward into a shapeless blob.

"Dad!" Bridget cried. She scrambled into the study. The dust hung in the air, no longer her father. Just dust. Just nothingness.

He'd been there all along, trying to help her. He was trying to show her something.

Bridget knelt on the floor. It wasn't fair. It wasn't fair that he was gone, that she'd been left with all this. The ache in her heart was back, sharp and cold like she'd just been stabbed with an icicle. She'd hidden the grief for so long, but she'd never really escaped from it, and now the full force of her father's death engulfed her. Bridget hung her head in her hands and wept.

Bridget wasn't sure how long she sat there, her chest heaving with each wretched sob, her eyes clenched tight against the raw, searing pain of loss. As her breath slowed, she felt a warm, furry body brush against her legs. It rubbed its face against her knee, then turned and pressed its whole body into her, just like Mr. Moppet used to do with Sammy.

Without opening her eyes, Bridget reached down and felt the soft fur of a cat. She stroked her hand down its back and up through the bushy tail, and she felt Mr. Moppet's throaty purr. In her memory, no cat had ever voluntarily been that close to her.

"I miss you, Dad." Bridget squeezed her eyes closed as she continued to run her fingers through the cat's velvety fur. "I miss you so much."

The cat let out a single meow, then the firm body faded to nothingness. Bridget was alone.

She sat with her eyes closed for a few moments. Her tears had stopped, her breath came calm and easy, and the tightness in her chest that had been with her for the last year evaporated. Her dad was dead, that would never change, but she'd gotten a second chance to say good-bye.

Bridget blinked her eyes open and realized she was staring directly at the spot at which the phantom cat had been clawing. The dust had settled back onto the floor, coating the wooden beams and gathering in the crevices to form little gray channels between the planks. But a few of them looked as if they had been broken. A horizontal line of dust bisected several of the wooden planks. Odd. Bridget leaned forward, drawing her nose to within a few inches of the beams. Something wasn't right: The broken line looked like it had been cut through with some sort of power tool.

She slipped a fingernail into the crevice and wiggled the board. The entire corner of wooden floor shifted.

Bridget dashed to her closet and grabbed a wire coat hanger, then unbent the hook and shoved it down into the crevice. It easily poked down several inches into a compartment beneath. Twisting the hanger so the curved end rotated beneath the broken floorboards, she carefully pulled up and out. The flooring popped up just enough for her to get her fingers beneath it, and she pried the compartment open.

It was a small space, no bigger than a shoebox, and it held a large yellow envelope.

THIRTY-ONE

TWENTY MINUTES LATER, BRIDGET SAT cross-legged on her bed. The envelope lay unopened before her, but she was ready to see what it held. Her laptop was powered up so she could listen to any recordings; she had a pen and paper for notes. All she had to do was open it.

Bridget picked up the yellow envelope gingerly, felt its weight in her hand, turned it over, and examined the seal. Just a simple piece of Scotch tape held the flap closed, and there was no writing on the outside to give a hint as to who placed it there or why. Not that Bridget needed a hint. There could be only one reason.

She slipped a finger beneath the flap, then stopped. What was she doing? Trusting the advice of a bunch of demons trapped in the body of a man who may or may not have murdered her dad? Or a demon cat that may or may not have been the incarnation of her dead father? Had she totally and completely lost her mind?

Rule Number Three: Do not engage.

Rule Number Four: Do not let your guard down.

Rule Number Five: They lie.

Fail, fail, fail. Not only had she engaged the demons, she'd purposefully sought them out at Sonoma State Hospital. She'd let her guard down when she tried to release the entities from Undermeyer's body. And now she was trusting what they told her to do. Trusting a demon, a minion of evil, instead of Monsignor Renault.

Exorcist-fail.

Maybe she should call Monsignor and ask his advice?

Bridget shook her head. She'd come this far on her own. She had to see what her dad had left hidden. She had to do it alone.

Bridget took a deep breath and broke the seal.

January 7
Patient: Milton Undermeyer
Session 1
Duplicate File
Severe case of demonic possession. Sensing anywhere from four to six entities. Repentants, I believe. Patient and his entities refuse to disclose why they broke into the sanctuary at St. Michael's. Something

tells me this is no ordinary crime. Not there. Contacting J from OSM for further instructions.

January 14
Patient: Milton Undermeyer
Session 2
Duplicate File
Patient's entities say they have a message for the Watchers, but there seems to be a disagreement among them in regards to sharing. Want to make sure they will be released afterward. Will decide once I hear their message. Still no answer about the break-in at St. Michael's.

January 21
Patient: Milton Undermeyer
Session 3
Duplicate File
Entities extremely agitated. Something spooked them. Possible they've had contact with the Emim. A threat of some kind. Which would mean the Emim are aware that the entities are attempting to pass a message to the Watchers. Unsure how Emim came by this information. J calling emergency meeting of the OSM. Awaiting word.

January 28
Patient: Milton Undermeyer
Session 4
Duplicate File

Stephen called. Undermeyer attempted suicide in his cell this morning. Had him brought to the house while Annie and the kids are at her mom's. Change of scenery made a difference. Entities have conveyed the following message:

Amaymon calling his servants. Attempting to regain the mortal world. Must not let him. Stop the priest. The Emim cannot conjure Amaymon without him. They need the priest. The priest wielding the sword.

Unsure if sword is physical or not. J researching. Suggested I contact Monsignor Renault at St. Michael's. Turns out the OSM was right in sending me to this parish after all.

Bridget's hand shook. It was true, it was all true, staring at her from the notebook pages in her dad's very own handwriting. He had been a Watcher, an ancient relative of a bunch of horny angels banished from Heaven. And she was too.

But she was no closer to discovering who killed her dad. The message Undermeyer had delivered to him was the same one they'd given her. Points for consistency at least, but there was nothing here that would prove who actually killed him.

The last entry, January 28. A week later her dad was dead.

She read through the notes again, looking for a hint she may have missed. The spooked entities looked promising, but she had no way of knowing why. Another dead end? It couldn't be.

Bridget's hand rested on the envelope, and she noticed

there was something else inside, something hard and circular.

She dumped the contents out onto her sheets. A CD. The missing audio? She slid the disk into her laptop and pulled on her headphones.

"All right, Mr. Undermeyer," Dr. Liu said. "I have stopped the recording."

"Not safe. Not safe. We are not safe here." Bridget heard several thumps, accompanied by frantic grunts from Milton Undermeyer. He must have been restrained and was attempting to get out of his chair.

"You're perfectly safe here, Mr. Undermeyer. And whoever else may be in there with you."

Undermeyer sucked in a breath. "He knows. The Watcher knows. Of course he knows."

"Yes, I do." Bridget could hear her dad's frustration bubbling below the surface. "I know who you are and I know why you're here."

"Liar!" Undermeyer taunted. "Liar, liar, liar."

"I know you have a message for me."

"Yesssss," Undermeyer hissed. "But they know it too. They know it too."

"Who is *they*?" Dr. Liu asked. "The Emim?"

More thumping.

"Do not say it!" Undermeyer's voice was twisted, distorted like it was coming through a bad loudspeaker. "Do not say it. Not safe. We are not safe here. Not safe. We are not safe here."

"I have dominion over the Emim," Dr. Liu said. "I will protect you."

"Not safe. Not safe here," Undermeyer muttered to himself over and over again.

Bridget heard her dad sigh, that sigh of exasperation she knew only too well. She couldn't help but smile: It was nice to know that she wasn't the only one who could make her dad sigh like that. Of course Dr. Liu was dealing with a demonically possessed madman, so maybe the comparison wasn't so great.

"I can't help you, Mr. Undermeyer, unless you help me. Tell me why you were in the Church of St. Michael. Tell what this message is you——"

A knock at the door.

"Come in," Dr. Liu said.

"Sorry to disturb you, Dr. Liu." Bridget knew that voice.

"No problem, Hugh. Is there something I can do for you?"

A shriek maxed out the treble on the record, and Bridget scrambled to turn down the volume. "Not safe!" Undermeyer screamed. "Not safe! Not safe! Not safe!"

The recording went silent.

It made perfect sense that her dad had hidden the duplicate files and the secret recordings, both of which exposed his abilities as a Watcher. Bridget almost laughed at the thought of Sergeant Quinn going over those materials. Would he have thought her dad was crazy? Probably. It's what Bridget would have thought herself if she didn't, unfortunately, know better.

"Contacting J from OSM for further instructions." Who the hell was that? A company? A religious organization? Whoever "J from OSM" was, her dad obviously had contact with him long before Undermeyer arrived on his doorstep. The OSM must be involved somehow with the Watchers.

Bridget hopped out of bed and shuffled down the hall to get a soda. She was wide awake now, antsy and anxious to find answers to new questions.

She pulled a can of Diet 7Up out of the fridge and popped it open. J from OSM. That was the key to the mystery. She had to figure out who or what it was. But how? She needed a database devoted to this kind of stuff . . .

She stopped midsip. Father Santos. Father Santos had a personal library in his office "borrowed" straight from the Vatican. That was as good as it got, right? The freaking Vatican library? Father Santos would let her look for whatever she wanted.

Don't trust the priest. The words came back to her like a punch in the chest. She didn't know who "the priest" was yet, but whoever he was, he was working for the Emim, working to raise Amaymon from the legions of Hell. Could it be Father Santos? Bridget laughed as she pictured the clumsy, stuttering Father Santos in league with the Emim.

Still, there was something about Father Santos she didn't like and didn't trust. The freak-out over her bracelet, for starters. At the doll shop, he "forgot" to finish securing the room by laying salt across the front door. Could it have been on purpose? And he was the one who suggested she directly engage the demons, inciting the doll riot. Was it intentional? Was he trying to get her killed?

Bridget trudged back to her room. No, she couldn't risk it, couldn't risk trusting anyone at this point. If she wanted to get a look in Father Santos's office, she'd have to do it on her own.

Her cell phone ring snapped Bridget back to reality. "Douchebag Quinn" was the incoming caller.

"Hello?"

"Is everything okay?" Matt asked.

"Matt." Bridget could barely keep her voice even. "I found it."

"You found it?"

"Yeah." She decided to leave out the part about the dead phantom cat. "There was a loose floorboard in the corner of my dad's study."

"Holy crap!"

"I know."

Matt dropped his voice. "What does it say?"

"It's kind of complicated. What time do you get out of practice?"

"You're home?"

"Yeah, I can hang out until—"

"I'll be there in fifteen."

"Wait, Matt. You don't have to . . . Hello?" Nothing. Had

he really just hung up on her?

Somehow, she wasn't really mad.

Bridget pulled a brush through her hair and applied some lip gloss. For the first time in her life, she actually cared what she looked like. It was a new experience to say the least.

The doorbell rang exactly thirteen minutes later, and Bridget tried to look casual as she opened the door.

"Hey," she said.

"Hey." Matt was breathless. Had he run all the way from Riordan? "Are you okay?"

Bridget smiled. Matt's hyperprotectiveness was growing on her. "Yeah."

Without thinking, she reached her hand out to him. The instant her fingers touched his, that God-awful tingling sensation raced up her hands through her body. She yanked her hand away.

"Bridge?" Matt looked stricken. She couldn't bear to see his pain and confusion, knowing she was the cause. Besides, she wanted to touch him so badly, to feel him protecting her from the things neither of them understood, to feel his lips pressed against hers, his arms pulling her to his body, to feel that delicious heat, that intoxicating energy flowing through her again.

She didn't care what it meant.

Bridget took a step toward him, holding the gaze of those hazel eyes. It must have been the invitation Matt was hoping for. He grabbed her hand and pulled her to him, wrapping his other arm around her waist. His kiss was gentle, but Bridget didn't want gentle. She wanted to feel those tiny explosions of pleasure racing up and down her body.

She kissed him hard, her tongue finding his as she pressed her body into him. The energy tore through her. It pulsed up her arms, down her legs, across her chest. She slipped a hand under Matt's shirt and ran her fingers over the taut muscles of his stomach. She heard him moan softly as her hand trailed down the front of his body. He belonged to her. Matt, this power, this feeling. They all belonged to her.

"Wait," Bridget said, breaking away. This wasn't why he was here.

"Wait?" he gasped.

Bridget put a hand on Matt's chest. His heart was racing, racing for her.

Focus! "Right, sorry."

Matt cocked his head to the side. "Huh?"

"Look, I need to do something, something that could get me in a lot of trouble."

"Why am I not surprised?"

Bridget rolled her eyes. "I mean it. And I don't want you to help me just because . . . well, because . . ." Her voice faltered.

Matt laced his fingers through hers. "Because of the way I feel about you?"

"Yeah."

Matt took a step closer to her. "I'm here for you, whatever you need."

Bridget held her hands up in front of her. "I'm talking about breaking and entering."

"Again, why am I not surprised?"

"Damn," Bridget said, pursing her lips. "You and your dad must really think I'm a total fuckup."

"Partial," Matt said with a sly grin. "Partial fuckup. But seriously, I'm in."

"You sure?"

"Totally."

Bridget couldn't help but feel relieved. She would have busted into Father Santos's office alone if she had to, but the idea of having Matt with her made the whole endeavor significantly less terrifying.

A soft beep came from Matt's pocket, and he dug down for his cell phone. "I've got practice in thirty. What time should I pick you up?"

Bridget wasn't sure what kind of cloak-and-dagger insanity she'd need to pull to get out of the house, but she'd think of something. "Eleven. Park down the street, though. I'll have to sneak out."

"Okay." He bent down and kissed her swiftly. "I'll see you then."

THIRTY-TWO

MATT CROUCHED IN THE SHADOWS, fiddling with the lock to the back door of St. Michael's Rectory. The air glowed a dull blue-gray as the beam from Bridget's flashlight dissipated into the thick, low-lying fog. She shivered and tucked her free hand into the pocket of her jacket.

"I thought you'd be better at this."

"Why?"

Bridget shrugged. "'Cause your dad's a cop."

"Right," Matt said, shifting his body so he wasn't blocking the light. "Why wouldn't he teach me Breaking and Entering 101?"

Bridget stifled a yawn. "Might be helpful now."

"Patience, grasshopper." Matt inserted a second metal

prong into the lock. "I know a few tricks."

Bridget heard a soft click, and Matt raised his eyebrows in an unspoken "I told you so" before twisting the handle. The door swung open.

"Slick, MacGyver," Bridget whispered, patting him on the head. "Remind me to give you a cookie."

Matt's face was serious. "You know where to go?"

Bridget nodded. He was right: enough with the crap, time to get what they came for.

They stepped into the rectory, and Matt pulled the door shut behind them, throwing the room into darkness. Bridget panned her flashlight: cupboards, butcher block table, stove. They were in the kitchen.

There was an open door on the far side of the room, and Bridget motioned for Matt to follow her. From the carpeted hallway, Bridget knew exactly where they were. Father Santos's office was on the second floor, third door from the end of the hall, just above the kitchen.

They crept up the staircase. Bridget tested her weight on each step before fully committing. The priests, including Father Santos and Monsignor Renault, would be asleep on the top floor and hopefully wouldn't hear the odd squeak or creak from the old rectory, but how the hell would she explain herself if the lights suddenly came on?

Her hand trembled so violently the flashlight beam shook. She wasn't so much concerned about herself as she was about Matt. What if this little stunt got him suspended? Ruined his pitching career? Made him hate her forever?

Bridget paused at the door of Father Santos's office. Hopefully, Matt wouldn't have to repeat his perp skills in busting a lock. She held her breath and turned the doorknob.

The door opened easily, noiselessly. Bridget and Matt dashed inside and eased the door closed.

"I'm not exactly sure what we're looking for," Bridget whispered. "But Father Santos probably has his books arranged—"

Bridget froze as the beams of their flashlights illuminated the office. It looked like an earthquake had hit. Books were pulled down from every shelf, strewn about the small room haphazardly. The chairs were overturned and Father Santos's desk had been toppled over, the contents of his drawers spilled onto the floor.

"Oh my God," Bridget said.

"Someone got here before us," Matt said. "Someone else had the same idea."

"That's impossible."

"No, it's not. What did Undermeyer tell you? The Emim are trying to raise some demon king, right?"

"Amaymon, thanks for listening."

Matt shone his light right in her face. "Hey, you threw a lot of info at me that day."

"You mean yesterday?"

"Oh, yeah." Matt swung his beam back into the upturned office. "Still, my point is, maybe the Emim or the priest working with them are looking for the same thing we are?"

"Maybe."

Bridget scanned the chaos of Father Santos's office. Every bookcase had been emptied onto the floor, creating a minefield of splayed books. Even if she knew what to look for, it would be impossible to find anything. Her beam moved past the cupboard behind the overturned desk, then zipped back to it. The door of the cupboard was open.

Bridget picked her way through the mess. "If you had something important, wouldn't you keep it locked up?"

"Probably. Hey, maybe we should just talk to Father Santos."

She gave him a look of disbelief. "Don't trust the priest, remember?"

"Yeah, but someone obviously broke in here. Wouldn't that mean Father Santos is on our side?"

She examined the cupboard. One of the doors stood wide open, the other was still locked. Neither showed signs of having been forced.

"Not necessarily," she said. "Look, this cupboard was opened with a key."

Matt stumbled through the carnage and peered down at the door. "Okay, fine. Someone used a key. But if they knew what they were looking for, why destroy the room?"

That situation had already crossed Bridget's mind. "To make it look like someone broke in. Father Santos could easily have done this himself to make it seem like he'd been robbed."

"But why?"

"To gain my trust, maybe?" It sort of made sense.

"I guess." Matt was clearly unconvinced. "What's in here, anyway?"

Bridget illuminated the contents of the cupboard. The wooden box was still there, unopened and unmolested; whoever had broken in clearly hadn't been interested in the Skellig Manuscript. The only other object was a set of books on the middle shelf, six leather-encased volumes, one of which appeared to be missing.

She clamped the end of the flashlight in her teeth and pulled the set of books out of the cupboard. The volumes weren't huge, maybe two hundred pages each, but the set weighed a ton.

"A widdle hewp," Bridget said through the flashlight.

Matt grabbed the books and eased them down on the side of the toppled desk. "See, I knew you'd need my help."

Bridget pulled the flashlight out of her mouth. "Oh, Matt, you're so big and strong. My hero."

"Your hero, huh?" Matt hooked a finger through a belt loop on her jeans and pulled her to him. "I'm going to remind you of that one day."

Bridget's heart fluttered as their bodies pressed lightly together. She had to fight the urge to reach her lips up to his. With a shake of her head, she turned back to the box on the table.

There was a label on the side of it. *"Les Grimoires des Rois*

L'Enfer," Bridget read awkwardly. "Oh, please tell me you speak French."

"Sorry," Matt said. "Spanish."

"Perfect. And I took Latin."

"Dead languages are so helpful. Any idea what it means?"

A voice answered them from across the room. *"The Grimoires of the Kings of Hell."*

THIRTY-THREE

BRIDGET DROPPED HER FLASHLIGHT. At first she thought it was a demon answering her from the darkness of the room, but then she saw the figure—the human figure—silhouetted in the doorway. It reached a chubby hand to the wall and flicked on the lights.

Father Santos's jaw dropped. "What in the name of G-God did you do to my office?"

Bridget looked sidelong at Matt. "It was like this when we got here, Father Santos. I swear."

"Are you s-sure?" Father Santos stepped into his office and closed the door behind him. He scratched his neck nervously as his eyes danced around the room.

Bridget snorted. "Pretty sure."

"Hmm." Father Santos bent down and began picking up books off the floor, examining their pages and spines, and stacking them on a nearby shelf.

Matt turned to Bridget and inclined his head toward Father Santos. "What the hell?" he mouthed.

"Um, Father Santos?" Bridget asked.

Father Santos didn't even look at her. "Yes, Bridget?"

"Any idea who would want to break into your office?"

"Besides you two?"

"Look, Matt only came because I asked him to. I don't want him to get in trouble."

"Actually, Father," Matt said. "It was my idea. Bridget was just trying to help."

"What are you doing?" Bridget whispered.

"Keeping you out of trouble," Matt said between clenched teeth.

Bridget set her jaw. "I don't need your help."

"Really? It doesn't seem that way."

"Um," Father Santos said. He was staring at them now, as if he were watching a pair of chimpanzees at the zoo. "Can you two save the b-bickering for later? We have more important matters at hand."

Bridget clammed up. She was keenly aware of how calm and patient Father Santos had been. No anger, no indignation. He wasn't calling the police or waking up the rest of the rectory. He just stood there, book in each hand, blocking the door, serenely shifting his gaze between Bridget and Matt.

They were so screwed.

"First off, I'd like you to tell me what you're doing in my office in the middle of the night."

Yeah, that would be first. Was there any plausible answer other than that they had broken in to steal something?

"Right," Father Santos said, interpreting their silence. "So you came here to find something. Do you even know what you were looking for?"

Bridget shook her head. At least that was the truth.

"And you found my office in this state, correct?"

"Yes."

"Any idea what they were looking for?"

Bridget glanced down at the volume of grimoires balanced on the side of the desk. "There's a volume missing."

"From *Les Grimoires des Rois L'Enfer*?" he asked.

"Yes."

"Hey," Matt said. He took a step forward so he was slightly in front of Bridget. "What are you going to do with us?"

Father Santos pulled his head back. "Do with you?"

"Yeah."

It took Father Santos a few seconds to realize what Matt was implying, then a look of utter surprise spread across his face. "You think I'm . . . I mean, that this . . ." His lips continued to form words but no sound came out. Father Santos shook his head in frustration, then stomped his foot on the floor. "Bridget," he said, his lips tight and drawn. "I think it's time you trusted me."

That's when Bridget lost it.

"Why should I trust you? I hardly know you, and since you showed up my whole life has turned inside out."

"Your life wasn't exactly p-perfect before I arrived."

Bridget scowled. "See, that doesn't help."

"Sorry. But still, you need to trust me."

"Trust *you*? Give me one good reason."

Father Santos sighed, long and low. "Because your father did."

Bridget's voice caught in her throat. "How did you know my dad?"

"Take one of the volumes out of that set," Father Santos said, pointing at the grimoires.

"What?"

"Please."

"Fine." Bridget pulled out the first volume. It was thin but solid, with thick, gilt-edged pages.

"Open the cover and read the inscription."

Bridget scowled but did what he asked. "'Property of Father Juan Santos, Order of Saint Michael.'"

"What does that have to do with Dr. Liu?" Matt asked.

Bridget gasped. "Oh my God. J of the OSM. Juan Santos of the Order of St. Michael. It was you!"

Father Santos inclined his head. "Yes."

"You knew my dad was a Watcher."

"Yes."

Matt grabbed her arm. "Bridget, what are you talking about?"

She turned to him and laughed, a wave of relief passing through her. "It was in my dad's notes, the ones I found in his study. He was waiting for instructions from someone—J of the OSM—when he was killed."

"The Order of St. Michael," Father Santos said.

Matt wasn't buying it yet. "Who?"

"The Order of St. Michael." Father Santos spoke quickly, with a fanatic's gleam in his eye. "An ancient order founded in the eighth century, after Michael the Archangel appeared to St. Aubert at Mont Saint-Michel. An order of warrior priests—"

"Warrior priests?" Matt said with a raised eyebrow.

Father Santos jutted out his chin. "As a matter of fact, yes."

Matt cast a glance at Father Santos's pudgy form. "Whatever you say."

"The Order of St. Michael is an order of the Vatican," Father Santos continued. He was obviously proud of his affiliation. "Entrusted with the task of protecting what is left of the Watchers."

"Including my dad."

Father Santos nodded. "Yes. Your father and a handful of other Watchers we've been able to make contact with over the centuries."

"There are more of us?"

"Oh, yes, but as I told you before, no one I've met whose abilities are as developed as yours."

"So you knew all this time what Bridget was?" Matt asked. He sounded less than impressed.

"I explained it to her."

"But left out the part about her dad."

Father Santos shrugged. "I was trying to protect her, just as you are now."

"Hey, guys, I'm in the room, remember?" Bridget was so tired of people trying to shelter her she was ready to scream. "And I don't need either of you standing over my shoulder, okay?"

Father Santos nodded. "Fair enough."

"Good. Now just tell me what's going on."

"All right." Father Santos clapped his hands together. "Let's start with the missing grimoire and work backward from there, shall we?"

With careful steps, making sure he didn't so much as nudge one of the books strewn across the floor, Father Santos made his way to the set of grimoires. He didn't touch them, merely bent at the waist and peered down.

"Bael, Paymon, Beleth, Gaap . . ." His voice trailed off, but his lips continued to articulate unspoken words as he ticked through the volumes. Then, with a start, he straightened up. "Oh my."

"What?" Bridget asked.

Father Santos paced in a tight circle. "My, my, my."

"What?" Bridget and Matt said together.

Father Santos turned to Bridget, his face draining of color. "Amaymon."

"Amaymon? That's the missing volume?"

Father Santos nodded. "The demon master from Mrs. Long's exorcism."

Matt leaned in to look at the grimoires. "Is that the demon king Undermeyer told you about?"

Father Santos's eyes practically popped out of his head. "What? What?"

"Oh, right." Bridget bit her lip. "You didn't know about that."

"You spoke with Milton Undermeyer?"

"Um, yeah. Yesterday."

"And?"

Bridget's eyes flicked toward Matt with an unspoken question: Can we trust him? Matt's brows drew together. He was clearly thrown by the odd, fumbly little figure of Father Santos. It took a moment before Matt slowly nodded.

Father Santos scratched absently at his neck. Her dad trusted this guy. Bizarre as it seemed. He was on their side. Time to take the plunge.

"Don't trust the priest. Those nonsense lines you gave me from the doll shop? It was an anagram for 'Don't trust the priest.' And Mrs. Long, she basically said it too, told me not to trust either of you."

Father Santos plopped down on the edge of the desk. "I see."

"And after what happened, I figured it meant you."

"W-what happened?"

"Yeah. You know. First you freaked out about my charm bracelet, then you didn't finish securing the door of the doll shop with salt. It seemed like you were trying to work against us."

Father Santos smiled wanly. "I was trying to protect you. I thought the doll shop might be a trap, and I was trying to leave a means of escape."

"Oh." Bridget hadn't thought of that. "And the bracelet?"

"A St. Benedict's medal *without* the image of St. Benedict? You don't understand how rare that is. It serves a very . . . specific purpose."

"An exorcist's amulet," Bridget said, clasping the charm between her fingers.

"Er, yes. Sort of." Father Santos hurried on. "What else have you kept from me??"

"I went to see Mr. Undermeyer, and he gave me the same message he gave my dad. That the Emim were using a priest—a priest wielding a sword—to try and raise Amaymon, to give him a human form so he could stay in our world and, well, I don't know. Do whatever it is demons do."

"Cause rampant destruction and suffering," Father Santos muttered.

"I guess."

"Shit," Matt said.

"Indeed." Father Santos started to stand up, then sat

back down again. Then, after a pause, he leaped to his feet. "Indeed. It all makes sense!"

"It does?"

"Absolutely. It's funny, really."

Bridget didn't see the humor in any of this. "You're kidding, right?"

Father Santos cleared his throat. "Oh, yes, I see what you mean. Catholic doctrine is just b-blown to bits, isn't it? It completely destroys the belief that fallen angels can think only of evil if they are attempting to warn us about . . . about one of their own."

"Um, that's not what I meant at all."

Father Santos angled his head, surprised that Bridget wasn't thinking about Catholic doctrine.

Matt slapped his forehead. "Tell us how it all makes sense." Even his infinite patience was failing the Father Santos endurance test.

"Oh, yes, of . . . of course," Father Santos twittered. He rolled back on the desk and lifted a volume from the set of grimoires. "The rise in infestations and possessions. Undermeyer breaking into the church. Your father's murder. It all makes sense now."

"Dude," Matt said. "No, it doesn't."

"Of course it does." Father Santos flipped through the volume. "You just haven't been paying attention."

The confused look on Matt's face begged Bridget for some sort of explanation, but all she could do was shrug. She was as lost as he was.

Father Santos popped up off the desk. "Ah ha! Here it is. Listen. *'Le sorcier peut gagner la dominance au-dessus de Beleth seulement à condition qu'il reste dans le cercle du——'*"

"Um, Father Santos?" Bridget interrupted.

"Wait," he said turning the page. "This gets really interesting."

"Father Santos, we don't speak French."

"French?" He examined the book to see if there was something wrong about it, then laughed nervously. "Ah, yes, yes, of course. So sorry. Let me translate."

"Is this guy for real?" Matt muttered.

Bridget poked him in the chest. "I would like to remind you that trusting him was *your* idea."

"Thanks."

Father Santos cleared his throat. "The conjuror may summon Beleth—that's another of the kings of Hell," he interposed by way of explanation, "by the ritual of blood. This ritual must take place on holy ground that has been rededicated to the Master—that would be Satan—with a relic of the old regime—those would be the archangels."

Something stirred in Bridget's mind. A relic of an archangel, holy ground that didn't exactly feel holy.

"The conjuror may hold dominance over Beleth only as long as he remains with the ring of silver affixed to the third finger of his left hand."

Bridget's fingernails dug into the soft flesh of her palm.

"A silver ring?" The words almost choked her.

Father Santos lowered the book. He was no longer smiling. "Yes, a silver ring."

"Like the one Monsignor wears."

"Exactly like that."

A priest wielding a sword. The hungry way Monsignor had questioned her about Amaymon. His avoidance of all Bridget's questions. He'd even been scheduled to meet with her father on the day of his death.

Matt's hand was around her waist before Bridget even realized she'd lost her balance. "Bridge, are you okay?"

"I'm so sorry, Bridget," Father Santos said. His voice was calm, and he spoke slowly, as if she were a child. "I didn't want to tell you until I was sure."

"But he taught me. He taught me what I was, how to do whatever it is I do."

Matt eased her into a chair and crouched down next to her while he questioned Father Santos. "Are you saying that Monsignor Renault is responsible for all this?"

Just like the son of a cop. He had to have it in black and white.

"If the Emim have been attempting to conjure Amaymon, it explains the rise in demonic activity recently," Father Santos said. "Remember, Bridget, I told you how a demon must be invited in? I've been looking into things. Monsignor Renault administered last rites to Mrs. Long when she was in the hospital with pneumonia, just last month. And

Ms. Laveau's father is an old friend of Monsignor's. She has him over for dinner at the apartment above the shop once a month."

"And he blessed the Fergusons' house when they moved in this summer," Bridget said mechanically. Her mouth felt dry and parched. "That's why Mrs. Ferguson called him after what happened."

Father Santos nodded. "All perfect opportunities to perform a ritual or introduce a curse."

Bridget's head spun. "But why? Why summon all these demons?"

Father Santos shrugged. "Practice. Conjuring a king of Hell isn't like placing a simple curse. I'd guess he was working his way up to attempting the ritual."

"Peter."

"Yes. But it didn't work. Even Peter's rage wasn't strong enough. Which is why I told you to be careful. To keep the bracelet on and to learn the mantra on the card."

Matt shot to his feet. "Why would Bridget need to be careful?"

Father Santos angled his head. "Don't you see? He needs a vessel, someone strong enough to hold a demon. No human is stronger than a Watcher. I thought he might come after you."

Monsignor needed a Watcher for the ritual. Bridget caught her breath. "Sammy!"

THIRTY-FOUR

BRIDGET SPRINTED DOWN THE HALL to Monsignor's office and threw herself against the door. Locked. Without thinking she reared back, cocked her knee, and kicked the door with all her strength. She wasn't sure if she actually expected it to give way, but with a crackling of timbers around the frame, the door to Monsignor Renault's office flew open.

"Bridget!" Matt bounded after her. "What are you doing?"

There was no time for explanations. Bridget knew exactly what she needed to find. She whisked the Pietà paperweight off the desk with one hand, then, crouching low behind the desk, she pushed up and out with her legs, tipping the heavy rosewood desk onto its side.

Tiffany lamp and plastic desk accessories crashed to the floor, but Bridget's eyes were fixed on the underside of the desk—the drawer Monsignor kept locked at all times, his private notebook stored within.

With a fierce swing of the Pietá, Bridget ripped into the flimsy wooden base of the drawer, punching a hole straight through. She flung the paperweight away and tore open the bottom of the drawer with her hands, the cheap wood splintering as she pulled half the panel away.

Father Santos jogged up behind Matt. "Wow," he panted.

Bridget thrust her hand into the drawer, searching frantically for the notebook. Monsignor wrote everything down—every note, every thought, every comment. If Father Santos was right, if Monsignor was in league with the Emim, the evidence would be here.

Her fingertips grazed a soft leather surface. "Yes!"

"What?" Matt asked. He was at her side in two strides. "What is it?"

Bridget twisted her arm and yanked a black notebook out of the underbelly of Monsignor's desk.

"Monsignor's diary," Father Santos said.

Bridget flipped to the back of the book and scanned for the last entry.

"'If I'd only known Santos had the grimoire all along,'" Bridget read aloud. "'No matter. The conjuration is almost ready. The girl would be too difficult, but perhaps the boy?'"

"Dear God," Father Santos gasped. He lifted the

notebook from her hand.

Bridget's hands shook. *The boy.* It had to be Sammy.

"NO!" she cried. Bridget fumbled in her pocket for her cell phone. She had to warn her mom.

Matt was a step ahead of her. "Yes, I'd like to report a kidnapping," he said, cell phone at his ear. "My name is Matt Quinn. My father is Sergeant Stephen Quinn, Central Station, and I need units to report to two four two six Ulloa."

Bridget's feet were rooted to the floor as her trembling fingers hit the autodial button on her cell phone. The home phone rang three times and went to voice mail. Her mom never let it get past two.

"Bridget." Father Santos's face was hard, and his eyes were keenly focused on her. "Bridget, if Monsignor has your brother, we don't have much time."

"Dad?" Matt said into his phone. "Dad, you need to get to Mrs. Liu's house right away. Look, I can't explain but something's wrong, okay? No, I'm with Bridget. We're down at St. Michael's."

"Bridget, are you listening to me?"

Her eyes drifted back to Father Santos. She noticed his knuckles turning white as his fingers gripped Monsignor's journal.

"The police won't be able to do anything if Monsignor has already started the ritual of blood. You are the only one who can save your brother."

Matt shoved his cell phone back in his pocket. "We're not

going anywhere until my dad gets here."

"What do you mean?" Bridget asked Father Santos. She'd never seen him so calm, so focused. His stutter was gone entirely, and he'd lost most of his fumbliness.

"I mean if the ritual works, once Monsignor begins the conjuration, once Sammy's blood mixes with the essence of Amaymon and the demon begins to take form, the police won't be able to stop it."

"What will happen to Sammy?"

Father Santos shook his head. "I'm not sure, but if Amaymon isn't banished, your brother will die."

"But you don't even know where they are," Matt said. "They could be doing this ritual anywhere."

"A relic of the archangels," Bridget muttered. "The sword of St. Michael."

"Yes," Father Santos whispered.

"And a church claimed by demons."

"St. Michael's," Father Santos said with a nod. "It's one of the reasons the Order of St. Michael asked your father to move into this district. We've always suspected that this church was built for a special purpose."

Bridget's eyes drifted to the three portraits of archangels that hung on the wall. Raphael, Gabriel, and Michael. Michael, the leader of God's army. Michael, whose sword hung in the church below. Michael, the patron of the Order of St. Michael, her protectors. Michael fighting the serpent on the rock. *Vade retro satana.*

Matt grabbed her shoulders and spun her around to face him. "Bridge, you can't be serious. If Monsignor Renault really killed your dad and your friend, he's dangerous. Like, homicidal. We should wait for the police."

"If you wait here, your brother will die."

"She's not going with you," Matt said through clenched teeth.

Father Santos ignored him, turning to Bridget. "You can save your brother."

"What if I can't?" Bridget stuttered. Panic welled up inside her. Never before had the stakes of a banishment been so high. And so personal. "What if I don't know how to save him?"

Father Santos smiled, restoring some of the goofiness to his face. "It's who you are, Bridget. You just have to accept it."

Bridget stared at her feet while Matt's grip on her shoulders tightened. It would be so much easier just to stay in the rectory, to let Matt take control and wait in his arms until the police arrived. But she knew in her heart that Father Santos was right, and if Sammy died it would be on her head.

She looked into Matt's eyes and wanted to cry. "Matt—"

"No," he said. "I won't let you. You're staying here with—"

He never got the last word out. There was a flash of movement behind him—a blur of white and black just above Matt's head. Matt stood stunned for a split second, then crumpled to the ground.

"I'm sorry," Father Santos said, dropping the Pietà paper-weight next to Matt's limp body. "But we were running out of time." He knelt down and examined Matt's head. "He'll be fine. Just a nasty lump tomorrow."

"You didn't have to knock him out."

Father Santos laughed. "Yeah, right. He cares for you too much to let you confront your dad's murderer with a strange priest in the middle of the night." He was serious again in an instant. "Are you ready?"

"Not really."

"Good. Then let's go save your brother, okay?"

THIRTY-FIVE

F ATHER SANTOS WAS MORE AGILE than he looked. Bridget had been half afraid he'd trip over his own feet going down the rectory stairs and topple ass over elbows into a broken mess on the landing. But in a stroke of surrealness not seen outside a VH1 reality show, Father Santos careened down the stairs like a Navy SEAL in boot camp and was ten strides ahead of Bridget by the time she reached the court-yard.

Maybe he was a warrior priest, after all.

There was a strange but familiar dance of lights in the St. Michael's courtyard. Bridget glanced up and saw a menacing collage of red and blue, green and gold lapping at the cobbled stone and masonry of the courtyard. Peter's murder scene flashed before her eyes: the sea of candles around the altar, the strange circle of figures and symbols, the body splayed within.

Only this time, the body would be Sammy's.

Father Santos sprinted for the door of the sacristy, whipping out a key and unlocking the priests' entrance without so much as a click of the bolt.

Bridget followed him into the church, but as soon as she stepped inside, it felt like she was passing through a wall of cobwebs, thick and sticky, clinging to her skin like a lattice of Silly String. She scraped her hands against her arms and face, but there was nothing touching her, just the sensation of hatred and malevolence weighing her down. Evil had attached itself to her, seeping through her skin.

"Bridget," Father Santos whispered. His fingers dug into her arms, and Bridget realized he was holding her up, preventing her from collapsing.

Bridget felt like she was drowning in the darkness. "I can't," she panted. "I can't."

"*Vade retro satana,*" he said under his breath. "Say it."

"*Vade,*" she said. That was all she could remember.

"*Retro,*" he prompted.

"*Retro satana.*"

Her St. Benedict medal lurched, and the darkness retreated.

"The motto of the Watchers," he whispered. "Why do you think I gave it to you?"

"Oh." Would have been nice if he'd mentioned that before.

Her head cleared. She felt herself again, strong legs, strong mind. Bridget took a deep breath. Time to find Sammy.

A doorless arch separated the priests' dressing area from the church altar. Bridget flattened herself against the wall and peered around the archway.

It was a scene she'd expected to see, a scene she had witnessed before. The church was awash in candlelight, black and white sticks of wax mounted in every sconce and on every surface around the altar. She could just make out the scribbles of symbols in a rough circle, and in the middle stood a small figure with hair sticking every which way, silhouetted against the candlelight.

"Where's the ice cream?" Sammy asked Monsignor. He wore his Justice League pajamas, rolled at the ankle because he was short for his age. "You said there'd be ice cream."

Monsignor crouched in the shadows behind Sammy. He held a sack in his hands from which he poured a stream of black sand, articulating the symbols in the circle. "Soon, Sammy. Very soon."

"Is Mr. Darlington bringing the ice cream? Is that where he went?"

Bridget frowned. Mr. Darlington? Had he been at their house that night?

"This stinks," Sammy said when Monsignor didn't respond. He sat down in the middle of the circle and rested his chin in his hands.

"If you sit there quietly for another minute," Monsignor said, straightening up. "I'll give you a surprise."

Sammy perked up. "Really?"

"Oh, yes." Monsignor dropped the sack and stepped behind the altar.

"Good, because I—" Sammy paused, then cocked his head as if he heard something. "Bridge?"

Bridget caught her breath. How could Sammy know she was there?

Monsignor reached behind the altar and retrieved a large object. "What did you say?"

Sammy turned to look at him. "I didn't know you brought Bridget here too."

Even in the dim light of the church, Bridget could see Monsignor's face harden. He didn't wait to question her brother but grabbed Sammy and hauled him to his feet.

"In the name of Amaymon," Monsignor bellowed. He lifted Sammy up by his wrists so his toes barely touched the ground. "In the name of the king of the west, the wielder of the silver ring."

Sammy kicked with his legs, struggling to free himself. "Lemme go!"

"In the place of the Master, I spill this blood for you!"

Bridget's eye caught a glimmer as candlelight flickered off something metallic in Monsignor's grasp. There was no doubt in her mind what he held: the sword of St. Michael.

Faster than Bridget could react, Monsignor drew the blade across Sammy's arms.

"No!" Bridget screamed, rushing from the shelter of the sacristy.

"Bridget, wait!" Father Santos hissed.

Bridget sprinted toward Sammy, who stood frozen in the middle of the circle. Monsignor spun around as her footsteps echoed through the church, but he made no move to stop her. Instead he stepped out of the circle and let Bridget blow past him. Why would he—

The air was sucked out of Bridget's lungs as she slammed into something hard and impenetrable at the edge of the circle. Her forehead smacked against an unseen wall, knocking her back as the rest of her body careened into the invisible barrier. There was a sickening crack, followed by a blinding flash of light. She hardly felt the impact against the frigid marble altar, only felt its coldness against the searing pain spreading outward from her chest.

A gravelly laugh reverberated through the sanctuary. "Always so hot-blooded," Monsignor said with a click of his tongue. "That's from your mother, I believe."

Bridget rolled onto her side and coughed, trying to catch her breath. Pain shot through her ribs. Her vision blurred and she gasped for air.

"Your father would have been more cautious. Of course, that's what got him killed."

Bridget forced her eyes open. She couldn't make out

Monsignor's features, with the exception of his eyes: They glowed a deep orange against the darkness of the church. She tried to speak, but the words caught in her throat.

"You're too late, anyway." Monsignor pointed to her brother. "The conjuration has begun."

Bridget propped herself up and gazed at her brother. It was Sammy, but it wasn't.

His eyes were entirely black. Ugly, empty pits of darkness where Sammy's dark brown irises used to be. He seemed larger; not taller or fatter, but as if he occupied more space than her little brother usually did. His shoulders were broad, his head thrown back, his palms turned upward as if he were supporting the weight of the church in his hands.

Then she saw the blood. It dripped from Sammy's wrists where two ugly gashes marred his flesh. His blood undulated, rippled, and spread through the arcs and lines of the circle like it had an intelligence all its own. Once the blood filled every crevice, completing its circular bond, it raced faster and faster through the maze of symbols until Bridget could hardly see the movement at all.

"You can come out now, Santos," Monsignor called.

Father Santos shuffled forward from the shadows of the sacristy. "We know all about your c-connection to the Emim, Renault."

Monsignor laughed. "If that were true, they'd have sent a real member of the order to deal with me, instead of the librarian."

"You're a librarian?" Bridget sputtered, finding her voice. Perfect. She glanced at Sammy, the blood still oozing from his body. Time was running out, and here she was facing a homicidal priest and a demon king, and all the Vatican had sent her was a librarian?

"Did he tell you he was one of the legendary warriors of the Order of St. Michael?" Monsignor sneered. "Look at him. Did you really think *he* could protect you?"

"W-w-well," Father Santos stuttered. "I—I . . . I mean. I'm not really. I mean, I am but I'm not. And I—I know a . . . a lot about . . . things."

They were completely screwed.

"The conjuring has begun," Monsignor repeated. He looked pointedly at Bridget. "You cannot stop it now. The circle of Amaymon will prevent even a Watcher from entering its domain."

Father Santos cleared his throat. Bridget looked up and saw him wiggling his fingers and jutting out his chin, trying to get her attention. His eyes flitted toward the sword, which lay discarded near the front of the altar, then back to Bridget. He gave a slight nod of the head, and Bridget realized what he was after. He was going for the sword, and he needed Bridget to keep Monsignor distracted.

Distracted. Okay . . .

"My dad," she began, grasping at straws. "My dad knew what you were."

"Your father consulted me on the Undermeyer case. He

thought he was so clever. Asked me to give the man a blessing." Monsignor smiled. "As if I would fall for that."

"Fall for what?"

"His little trap. He guessed the janitor had broken into the church to steal the sword before I could use it." Monsignor pointed at her. "Your father hoped that if he put Undermeyer face-to-face with me, he'd be able to figure out why the sword was so important."

Bridget gritted her teeth. "You killed him."

"Of course I killed him. The Emim have the power to obscure the minds of men. With their help, I outsmarted your father, that fool of a police sergeant, all of you."

She wanted to throw herself on him, tear at his face with her fingernails, strangle him with her bare hands. She tried to stand, but the pain in her cracked ribs shot through her body. She stumbled into the altar and clung to it to keep from sinking to her knees.

A movement from above caught her eye. The stained glass windows were moving. Not a trick of the eye from the quivering light of a hundred candles, but moving of their own accord. The angels, those menacing, nightmarish angels with their empty eyes and blood-tipped swords, had come to life.

"To the Master!" they cried, dozens of swords lifted to the heavens. She could hear the clattering of steel as the stained glass angels clamored around their panes. *"The Watchers will perish. The Watchers will perish."*

"By the ritual of blood I will conjure Amaymon."

Monsignor spun around, addressing the angels in the windows. "In this holy place, built by the Emim, built for the Master. I shall use the archangel's sword against him. The Master will rise and I will take my place at his right hand, his beloved servant."

The church, built by the Emim. The sword, used to raise a demon king. It made sense, all of it. Except for one thing.

"Why did you train me?" Bridget asked. It didn't really matter, but after all they'd been through together, Bridget needed to know. "Why teach me how to use my powers?"

Monsignor laughed. "Once your father was out of the way, I had a clear path before me to conjure the Master. Until that call from Mrs. Ferguson. I needed to know for sure what you were, what I might be up against."

"Up against?"

"How powerful you were as a Watcher. And you *are* powerful, Bridget. Too powerful. I originally planned to use you for the conjuration, but thankfully—" He glanced at Sammy, and the ugly curl of his lip returned. "Thankfully, there is another Watcher in the Liu family."

Bridget turned her face away, appalled she'd never before seen Monsignor for what he was, ashamed at her own bad judgment. What an idiot she'd been.

Sammy's body lurched. In the circle, the blood had reversed its course. Instead of pouring out of his body, it was now crawling up his feet and legs, back to the slashes in his arms. The blood was flowing back into Sammy's body.

"Ah," Monsignor said, following her eye to Sammy. "Very soon, now. Very soon we shall—"

In a blur of movement, Father Santos kicked the sword and sent it sliding into the center of the circle. As it careened across the marble floor, it cut a swath through the symbols, scattering the blood in its wake.

"No!" Monsignor raced into the circle, but the damage had already been done. Sammy slumped back on his heels, teetered like a drunken man, then crumpled to the ground amid the remnants of blood.

"Bridget," Father Santos yelled. "Run!"

Bridget pushed off from the altar and staggered toward the limp body of her little brother. Monsignor was already at Sammy's side, rolling him over onto his back.

"Master," he cried. "Master, speak to me."

"Sammy," Bridget mumbled. The pain in her ribs burst fresh through her, but she had to get Sammy away from that murderer. Had to.

Father Santos gripped her wrist and pulled her down the stairs into the sanctuary. "Move. Now."

A monstrous gust of wind raced through the sanctuary from the front of the church, extinguishing all of the candles. Bridget and Father Santos froze halfway down the aisle as a deafening growl shook the stone floor beneath their feet.

Moonlight filtered in through the stained glass windows. In the near darkness, Bridget could hear Monsignor's choking sobs. His voice cracked. "Master?"

"Sammy?" Bridget whispered.

A voice like nails on a chalkboard answered. "No."

Another blast of air rushed through the church, down one wall, around the back and up the other side. In its wake, the candles reignited and shadows emerged, dancing along the walls of the church—erect, menacing figures at once human and animal, their bodies darting and racing around Bridget and Father Santos. The angels in the stained glass windows began to dance and jabber, the words at first strange and foreign as they were shouted forth from all corners of the church at random, but as the words came together into a demonic chant, Bridget could clearly make them out:

"Amaymon, Master. The Master is here!"

"That can't be good," Bridget said.

"Master," Monsignor said, his voice raw with crying. Bridget could see him now, kneeling by the altar. "Master, you are not at full strength."

"I am strong enough," Amaymon said through Sammy's body. "For them."

Sammy stood at the front of the church. He pointed directly at her.

"Watcher," Amaymon snarled. "Your time is over."

Before she could respond, Sammy bent at the waist, gripped the front pew, and with a crackle of splintering wood, ripped it from its foundations.

"Move!" Father Santos yelled. He pulled her down the aisle. "Move, move, m—"

Sammy lifted the pew over his head like it was a cardboard box and, with a heave, sent the entire thing flying in their direction.

Father Santos pushed Bridget into the aisle, then dove after her. Her broken ribs cracked again as she slammed into the kneeler, and her ankle wrenched in agony. The pew missed Father Santos's head by inches, landing two rows behind them.

The angels in the stained glass windows erupted in cheers and shouts as Father Santos scrambled to his feet, hauling Bridget after him. "Come on."

"There is no escape, slave," Amaymon said. "There is no escape from my house."

Bridget stumbled after Father Santos, down toward the back corner of the church. The pain from her ribs and twisted ankle were blending together so that every movement, every breath brought renewed agony. Just when she thought she couldn't take another step, Father Santos threw open the confessional and dragged Bridget inside.

"NO ESCAPE!" Amaymon roared. He grunted as the sound of cracking wood echoed overhead. Then, with a heave, another pew came flying through the air and crashed through the crying room window.

Bridget propped herself up with one arm, the other wrapped tightly around her rib cage. "Please tell me," she said between gasping breaths, "that you have a plan."

Father Santos peeked through the confessional window.

"Other than fleeing for our lives? No."

Bridget's breaths came shorter and shorter. She was light-headed from the shallow panting, and the pain had spread from her chest down to her hips and up through her shoulders.

Another roar. Another splintering of wood as the demon king possessing Sammy's body ripped a pew out of the floor and heaved it across the church like it was made of Styrofoam. This time it crashed into the wall right above the confessional door, sending Father Santos ducking for cover as the tiny room reverberated from the impact.

"The Master is strong! The Watcher will perish!"

"This is hopeless," Bridget said.

Father Santos shook dust from his hair. "Bridget, listen to me."

"What?" In her final moments on the planet, she rather relished the idea of wallowing in her own misery.

"Look, I know—" He crouched down before her, cradling his knees in his arms. "I know you're hiding something."

"Huh?"

"I've been watching you. At Mrs. Long's, at the doll shop. You were holding something back, something that bothered you."

Bridget sat bolt upright.

"I've seen other Watchers banish demons, and there's something, a feeling, an energy, that overtakes them. Whatever it is, you've been fighting it."

He knew? "You've seen it before?"

"Yes."

Bridget bit her lip. There were others like her, others who had felt the strange burning in their bodies, the tingling deep within. Maybe even her dad? Maybe he'd felt the same thing? Accepted the same thing?

"Bridget, in about thirty seconds we're both going to die. If there was ever a time for you to come to terms with your destiny, this would be it."

He said it like it was easy, like taking a stroll down the street or ordering a latte at Starbucks. Come to terms with your destiny, Bridget. It only means you're part demon.

"Emerge, slave," Amaymon roared. He was right outside the confessional.

Father Santos scrambled to his feet and took a quick glance out the window. He turned back to her and spoke quickly. "I have a plan, but it will only succeed if you're strong, Bridget. Stronger than you've ever been."

"Give up the Watcher to me," Amaymon continued. "And I will spare your life, priest."

Father Santos grasped her hand. "Amaymon is not at full strength. I interrupted the conjuration when I scattered your brother's blood, but it's only a matter of time before Monsignor rearticulates the symbols to complete the process. And then your brother will be lost forever."

"I lose patience, slave," Amaymon snarled. "I shall crush your bones to dust if you disobey me."

"But if I can get the ring off Monsignor's finger, we might be able to stop the transfer."

Bridget cocked her head. "The ring?"

"It controls the conjuration and protects him from Amaymon."

"Will that save my brother?"

Father Santos shook his head. "No."

"Then—"

"You, Bridget. You're the only one who can save Sammy."

Bridget dropped her eyes. "I can't."

"You can."

"Now, slave!"

"Bridget, it's time to accept who you are."

"Easy for you to say."

Father Santos sat back on his heels, then rose majestically to his feet. "On the count of three, I'm opening that door and making a run for Monsignor. You can either follow me, or die here. The choice is yours."

With one arm wrapped around her ribs, Bridget hauled herself to her feet. "That's a choice?"

Father Santos ignored her. "One. Two. *Three!*"

THIRTY-SIX

FATHER SANTOS SLID THE CONFESSIONAL door open and bolted down the aisle. Bridget could hear his rapid footsteps retreating until the sound was masked by a rumbling laugh.

"Your priest forsakes you, Watcher," Amaymon growled.

Bridget limped into the doorway. Sammy, or the thing possessing Sammy's body, stood in the center aisle of the church. She could see the tousled black hair, the thin, delicate neck, the blue-and-white Justice League pajamas. But the faint light from the flickering candles illuminated his features enough for Bridget to know that this thing, this creature, was no longer her little brother.

The muscles of his face had completely rearranged themselves beneath Sammy's skin. His flat nose was now sharp, and his normally weak chin squared. The lips were thin, almost nonexistent, and parted to reveal jagged, broken teeth. Sammy's brows protruded over his eyes, which were sunken far back in his skull.

"Well, Watcher?" Amaymon didn't move. "Do you not wish to challenge me? Banish me?"

"Banish. Banish. Banish the Master," the stained glass windows mocked. *"The Watcher cannot. The Master is strong."*

Bridget's heart ached. Sammy. This was her fault. She should have been able to predict this. She should have been able to protect him, and now here he was, with a demon's soul sucking the life from his body. Poor Sammy.

Who's been ripping pews out of the ground and launching them across the room.

But it was still her brother, who did her math homework for her when she didn't feel like doing it herself and who still crawled into bed with her when he'd been spooked by a nightmare. Amaymon was not fully conjured. Not yet. He was still Sammy.

If that's half strength, you're seriously screwed, Bridge.

True, but if she was going to die, she was going to do it trying to save her brother's life.

"I banish you, Amaymon."

Laughter rippled through the windows above.

"Finish her, Master." Monsignor's voice was harsh, empty. She couldn't believe she'd ever trusted him. "Finish her so we can complete your conjuration."

"I banish you from this church," Bridget continued.

"Do you?" Amaymon growled. Still he did not move.

His calmness unnerved her. "I banish you from this world."

"Yes?"

"I—I . . ." Her words seemed to have no effect, and that tingling feeling had completely abandoned her.

Monsignor's voice boomed from the altar where he stood. "The Watcher is weak."

"Yes," Amaymon growled.

"Show the Watch—"

Bridget heard a high-pitched scream, then watched as Father Santos barreled across the altar like a free safety and tackled Monsignor.

"You cannot stop me," Monsignor yelled as Father Santos attempted to pin his hands to the ground. "It's too late."

"Hurry, Bridget," Father Santos cried.

Hurry and do what? So far, nothing she said had affected the demon king in the slightest.

"The slave is foolish," Amaymon said, his full attention turned back to Bridget. "It is time for you to see what real power is."

Bridget never saw what hit her. One moment she was leaning against the confessional, and the next she was dangling six feet off the floor, grasping at an invisible hand that squeezed her throat. A cacophony of shrieks and screams filled the church, and the menagerie of shadows lining the wall erupted in a frenzy of thrashing limbs and bodies. In the distance she could hear Father Santos and Monsignor wrestling on the altar.

The invisible hand that gripped her was massive, the fingers long enough to wrap all the way around her neck. As her senses began to dull, Bridget could have sworn she heard laughter. Not the deep, cacophonous laughter of demons, but a girlish giggle. She pried at the cold, scaly flesh at her throat, and out of the corner of her eye she thought she saw two figures in the darkened corner of the church: a tall, slender man and a girl with a halo of curls around her head, both with glowing green eyes. They looked so familiar, but as the hand continued to squeeze, Bridget lost sight of them. Her windpipe closed off, her lungs seized up from lack of air. She felt herself slipping into the darkness.

"Let her go!"

It took Bridget a moment to realize who had spoken.

"I said, let her go!" Matt yelled.

The hand released her. Bridget crashed onto a pew, her feet sliding out from underneath her as she collapsed like a marionette whose strings had been cut.

"Bridget?" Matt called. She heard his footsteps thundering down the aisle. "Bridge, are you okay?"

She hoisted herself onto the pew and held her arms out before her, trying to keep him away. "Matt, don't. Get out of here."

"Fool!" Amaymon cried.

Matt's sneakers screeched to a halt. "Sammy? Sammy, is that you?"

Bridget caught a gleam in Amaymon's eye. She heaved herself into the aisle and pointed toward the door. "Matt, get out. Get—"

A guttural roar from her possessed little brother froze the words on her lips. Amaymon shot his hand forward. Matt's body flew through the church, over the altar, and hit the wall next to the crucifix.

"No!" Bridget screamed. She stumbled forward, her eyes fixed on Matt's crumpled body.

She didn't make it ten steps before the invisible hand grabbed ahold of her hair and yanked her to the ground. Her skull cracked against the stone floor; sickening pain engulfed her. She wanted to vomit, but the pain in her chest was so crippling it stopped her heaves.

Amaymon stood before her. "Stand, Watcher." The angels in the windows cheered him on. "Stand and meet your death."

Tears streamed down her face. Peter was dead. Matt was dead. Sammy and Father Santos would die. It was all her fault. She should just let the demon kill her and be done with it. At least then she'd be free. No more pain, no more suffering. And maybe she'd see her dad again.

Vade retro satana.

The words came to her as soon as she thought of her dad. *Vade retro satana.* Step back, Satan.

The St. Benedict medal trembled, then her hands and arms, her feet and legs began to vibrate. She'd never felt it this strong before, racing through her like lightning, buzzing and churning, awakening every last inch of her body with its energy, its heat, its life.

"*Vade retro satana,*" she murmured.

She heard Amaymon catch his breath.

"*Vade retro satana.*" Her voice was stronger, more powerful. The sensations in her body intensified in waves. She got to her feet; her ankle no longer throbbed with pain. The energy rose to a fever pitch. Bridget reached the tipping point. If she didn't force the feelings back, they would take over, swamp her, consume her.

Amaymon growled and lowered his head, his orange eyes filling the darkness beneath his brows.

"Bridget!" Father Santos yelled above the fury. "This is who you are. This is who you—" His voice choked off.

"Shut up, fool," Monsignor snarled. "You cannot help her now."

This is who you are. This is who I am. I'm Bridget Liu and I'm a Watcher.

"*VADE RETRO SATANA!*" she screamed at the top of her lungs. She spread her arms wide, closed her eyes, and let the vibrations wash over her.

She was floating on water, her body buoyed, enfolded by warm, tropical waves. She no longer felt the cold interior of the church, the lacquered wood of the pew, the harsh marble beneath her feet. The screams of the demons, the clash of Monsignor's sword, the growling form of Amaymon: None of it existed.

Every inch of her body seemed alive, crackling with energy. The pain in her ribs and ankle was gone. She ran her fingers through her hair, down the sides of her face, across her chest, down to her hips and back up again. Her fingertips lingered at her neck, caressing the soft skin, indulging in the teasing stings of electricity at each touch.

"Oh my God," Father Santos said.

Bridget opened her eyes to find the chaos of the church had ceased entirely. The stained glass angels stared at her, motionless. The shadows stood frozen on the wall. Monsignor had one arm around Father Santos's neck and the sword of St. Michael in the other.

And Sammy.

She could still see Sammy, the real Sammy, standing small and docile in his Justice League pajamas, his eyes closed as if sleepwalking. Surrounding him was a new creature, a figure defined in black smoke, its indefinite shape illuminated by silvery light that shifted and seethed. This was the entity she'd caught a fleeting glimpse of at Mrs. Long's. This was the invisible hand that choked her, the unseen force that threw pews, that attacked Matt. This was Amaymon, the real Amaymon, a demon king of Hell.

Then she realized something else. She was staring this creature—this towering shadow of evil—dead in the eye.

She looked down at her body. The silver light was coming from her. Through her. *Was* her. The outline of her hands and fingers was obscured by a blur of intense light. She couldn't even see her jeans and sneakers, just a pillar of light extending ten feet down to the floor.

Well, that was new.

She should have been afraid. She should have closed her eyes and wished she was safe in her bed at home, but she didn't. She should have looked to Father Santos for advice on what to do next, but she didn't need to. Somehow, she just knew.

"Amaymon, fallen from Grace." Her voice sounded huge.

Amaymon backed away from her. "This cannot be. This cannot be."

She followed him. "The Watchers were given dominion over you and your kin."

"We are strong." Amaymon sounded anything but. "We are many."

"I banish you."

Groans and howls of agony pierced her eardrums. Father Santos and Monsignor must have heard them as well; both sprawled on the floor, hands clamped to their ears. The glow of Bridget's skin intensified. The stained glass angels shielded their faces from her light, and the shadows on the wall faded into the dappled stone.

From the back of the church, Bridget heard running foot-steps, followed by a door opening, then slamming shut. Had there been someone else in the church with them? She pushed the thought out of her mind. She had more pressing matters to deal with, and whatever she was doing, it was working.

Bridget held out her arm and pointed at Amaymon. It was

just a shaft of light, and it penetrated the wavering smoke of his being. "I banish you, Amaymon. I banish you to Hell."

"Bridge?" It was Sammy's voice. Bridget gasped; he sounded terrified. "Bridge, you're hurting me."

"Sammy?" He was still there, beneath the wavering smoke figure of Amaymon, eyes closed, body rigid. Was it really him or just a trick? "Sammy, are you okay?"

Sammy began to cry. "Bridge, you're hurting me."

Father Santos rolled onto his knees. "Don't listen to him, Bridget."

"Stop it," Sammy wailed. "Stop it!"

"It's still Amaymon," Father Santos said.

"No!" Monsignor launched himself at Father Santos. "The Master will see you burn."

Bridget reached her arm of light toward the small, sleep-walking figure of Sammy buried deep within the shadow of Amaymon. She willed her fingers to curl around Sammy's arm.

"Let me go, Bridge!" Sammy was hysterical. "Let me go!"

"Finish the exorcism, Bridget!" Father Santos yelled. "Finish the banishment."

Bridget set her jaw. It wasn't Sammy. Sammy was only the vessel. If she didn't get Amaymon out of his body, he'd be lost forever.

Her grip on Sammy's arm tightened. No, she wasn't going to lose her brother now. He and the demon weren't inseparable. Not yet. She turned her attention to Amaymon, focusing on his being, his essence, the aura of evil in the church. Separate from Sammy. Separate from her brother.

"I banish you."

"No!" Sammy screamed. She tensed, keeping his arm in a death grip.

"I banish you from this church, from this land, from this—"

"No!" Amaymon's voice this time, booming forth from her brother's mouth.

"I banish you from this world of men."

Bridget held on to Sammy's arm with all her strength. There was a moment of strain as the demon king tried to wrest his human host away. Then Bridget felt the snap. Amaymon had given up, leaving Sammy's limp body in Bridget's arms.

"Sammy?" she said. She lowered his body to the ground. His face was tinged with gray as if the life had been drained from him.

He was dead. He was dead, and all this had been for nothing.

"Master!" Monsignor stretched his hand in supplication, and Father Santos was on him in an instant. He wrenched the silver ring from Monsignor's finger and threw it to the back of the church.

Monsignor's face blanched. "What have you done?"

"Now, Bridget!" Father Santos said. "Finish it."

Amaymon's form swelled, doubling in size. He was gathering his strength.

"Bridget!" Father Santos called again. "What are you waiting for?"

She looked down at Sammy's motionless body. They'd taken her father. They'd taken her brother. It was time to take something in return.

"By the power of the Watchers," Bridget yelled as the tears streamed down her face. "Amaymon, king of the west, I BANISH YOU!"

Amaymon whirled into a vortex of swirling blackness. The force of the tornado was so fierce it sucked the words right out of Bridget's mouth. The swirling mass lifted up off the ground, and the floor beneath the circle crumbled away. As Amaymon sank into the hole, a tendril of smoke shot toward Monsignor and wrapped around his outstretched hand.

"NO!" Monsignor screamed. He slid across the floor, pulled by the last gasp of strength from his master. He clawed at the broken ground at the mouth of the hole, trying to keep from falling in. "Help me, Bridget. Help me."

Bridget looked down at Monsignor. She should have reached out, kept him from falling, allowed him to face his fate for the murders of her father and brother. It would have been the good thing to do.

But Bridget didn't care. "Rule Number Two, Monsignor. Do not show pity."

His red-rimmed eyes grew wide. He tried to pull his way to her, his fingertips inching across the broken marble. He lost his grip, and with a terrified scream, Monsignor Renault was gone.

THIRTY-SEVEN

B EFORE MONSIGNOR'S CRY DIED AWAY, a blast rocked the Church of St. Michael.

The marble altar cracked right down the middle and enormous fissures formed in the floor, emanating outward from the hellhole in jagged lines. Chunks of the tile and stone nearest the hole rocked free and plummeted downward. The chasm doubled in size.

Father Santos grabbed her hand and pulled her away from the widening fissure.

"We have to get out of here," he said.

"Right." Bridget looked down at her body—five and a half feet of nonglowing, nonangelic high school sophomore. She was glad to be normal again, and yet she almost missed that electric power of her Watcherness.

Father Santos picked up Sammy, cradling him. Her brother looked unnaturally pale.

"Is he dead?"

Father Santos opened his mouth, but she never heard what he said. With an earsplitting crack, one of the huge ceiling beams in the middle of the church broke free and collapsed to the floor. Broken bits of plaster and splintered wood flew in every direction. Another beam, closer to the altar, followed suit.

Father Santos pointed to the back of the altar. "Matt."

Matt! She'd totally forgotten about him. She sidestepped a fallen candelabra and found Matt's body behind the altar. She gently rolled him onto his side and brushed his sandy blond hair from his face. There was a gash over his left eye, already crusty with dried blood, but his body was warm and he was breathing.

He was still alive.

She stroked his cheek with the back of her hand. "Matt? Matt, can you hear me?"

She felt his body shift, and his eyelids fluttered. "Bridge?" he said slowly. He squinted at her. "Bridge, are you okay?"

"Thanks to you."

He reached a hand up to her face, then winced. "What happened?"

Father Santos crouched over them. "We'll explain later. Can you stand? We need to get out of here. Now."

Matt grunted as Bridget helped him to his feet. His left arm hung limp at his side, and his knee was twisted. She draped Matt's good arm around her neck and started for the sacristy.

Another jolt rocked the church as one of the giant pillars flanking the back wall severed from its foundations and toppled forward. Bridget hauled Matt out of the way and scrambled down the altar behind Father Santos as the pillar slammed into the wall, blocking the sacristy door.

Father Santos lost no time. He heaved Sammy over his shoulder and headed right down the center aisle. Bridget and Matt limped behind as glass exploded overhead. One by one, the stained glass windows shattered into millions of colored shards that rained down on them like confetti. Broken glass crunched beneath their feet. Plaster and tiles, glass and iron, pieces of the church crashed around them as they shimmied over a fallen ceiling beam. Father Santos dripped with sweat and Bridget's heart pounded in her chest, but they were almost there, almost to the main entrance.

As a sickening roar erupted from behind them, Bridget craned her neck and saw that the hellhole had enveloped the entire front of the church. The altar and sacristy were already gone. The back wall collapsed, and the ceiling began to crumble.

They weren't going to make it.

"Keep moving," Father Santos puffed. "Don't look back."

Ten more steps, and they made it to the door. Father

Santos threw it open, and Bridget and Matt came barreling through behind him. The earth shook again as they careened down the steps and collapsed on the front lawn of St. Michael's.

Bridget looked up in time to see the entrance of the church crumble in on itself. The last of the roof disintegrated. The walls tumbled inward. In the building's final death throes, an enormous mushroom cloud billowed up from the ruins. It surged into the sky, making one last affront to Heaven. Then the entire cloud was sucked down into the sinkhole.

Bridget blinked as she watched wisps of smoke and dust filter up. They'd done it. Somehow she and Father Santos had defeated a demon king, defeated Monsignor Renault, defeated the evil that slept within the church itself. And saved Sammy.

"One—two—three—four—five—six—seven—eight—"

Bridget spun around. Father Santos hunched over Sammy's body, his arms locked straight, his hands compressing against her brother's chest as he counted out loud.

"What's wrong?"

"—nine—ten—eleven—twelve—thirteen—fourteen—fifteen." Father Santos bent down, grasped Sammy's chin and pinched his nose closed, then breathed heavily into his mouth.

Bridget scampered across the grass to her brother's side. "What's *wrong*?"

"Not breathing," Father Santos panted between chest compressions.

Matt grunted as he pulled himself up behind her. "Bridget, maybe you shouldn't—"

"He's my brother," she said, whirling on him. "And this is my fault."

"It's not."

Her voice cracked. "Of course it is."

Matt slipped his hand over hers but said nothing.

"One—two—three—four—five—six—seven— eight—"

The tears spilled down her cheeks as she turned back to Sammy. His limp, lifeless body jolted beneath the force of Father Santos's compressions. As Father Santos began another round of mouth-to-mouth, Bridget reached out and took Sammy's small hand in her own.

Come on, Sammy, she thought. *Breathe.*

Her fingertips tingled. Not the same. It was a different feeling. It wasn't coming from inside of her.

It was coming from Sammy.

Bridget pushed herself up on her knees. "Stop."

"—twelve—thirteen—fourteen—"

"I said *stop*!" She pushed Father Santos away from her brother. The priest rocked back, his face tomato red and caked in sweat-soaked dust and grime.

"Bridget," he panted. "What are you doing?"

"Bridge?" Matt said.

She held up her hand. Slowly, she crouched over Sammy's body, not quite sure what to do next. The tingling, the vibrations, they were coming from him. There was life inside her brother. She just needed to figure out how to spark it.

Bridget took both of Sammy's hands and repeated the words that had elicited the reaction. "Breathe, Sammy," she whispered. "Breathe."

Her palms vibrated. There was no mistaking the sensation, no pretending that it didn't come from her brother's hands.

"Breathe," she said, louder this time.

The vibrations pulsed beneath her grasp. It was as if Sammy's Watcherness was only stimulated where she touched him.

Bridget whipped Sammy's pajama shirt up over his head, then pulled off her own T-shirt. She barely registered that she was kneeling on the lawn in jeans and a bra in front of a priest and her almost-boyfriend. Her mind was fixed only on Sammy.

She wrapped her arms around her brother and held him tight, cradling his head with one hand. "Breathe, Sammy," she said softly into his ear. "Breathe. I know you're in there. I know you are."

Her chest and abdomen, arms and hands began to vibrate. She tucked her head into the crook of Sammy's neck and pressed her cheek against his. The sensations were widespread, but they weren't strong enough. Not yet.

"You want to live, Sammy. You want to. Don't leave

me. Please don't leave me."

Bridget closed her eyes and concentrated on her own body while she clutched her brother to her. She recalled the feeling that she'd allowed to overwhelm her in the church, swamp her, engulf her. There had always been a catalyst before, a demon who provoked those feelings in her. But this time she was willing the Watcher to take over. It had to. She had to save her brother.

Beneath her, Sammy gasped.

Her eyes flew open. "Sammy? *Sammy?*"

She never even heard the sirens.

"Matt!" Sergeant Quinn raced across the lawn. "Matt, are you okay? Bridget? Oh my God. Oh my God, what the hell happened?"

Sammy still looked gray and lifeless, but she'd felt him breathe. She'd felt it!

"Bridget!" Her mom slid to her knees in front of Bridget. She took Bridget's face in her hands and kissed her forehead. "My baby girl. My baby. What happened?" Her mom's eyes drifted to Sammy's body. "Sammy?"

"Mrs. Liu," Father Santos said. "Bridget did everything she could. I'm terribly sorry."

Her mom lifted her son's head into her lap. "Sammy?" Her voice was calm. Too calm.

A team of EMTs sprinted across the lawn and Matt's hand slipped around her waist, bracing her for the inevitable.

No one expected the yawn.

As if someone had thrown his on switch, Sammy arched his back and stretched his arms up over his head. Color ebbed back into his face. He opened his mouth and let out a heavy yawn, then rubbed his eyes.

"Bridge?" Sammy said, blinking his eyes open.

"Sammy!" Bridget's mom choked back a sob and pulled her son to her, smothering him with kisses. "My Sammy, my Sammy. Oh, thank God."

"Mom, stop it!" Sammy wrenched himself free and crawled over to Bridget. She tried not to notice that her mother immediately sank into Sergeant Quinn's arms.

"Bridget, are you asleep?"

She smiled and wiped the tears from her cheeks. "Nope."

"Good."

"Elephants again?"

Sammy shook his head. Bridget's eyes almost popped out of her head as Sammy lightly placed his small hand on top of hers. "Angels."

"Angels?"

His fingertips grazed the top of her hand as he pulled away. "Angels. Mr. Moppet brought them to save us."

Mr. Moppet. "Yeah." Bridget smiled. "Yeah, he did."

THIRTY-EIGHT

BRIDGET MARCHED RIGHT UP TO the Darlingtons' Sea Cliff mansion and rang the doorbell. A maid answered and Bridget asked for Alexa, saying she was a friend from school. Instead of inviting her in to wait, the maid asked her to stand outside, then closed the door in Bridget's face while she went to fetch Alexa. Yeah, that was about right.

It took a full five minutes for the door to reopen. Despite the fact that it was nine o'clock on a Sunday morning, Alexa's hair was perfectly curled, her makeup expertly applied.

When she saw Bridget, her eyes narrowed. "What are you doing here?"

"Listen up, Alexa, because I'm only going to say this once. I know what you are, you and your dad. And more importantly, I know what *I* am."

"I don't have to listen to this." Alexa started to close the door, but Bridget wedged her boot inside the frame.

"The Watchers were given dominion over the Emim," Bridget said, quoting Father Santos. "So you'd both better watch your step, get it?"

From the darkness on the other side of the door, Bridget could see Alexa's eyes glow bright green. "Is that all?" Her voice sounded like she was barely controlling her rage.

A sly smile crept up Bridget's cheeks. "For now." She pulled her boot out of the door. "See you at school."

Bridget trotted down the front steps as Alexa slammed the door behind her. The Crown Vic's motor was still running as she opened the passenger door and got inside.

"H-how did it go?" Father Santos asked.

"Awesome."

"And you're positive the Darlingtons are Emim?"

"Yep," Bridget said. "I saw them in the church the night I defeated Amaymon, and I'm pretty sure Mr. Darlington lured Sammy out of the house. Plus Alexa can hear the same voices I do." Those glowing green eyes. Mr. Darlington's presence in her father's office, which seemed to send Undermeyer into a paroxysm of fear. Their reluctance to touch Bridget. It all made sense.

"Just remember, the Emim are extremely dangerous. They may not be able to harm you physically, but the Emim have spent centuries influencing men to destroy the Watchers.

Now that they know you're on to them, they'll be even . . . even more devious next time."

Bridget shrugged. She felt invincible, the high from defeating Amaymon still coursing through her. "Then we'll have to be a step ahead of them. That's what you're for, right? You and the Order of St. Michael?"

Father Santos put the car in gear but kept his foot on the brake as he turned to look at her. "There's much you still have to learn, about your abilities and about your enemies. Are you up for it?"

"Do I have a choice?"

"Not really."

She knew that would be the answer, but she didn't care. She wasn't afraid anymore. This was her dad's legacy, and she was going to see it through.

"When do we start?" Bridget asked.

Father Santos eased the car away from the curb. "This afternoon?"

"Better make it tomorrow," Bridget said. She pulled out her cell phone and texted Matt. "There's something I need to finish first."

Matt parked in a visitor's spot and cut the engine. "Are you sure you don't want me to come in with you?"

Bridget shook her head. "I need to do this on my own."

"Okay."

The stitches above his left eye were partially covered by a

butterfly bandage, and his arm hung from a sling around his neck. At least it wasn't his pitching arm, but he'd still be out of commission for several weeks leading up to baseball season. That was the cost of trying to help her. She wasn't going to let anything like that happen again.

"Did you tell your mom where we were going?"

Bridget nodded. "She understands, but she still didn't want to come with me."

"Do you blame her?"

"Nope." Her mom would never be able to separate her husband's death from Milton Undermeyer, even if he had been innocent all along. But that was okay. She didn't need her mom witnessing what she was about to do.

"And Sammy's okay?" Matt asked for the fourth time.

"He's fine," she said. "Doesn't remember a thing."

Matt scratched his forehead above his stitches. "I don't remember much myself."

"I know." It's better that way. Trust me.

She started to get out of the car, but Matt grabbed her hand. "You're sure you'll be okay?"

"I'll be fine," she said with a smile. "Don't worry. It's okay now."

Bridget checked in at the main security desk of Sonoma State Hospital. Her mood was so different now than it had been the last time she came here. She smiled as she showed her ID and pinned a visitor's badge on the front of her hoodie.

A woman in a brown tweed suit clacked down the long

hallway. "You must be Miss Liu."

Bridget took the outstretched hand and shook it, strong and confident. "I am."

"Excellent. I'm Ms. Parker, the lead administrator for Sonoma State Hospital. We've been anxiously awaiting your visit."

"Thanks." *I just bet you have.*

Ms. Parker motioned for Bridget to follow, and they hurried down the familiar corridor. "A meeting like this is highly unusual."

Bridget didn't say a word, just waited for Ms. Parker to continue her spiel.

"A patient with Mr. Undermeyer's history," she paused. "If the district attorney's office hadn't arranged it, an unsupervised visitation would not have been permitted."

Bridget remembered her last encounter with Milton Undermeyer and smiled grimly. "Oh."

Ms. Parker stopped at the elevator and pushed the up button several times. "I must tell you, Miss Liu, I find this whole arrangement to be highly irregular."

Bridget held her smile. Ms. Parker's annoyance bled through every gesture: the tapping foot, the repeated pushes at the elevator button. Bridget guessed the real reason for her irritability was that no one had consulted her on the day's "arrangement." *Too bad, so sad, Ms. Parker.*

"It's true?" Ms. Parker continued. "They've reopened your father's murder case?"

A few weeks ago, the mention of her dad's murder would have been a kick in the gut for Bridget, but she felt a new sense of calm about it. "Yes. Mr. Undermeyer is innocent."

Ms. Parker stepped into the elevator. "Hmm. Perhaps he can be moved to another facility then."

"Oh, I have a feeling you'll be able to release him entirely."

Ms. Parker turned to her with a look of horror on her face. "I doubt that very much. Mr. Undermeyer suffers from one of the most acute cases of paranoid schizophrenia and multiple personality disorders I've ever seen."

Bridget smiled to herself. Not for long.

Milton Undermeyer sat at a table in the recreation area. He was still in his straitjacket, and he stared with unseeing eyes at a small television mounted on the wall. She wondered how many hours a day he was confined in that thing. Maybe this would be the last time.

Ms. Parker stood at Undermeyer's shoulder and addressed him as she would a small child. "Mr. Undermeyer? There is someone here to see you."

His eyes never left the television, and he gave no indication that he'd heard a word she said.

"Mr. Undermeyer?"

"It's okay," Bridget said. As soon as she spoke, she saw Undermeyer's eyes flicker in her direction. "I'll take it from here."

Ms. Parker looked from Bridget to Milton Undermeyer and back, then shrugged and clacked her way back to the nurses' station. Bridget watched her go. What was about to happen would throw that woman's years of study and research right out the window. Oops.

Bridget pulled a chair close to him and sat down. "Mr. Undermeyer, do you know who I am?"

It took a moment for his eyes to focus on her face. He sucked in a quick breath and his eyes unclouded.

"That's right. I'm Dr. Liu's daughter. I'm a Watcher."

Tears welled up in Undermeyer's gray eyes, spilling down his ashen cheeks. "You're—you're here to release us?"

Bridget smiled. "A deal is a deal. You delivered your message."

"Amaymon?"

"Defeated."

Undermeyer closed his watery eyes and sighed. "Yes. It is now time."

Bridget leaned forward and placed a hand on either side of his sunken face. "Your service to the Watchers is complete. Your penance is done."

Bridget paused. She could feel the demons inside, their joy and their longing. Instead of banishing malevolent demons back to Hell, this time she was releasing something good, something repentant. It felt nice.

"I release you."

A shudder rippled through Undermeyer's body; he went rigid, then he crumpled. Bridget caught him as he slumped forward, pushing his shoulders back against the chair. Two orderlies came running across the room.

"It's okay." She could sense it in his touch. The demons had left, back to wherever they'd come from or perhaps someplace better. Bridget had no idea; she only knew that the body and mind of Milton Undermeyer were now free.

The orderlies kept their distance, confused by what was happening. As Bridget held him upright, Undermeyer's lids flitted open. His eyes darted around the room—to the orderlies, to the television, to the straitjacket that held him, taking in his surroundings for the first time. Finally they landed on Bridget.

"You."

She smiled. "Yes."

"They're gone?"

"Yes."

Undermeyer's chest heaved. "I didn't kill your father."

"I know. I know it was Monsignor Renault. You'll be getting out of here soon, I promise."

"How can I ever thank you?" His voice sounded so old, so frail. Bridget caught the orderlies exchanging glances.

Bridget winked. "Just don't tell anyone."

Matt was leaning against the truck, waiting for her. He had taken his arm out of the sling and was slowly flexing and bending it in front of him. When he saw Bridget coming down the stairs, he straightened up.

"Well?" he asked.

Bridget nodded. "Done."

He reached his good hand toward her. "What did it feel like?"

"It felt . . ." She laced her fingers through his, and a feeling of comfort and love and hominess enveloped her. "It felt right. Like this."

"It does feel right." Matt pulled her close. "I'm glad you don't hate me anymore."

"Me too."

He gazed down at her, and the longish strands of his hair hung in front of his eyes. She reached up and brushed them off his forehead, then stood on her tiptoes and kissed him playfully on the lips. The tingling began immediately, but Bridget didn't pull away. Instead she relished the sensation for a moment, letting her tongue graze Matt's upper lip. Then she pushed the feeling away, relegating it to the other part of her, the Watcher part. Separate.

"I'm still going to keep an eye on you," Matt said. "You're trouble."

"Tell me something I don't know."

"From now on, consider me your guardian angel."

Bridget snorted. More like the other way around.

Matt pulled his head back. "What's so funny?"

Bridget ignored him. "So what duties go along with being a guardian angel?" she asked.

"Well, for starters," he said, wrapping his arm around her waist, "I'm never leaving your side."

"That'll make gym class a little awkward." Bridget smirked.

But Matt's face was serious. There wasn't even a hint of levity in his eyes as he held her body firmly against his. "Bridget, I mean it. I want to be there for you. I want to be with you."

"You are."

"I mean forever." He paused and Bridget's stomach got all fluttery. "I love you, Bridget Liu."

He loved her. She'd known it somehow, known it since before her confrontation with Amaymon, before he helped her unravel the mystery of her dad's death, before they shared that first kiss. But the warmth spreading throughout her body told her something even more important.

"I love you too," she said. She didn't care if she was going soft. She loved Matt Quinn.

He leaned down and kissed her. Bridget closed her eyes and reveled in the feeling of his soft lips against her own. It was a sensation she wanted to feel every day.

Matt was the first to break the kiss. He brought his hand to her cheek and caressed it. "Now what do you say we get the hell out of here? This place gives me the creeps."

"Agreed." Bridget smiled and opened the passenger door. "Besides, we've got to get home. Sunday night. Shepherd's pie."

"I wouldn't miss it."

Bridget took one last look at the Sonoma State Hospital

as Matt circled out of the parking lot. She had no idea what the future would bring them, and even though she felt a slight pang of guilt for bringing Matt into her world of angels and demons, of Watchers and Emim, she couldn't for one moment picture going forward without him.

Good or evil, they'd face it. Together.

ACKNOWLEDGMENTS

To Ginger Clark, my fearless, amazing, ballsy agent. She's been a friend and ally, and she's never given up on me. I count myself lucky to be one of her clients.

To Kristin Daly Rens, my wonderful editor, who understood this novel from the get-go, whose notes and vision totally resonated with me, and who loves Bridget as much as I do. Again, I'm a lucky girl.

To the entire Balzer + Bray and HarperCollins team who have been so supportive throughout this process: Alessandra Balzer and Donna Bray, Sara Sargent, designers Sarah Hoy and Amy Ryan, copyeditors Kathryn Silsand and Laaren Brown, Emilie Polster and Megan Sugrue in marketing, and Allison Verost in publicity.

To the fabulous Holly Frederick and Dave Barbor at Curtis Brown, Ltd., who have worked tirelessly on behalf of this novel.

To my expansive support network of Inkies, Hopefuls, Purgies, Apocalypsies, and Bookanistas, especially Cindy Pon, Sarah Eve Kelly, Chandler Craig, Lisa and Laura Roecker, Deborah Gray, Wendy Cebula, Emily Kokie, Amy Dachtler, Yadira Taylor, Jake Gilchrist, Rachanee Srisavasdi, Tara Campomenosi, and Jessica Morgan. And of course, my comrades-in-arms, YARebels Jen Hayley, Leah Clifford, Scott Tracey, Victoria Schwab, Hannah Moskowitz, and Karsten Knight.

To a group of readers whose collected awesomeness surpassed all expectations—Jen Hayley (again), Courtney Allison Moulton, Amy Bai, Debra Driza, Mónica Bustamante Wagner, Jennifer Donahue, Sue Laybourn, ChristaCarol Jones, Nadine Nettmann, Juliette Dominguez, Rebecca Burrell, L. K. Herndon, Tracey Martin, Bryn Greenwood, Lisa Brackmann, Laurel Hoctor Jones, Shveta Thakrar, Karen Latham, P. J. Hoover, Kiki Hamilton, Keely Parrack, Holly West, Jill Myles, Rachel Hunter, Kitty Chiu, and Mark Uhlemann, who also gets some credit for the title.

To the amazing Pixie Spindel of Pixie Vision Productions, who made magic happen with that author photo.

To my "other" family at Cirque Berzerk, who have been endlessly enthusiastic about my "other" artistic endeavor. Rock on.

To Carrie Policella, boss and friend, who always turned a blind eye when I was writing on the clock.

To Roy Firestone, my brother from another mother, without whom I would surely be completely insane. He's my rock, my sounding board, my dog sitter, my happy hour partner, my reality check, my cheerleader, and clearly the best friend a girl ever had.

To Peggy McNeil, my mom, who raised me to believe that I could do and be anything I wanted. I'm not sure she was thinking "opera singer–circus performer–writer" at the time, but it all worked out.

Much love.

"THAT'S SO WEIRD," MEG SAID. "I DIDN'T PUT ANY
nuts in. I swear."

Vivian planted her hands on her hips. "You must have."

Once again Meg felt nine pairs of eyes boring into her. She
wished the floor would just open up and swallow her whole. Her
mouth was suddenly parched, her throat tight. She knew she
hadn't added the nuts to the salad. Absolutely positively not. She
wanted to defend herself, but she couldn't even think of what to
say.

"Hey!" Minnie said sharply. "If Meg says she didn't do it, she
didn't do it."

Meg could have hugged her. It was comforting to know Minnie had her back.

Vivian clicked her tongue. "Well, someone must have."

Mumbles of "I didn't" and "Not me" rippled around the table.

Meg sat down in the nearest chair. She knew she hadn't added
almonds—which meant one of the others must have. But why
would anyone do something as mundane as add nuts to a salad

and then not cop to it? It had to be a mistake. Someone accidentally added them, then after Ben's attack was too embarrassed to fess up.

Meg felt a hand brush against her back. "No one's blaming you," T.J. said.

"Oh, my God, no," Ben said. He grabbed Meg by the shoulders. "You totally saved my life. I don't know what would've happened if you hadn't been here."

Ben stepped away and Minnie practically tackled Meg with a ferocious embrace. "Thank you, thank you, thank you," she said, planting a kiss on Meg's cheek between each repetition.

Meg smiled. That was the Minnie she knew and loved. It was good to see her again. "You're welcome."

Silence descended over the dining room table as everyone wandered back to their seats. A few people picked at the food on their plates but it seemed no one had any appetite left.

Ben was the first to break the silence. "It's no big deal, guys. Seriously. Happens all the time."

"Sorry," T.J. said. "It was just kind of a shock, you know?"

Ben piled his utensils on his plate and stood up. "Forget it. Let's go watch TV or something, huh? You guys are bumming me out."

He bussed his plate into the kitchen, and Minnie quickly followed, leaving her mostly untouched dinner on the table. One by one they gathered up plates and serving trays, and hauled everything to the sink. Nathan and Kenny didn't hang around to get roped into clean-up duty. Lori followed close behind Kenny, and

Vivian, after a few instructions on how the dishwasher should be loaded, joined the group in the living room. But Meg lingered.

While Gunner and Kumiko rinsed plates and loaded them in the dishwasher in the exact opposite way Vivian had recommended, Meg checked the cupboards for signs of the slivered almonds. When she came up empty, she pulled out the trashcan and used a long wooden spoon to pick through the table scrapings, looking for an empty bag.

"I already checked," T.J. said. "No bag of almonds."

"Oh." Meg stood up and tossed the spoon into the sink.

"Weird," Gunner said. King of the Obvious.

Kumiko added detergent to the dishwasher and closed it up. "Don't worry about it. Ben's fine. Just put it out of your mind."

"Exactly," T.J. said. "You need to relax. That's what this weekend's for, right?" He disappeared onto the patio and returned with four beers. He handed two to Gunner, then popped the other two with an opener on his key ring. "Seriously, have one. I know you don't really drink but it'll help you relax."

Meg took the bottle gratefully. T.J. was right. She just needed to relax and have some fun. Stop worrying about who put almonds in the salad. This weekend was supposed to be fun.

Beers in hand, T.J., Gunner, Kumiko, and Meg joined the rest of the party in the living room. Meg expected to see a movie on the huge flat-screen television, but instead it was blank and blue, bathing the living room in a dullish cerulean light. Nathan and Kenny stood at a bookcase. They yanked DVD cases off the shelf and tossed them to Ben and Minnie on the sofa.

Minnie pried open *The Hangover*. "Empty," she said before flinging it in a large pile on the floor.

"Empty," Ben said, and added *Trading Places*.

"Empty?" Meg asked.

"Empty," Ben and Minnie said in unison.

Kenny didn't even turn around. "All of them."

"It doesn't make sense." Vivian examined the discarded cases as if she didn't entirely trust anyone else's opinion. "Why would someone put empty DVD cases on the shelf?"

T.J. picked up the remote and flipped through input devices. The result was always the same: blue screen of death.

"The satellite's out," Kenny said.

A gust of wind blasted the backside of the house as if in agreement. It wasn't the least bit cold inside, but Meg shivered.

"Must be the storm." Ben jumped to his feet and headed to the kitchen. "I'm getting more beers. I think we're gonna need them."

"We can always play board games," Lori said. "I saw some stacked in the—"

"Here's one!" Minnie squealed. She held up a shiny DVD like she'd just found Willy Wonka's last golden ticket.

"What is it?" Vivian asked.

Nathan plucked the disc out of her hand. "It's homemade." He held it up to his face and read the label: "Don't Watch Me."

"I don't know that movie," Gunner said.

Minnie snorted. "It's a burned disc, Gun Show. Not a real movie."

"Oh."

Ben handed beers around. "It's probably lame vacation footage or something."

"Or porn," Nathan volunteered.

Lori wrinkled her nose. "Why would someone label porn *Don't Watch Me*?"

Nathan shrugged. "Why not?"

Vivian sat in one of the winged chairs and crossed her legs. "I don't like this."

"You know what?" Minnie said with a dramatic pause. "This is how horror movies start."

"We've already had one near-death experience," Kumiko said.

Ben laughed. "Just an accident. Nothing sinister."

"Dude!" Nathan pointed at T.J. "You'd better watch out."

T.J. arched an eyebrow. "Why?"

"Well, if this is a horror movie, you're the first one to go. The black dude's always the first one to die."

Words flew out of Meg's mouth before she even knew what she was saying. "Really? You really needed to go there?"

"What?" Nathan looked around the room. Everyone avoided his eyes. "It's true."

Focus shifted back to Meg. She felt her throat start to tighten up, the usual shyness creeping over her. "I, uh . . ."

"Come on," Nathan said. "Say it."

Meg saw the bully come out in Nathan. And there was nothing she hated more than a bully. It pissed her off that he was trying to intimidate her, and suddenly, Meg was able to say exactly what she meant.

"Racist much? Are you going to ask if Kumiko can help you with your math homework next?"

Kumiko laughed. "Good one."

Meg smiled, surprised by her own words. She usually wasn't this confrontational. Must be the booze.

"Whatever." Nathan snatched the disc out of Kenny's hands. "Are we watching this or not?"

"Why not?" Ben handed Minnie a beer and sat down next to her. Meg saw him drape a long arm around Minnie's back. "Better than board games."

"Dude," Gunner said, his eyes wide. "Don't do it."

Minnie laughed, light and airy, as she leaned into Ben's arm. "Oh come on, it's just a video." She pointed at Nathan. "Hurry up!"

Nathan put the disc in the machine and hit Play.

The number "10" appeared on the screen. It was animated as if it had been written by hand, and then a red slash crossed right through it. "9" and "8" were drawn and slashed through in the same manner, then three images of a beach at night cycled through in rapid succession, all different locations, it seemed, but all with a prominent starry sky and waves breaking across an expanse of sand.

The numbers started again: "7," "6," "5," all with the same red slash marks crossing them out as if they were being counted down. Then more images. This time it was a collage of students in class—taking a test, arguing in some sort of mock trial, doing science experiments, running around a track, glee club.

"4," "3," "2," "1."

The screen went black and a low soundtrack kicked in. Just a few solo piano chords at first, then a soprano voice began to sing.

"Sure on this shining night . . ."

Words faded onto the screen.

When you hurt someone . . .

. . . with intent . . . with cruelty . . .

The screen went black as the song continued, then more words faded into view.

To steal someone's soul.

To break someone's heart.

The screen flashed, then filled with a quick montage of totally random images—a lightbulb turning on, a judge's gavel striking a sound block, a bonfire.

`To lie, cheat or steal.`

`To destroy a reputation.`

More random images. Math equations scrolling across the screen. People dancing. A girl and a boy making out.

`Your actions are a crime.`

Now it was capital punishment. An electric chair. A firing squad. A gallows.

`Even if the law does not recognize it.`

Flames filled the screen.

`Your betrayal, your backstabbing, your character assassination.`

The music stopped.

`Steps must be taken to protect the innocent.`

`Those steps begin right here, right`
`now.`

Suddenly the screen exploded with light and sound. The images flashed at a manic pace, moving backward as if the movie had been switched into rewind. The music was no longer a languid song but a dissonant cluster of screaming chords. The noise crescendoed as the video reached the countdown again, flying rapidly in reverse from one to ten. There was a massive explosion, along with matching sound effects, then a single line of text faded into view.

`Vengeance is mine.`

The screen went black.

STATIC FIZZLED ON THE SCREEN WHILE EVERY-one sat frozen in their seats, unable to move.

Kumiko was the first to break the spell. She jumped up and turned off the television with a shaky hand. "What the hell was that?"

Gunner scratched his knee. "Maybe Jessica's messing with us?"

"Backstabbing? Character assassination?" Vivian's voice seemed to have gone up an octave. "What does that even mean?"

"I can honestly say that was the weirdest thing I've ever seen," Ben said.

"Math problems?" Nathan said with a tense laugh. "And a noose? I mean, it's just a joke, right?"

"Sick joke," T.J. said. He was still staring at the dark television screen, his jaw muscles clenched tight.

"It couldn't mean anything," Vivian said.

From the corner of the room, someone sobbed. Everyone turned. Lori sat on the window bench, frantically rubbing the side of her face. Her eyes were red and swollen, and heavy tears streaked down her cheeks.

"Lori, are you okay?" Kenny asked. He heaved himself off the sofa with more agility than Meg thought possible and was across the room to her in an instant.

He placed his hand on her shoulder, and Lori started as if she'd been woken out of deep sleep. There was a look on her face that Meg could only describe as panic. Without warning, she balled up her fists and pounded them against the wooden bench. *"Who did this?"*

Everyone froze. Stunned.

Nathan glanced at the blank television screen. "Huh?"

"One of you did it. To scare us." Lori looked around aimlessly. "I need . . . I need . . ." She spotted the beer Ben had placed next to her and polished it off.

"I'm sure it's nothing," Vivian said. She sounded less than sure. "Calm down, okay?"

"Calm down?" Lori grabbed Vivian by the shoulders. "Someone's trying to scare us. Someone's out to get us."

Meg's eyes grew wide. Did she mean everyone or just her and Vivian?

Vivian shook herself free. "That's ridiculous."

"Is it?" Lori wobbled a bit and steadied herself against the wall. "You think this is a coincidence? I know what that means. I know what you did."

"Excuse me?"

"What you did to that girl last year. Everyone knew about it."

Vivian flinched. "I don't know what you're talking about."

"Really? Please. You'd stab your own mother in the back to win that competition."

Gunner leaned into Kumiko. "What's with the freak-out?"

T.J. shook himself, then stood up slowly. "I think we all need to calm down," he said. "It's been a long day and we're probably all tired. Maybe we should call it a night?"

"I'm getting out of here. First thing in the morning." Lori stumbled down the hallway. "I'm not staying here with you liars."

Meg listened to Lori's staggering footsteps as she ascended the stairs. She'd only seen Lori drink one beer, so she couldn't be drunk. Was she *that* upset?

As soon as Lori was gone, Vivian dashed down the hall after her without saying a word. Meg was pretty sure she was crying.

"Damn," Minnie said. "What is wrong with everyone?"

"I'm sharing a room with Lori," Kumiko said. She sounded genuinely concerned. "I'll make sure she's all right."

"Okay," T.J. said. "Good."

No one spoke as they filed out of the living room. No one looked anyone else in the eye. There was zero interest in discussing what they'd just seen.

They trudged up the stairs, single file, like school children marching off for detention. At the second floor, everyone disappeared into their own rooms. The door to Vivian's room was already closed. At the other end of the hall, Kumiko approached her bedroom door, knocked softly, then entered.

The oppressive silence lingered as Meg and Minnie ascended

the stairs to the garret. They didn't speak while they got into their pajamas, they didn't speak while they climbed into bed, they didn't speak as Meg turned off the light.

Meg stared at the roof, listening to the sharp tapping of the rain as it was catapulted into the windows by a ferocious wind. She'd been so excited to stay in that room but now everything felt odd. Off in a way she couldn't explain.

Meg shook her head. Jessica would be arriving in the morning with more guests. The storm would probably blow over during the night and tomorrow things would be different. She was being silly; she just needed some sleep.

"We should see about getting out of here tomorrow," Minnie said softly. The nearest guest room was down on the second floor, yet she still whispered.

"Really?" Meg asked. "But I thought you were having a good time?"

"Yeah . . ." Minnie's voice trailed off, then she fell silent. Meg could hear her turning over in bed. "Meg?"

"Yeah."

"Will I be okay? When you're in LA?"

"Mins, you'll be fine."

A rustle of sheets and bedding. "Sometimes, I don't think I can, you know? Be fine without you. I'm not sure I can do it."

"We'll talk about it later, okay?" Meg said. "When we're home." She didn't want to have that conversation at all, let alone in the pitch-black garret at White Rock House with T.J. sleeping in a room downstairs. It made her feel even more like a traitor to her friendship with Minnie: First she was running away to college, then she was rekindling her feelings for T.J.

"Promise?" Minnie said. More promises no one expected her to keep.

"Promise."

A roar of wind rattled every window in the garret and the rain lashed at the glass so fiercely it sounded as if someone had thrown a handful of pebbles at the side of the house. The light filtering through the white gauze curtains was muted and dull, and Meg's first thought as she squinted her eyes open was that the storm must have raged all night without letting up. Judging by the wind and the rain, they were in for another dark, damp day on Henry Island.

She shivered and pulled the quilt up around her ears. Damn, the house was freezing. Had someone turned off the heat? She rolled on her side to check the time on the alarm clock but the digital face was completely blank. No wonder it was so cold in the house. The storm must have knocked out the power during the night. No power, no heat, no satellite. Minnie was right—they needed to catch the first boat out of there.

Meg listened for other noises in the house, but there was only the sound of Minnie's rhythmic breathing. She lay there for a moment, eyes squeezed shut against the encroaching daylight, and wondered if she should get up and tell someone about the power outage. Eh, what could they do? No point in leaving a warm bed. She snuggled under her covers, hoping she'd drift back off to sleep.

Except she had to pee. Small bladder and too much beer. She swung her legs over the bed and tested her toes on the frigid floor, silently cursing her decision not to pack slippers. With the giant comforter wrapped around her, Meg tiptoed across the garret and down the stairs.

There was a slight breeze in the open stairwell of the tower that sent a chill racing down Meg's neck. She hitched the comforter up over her head—sympathizing suddenly with Eskimos, mummies, and women in burkas—and quickened her pace.

Pat, pat, pat. The sound of her bare feet was distant and fuzzy as it permeated the layers of thick down wrapped around her head. Her toes were so cold she could barely feel the smooth wood of the stairs, and the comforter cocoon was like having blinders on: She could only see a small oval right in front of her. She moved as quickly as her bulky wrap would allow, praying she didn't trip and send herself careening down the stairs or worse, over the railing. That fall would certainly end in a broken neck.

Why was she always thinking of the most morbid scenarios? Sheesh. Just go down to the bathroom then back to a warm, comfy bed.

Pat, pat, pat.

Creeeeeak.

Meg paused. Was that the stairs creaking? It sounded like it came from somewhere above her. Maybe the old house was straining against the storm? She rounded a corner of the stairs and heard it again.

Creeeeeeak. A shadow on the white wall of the tower caught her eye. There was something odd about it, something familiar and yet there shouldn't be a shadow there at all. The windows in the tower didn't have any curtains, nothing to cast a shadow. Meg started at it for a second and noticed the shadow was moving, swaying slowly from left to right.

Creeeeeak.

Meg froze, her eyes locked on the shadow. The heavy form, oblong and amorphous except for the dangling appendages. . . .

Legs. Holy crap, they were legs.

Meg turned her head and came eye-to-eye with a face hanging in the stairwell. The noose around the neck. The purplish-blue hue to the skin.

Meg opened her mouth and screamed.